into the sea

a novel by **jay laurie**

Into the Sea

ISBN 978 0 646 59348 7

Cataloguing in Publication details are available
from the National Library of Australia.

Cover design by Salty Studios Pty Ltd.
www.saltystudios.com.au.

For P

1.

The old man sat cross-legged on the sand in the shade of a palm tree. Smoking, squinting into the glare of the morning sun glittering off the sea. Loose skinned brown legs protruded from under a faded sarong tied around his waist. Below the knees, his legs lay placidly on top of each other at rest. Wide calloused feet merged into the sagging muscle of his calves.

Selamat pagi.

Pagi, the old man replied.

Apa kabar?

Baik baik terima kasih… anda dari mana?

Saya dari Australia.

Australia… mmm, the old man smiled. His watery eyes slowly blinked. He drew thinly on his skinny crooked cigarette and looked peacefully out across the sea: apa pekerjaan anda di Indonesia?

2.

In the distance the straight black road shimmered under the scorching sun. Each time they neared a watery mirage, falsely heralding respite from the unrelenting dryness, it vanished and a new fool's pool formed further down the way. On either side, camel coloured earth baked and cracked in the midday furnace. Now and then its upper crust whipped across the barren plains in a dusty haze. Occasionally a spiralling willy-willy formed and pirouetted across the desert. Hawks patiently circled on high for limited prey above the ragged saltbush. Mallee trees tenaciously clawed into the dirt, surviving on meagre drops of dewfall when it came. It never rained.

The old four-wheel drive panted along in the heat with windows and vents flaring. Hot air blasted around the cabin from every direction, threatening the books and papers strewn across the dashboard. The side windows had seen better days. They only worked if the handle was wound slowly while the glass was coaxed with the outstretched fingers of the other hand. Otherwise they fell off the winder and packed it in until the whole door was stripped. In the daytime heat the triangular windows in the corners were the saviours, funnelling a stream of air across sweat-drenched skin until the cool of the desert night.

Heaving trucks blustered past in both directions, thundering by, trailer after trailer. Each time a semi came at them head on, they put a hand up to the cracked front windscreen to soften the impact of the raining stones flicked up by the truck's wheels. After it had passed by, they peered nervously in the mirrors at the road behind and pressed their foreheads up against the windscreen to see if the boards were still on the roof.

Clean white cars, commanded by white-haired seniors with sun hats and cushions cosily stationed on carpeted perches above back seats, carefully indicated their way at length past them. Everything did. The only overtaking they'd done was a lone cyclist, pedalling along in shorts and long socks in the middle of nowhere, grinning out from under a white cap, neck flap streaming, his essentials packed in bulging panniers strapped on either side of his back tyre and a German flag on his bouncing backpack.

It didn't matter. They had nowhere else they had to be. No schedule. No time limits. Just an open road and a roof full of boards.

Since stopping at the border early that morning, where a khaki clad female customs officer had suspiciously inspected their car and sternly confiscated without debate all of their fresh fruit and vegetables except the stash hidden underneath the spare tyre, the road east had been straight for over a hundred kilometres. Not a single bend. There'd been a long stretch where they didn't even see a tree. To relieve the monotony, they had pulled over at one of the lookouts on the south side of the road and watched in awe as the ocean swells rolled gravely in over the deep water, clean and blue in the offshore wind and then smashed against the layered cliffs of The Bight hundreds of feet below. Knowing that there were none, they had both silently surveyed the coast for a deep cove or an elevated reef which might have a rideable wave until the Nullabor sun seared their heads and prickled their skin and drove them back to the barely greater comfort of the car.

Bleached and tattered copies of Mark Warren and Nat Young's guides to surfing in Australia lay on the dashboard in the sun along with poorly refolded maps, scraps of torn paper with phone numbers and reminders long since forgotten and an old red pocket knife. A battered cardboard box of tapes shared the passenger floor with empty chocolate milk cartons, chip packets and a dank carpet of crumbs and sand that had built up over the years.

Riley picked up the box and clicked slowly through the cassettes. He pulled Hunters & Collectors out and tightened the strip of tape with his forefinger in the spokes, pushed it into the tape deck and turned the volume up loud to reach over the noise of the wind.

Good choice mate, Will said and beat a few drums on the wheel, haven't heard these guys all trip.

They sang along with some of the tunes, sometimes getting the words right and not caring when they didn't. A few tapes later on, with the mid afternoon sun behind them but the landscape little changed and the heat undiminished, they pulled over to top up the radiator again.

Might check the roof racks to see if the boards are still ok... you all right to drive for a bit? Will asked.
Sure, Riley said.

Will climbed up on the side step of the car and tugged at the old occy straps and checked that the rusted brackets were still holding tight in the door jam. He scuffed around and did the same on the other side. The bits of cardboard, shoved in for protection between the straps and the edges of the boards at the last minute, were still in place. The boards were their most important cargo. They had three each piled in two stacks on the roof in flimsy striped covers stiff and crusty from years of melted wax, ingrained sand and salt. The longest board on the bottom, fins to the back and the next two sat with their tails just inside the fins of the board below.

Riley had had the car for a few years. He'd picked it up in the South West off a dairy farmer. It had gone a long way even then but diesels went forever. Here and there remnants of white paint peered through the rust and dust and dirt. The back seat had been folded down for their gear. It'd had some sort of order when they had set off but was now a shambles. Tents and fold out chairs, sleeping gear, wetsuits, leg ropes, towels and clothes, boxes of food, water containers, a gas bottle and cooking gear, a blue plastic box of plates and cutlery and cleaning stuff and fishing rods, an esky and other things all jostled about on top of each other in the back.

Riley finished topping up the radiator and shut the bonnet hard amid a cloud of dust. It only stayed shut if it was slammed down. He climbed up into the driver's seat and they headed off again. They were in the home stretch of the long journey across half the country now. They'd probably be there at dusk if nothing went wrong with the car.

Part I

3.

Billie Saunders and Riley met in the schoolyard at lunch on the first day of high school. Standing around on the edge of the mayhem unfolding on the oval, lost and a bit empty and trying hard not to show it. The long Summer holidays which at their beginning had no end, stretching way into the never never, to some date long past Christmas, too far away to fathom, were really over.

Clusters of boys and girls in dishevelled grey uniforms and bare feet ran riot across the grass after tennis balls and footies and leapt about under skipping ropes and frisbees in the February heat, scattering seagulls prospecting for lunch scraps near discarded shoes and socks.

Billie looked over at the bigger kid standing near him with a woolly mop of brown hair, gnawing steadily on his fingernails and, above the continuous cheer of the schoolyard, asked: You new here?

Yeah, the other kid said, glancing quickly over, his finger still in his mouth.

Me too... what's your name?

Riley, he said taking his finger out of his mouth.

What kind of a name is that? Billie asked with a grin.

The other kid's face flushed and he looked away and started on his fingernails again.

I'm Billie Saunders, he said to the side of Riley's head, I'm actually Will but everyone calls me Billie.

Riley's hunched shoulders dropped a bit.

Wish I was at the beach today, Billie said rooting around in his nostril with a forefinger.

Me too, Riley replied.

Do you surf?

Yeah, a bit, Riley lied.

What's your board like? Billie asked and flicked a crusty flake off his finger.

I'm getting a surfboard for my birthday, Riley lied again and then hurriedly confessed more quietly: I just go out on a surf mat at the moment. He looked away and flushed again, waiting for derisive laughter from Billie who he imagined was a real surfie like the kids with proper boards his Mum and Dad told him to stay away from at the beach.

I've got one of those as well, Billie said smiling. I ride it sometimes, my stomach kills for ages afterwards... mostly just ride my surfboard now... maybe we could go to the beach one day.

Yeah that'd be great, Riley grinned.

*   *   *

Billie lived a couple of streets back from the beach in a small sky blue fibro house with his parents, his sister and little brother. It was a distant suburb. They rarely went to the city. Mr Whippy dawdled along the streets on weekends from time to time, pied-pipering the kids with Greensleeves on continuous play out of the megaphone fixed onto the roof and setting off a flurry of pleading and tugging at dress hems for a choc top with a flake and nuts or alright just a plain vanilla ice cream (with nuts).

He was younger and smaller than a lot of kids in his year. At the start of Year 8, he was still 12. He had watery blue eyes that made him seem elsewhere. He mostly was if he wasn't at the beach. His face was brown from months on end in the sun over Summer and speckled with freckles and peeling skin which he worked at patiently hoping to get a long bit. He knew he had to time it right. If he waited too long to peel it off it became itchy and flaky and came off in small wispy shards. If he tried too early, it hurt as the soft unripe pink skin underneath became exposed.

Straight, bleached hair ran horizontally across his forehead above his barely discernible blond eyebrows and in short neat lines across his ears, leaving only the lobe exposed. Despite his protests about looking like a roman helmet again, his Mum had cut it the week before, ready for school. She had sat him down shirtless on a chair on the grass and leaned in close while she moved her dress making scissors along his forehead and asked him to sit still when she cut the hair near his ears. Then she'd combed it down straight to make sure it was even. After she'd finished he'd bent right over and rubbed and slapped at his head and shoulders to get rid of the itchy loose hair and then run down to the beach and across the sand whipping at his ankles in the stiff sea breeze and plunged into the short peaked chop to mess it up.

Billie's father went up north to the mines for work for long stretches at a time. Each time he left Billie had a lump in his throat for a day. While he was away, the bigger kids chipped in a bit more at home and Billie's Mum showered the three of them with evenly distributed affection. She had olive skin and bright blue eyes. She wore colourful skirts and dresses and bright headbands in her honey coloured hair and walked with a light dancing sway. Some nights, as the days his Dad had been away mounted up, when Billie and his sister should have been in bed, they peaked out from behind the curtain and watched her hosing the garden out the front for a long time and talking in low voices and laughing with different men who seemed like they wanted to be Joe.

Their house was raised off the ground on low wooden stilts. The space underneath provided shelter for creatures from the nearby bushland and so an almost fool proof hiding place during games of hide and seek. Across the front lawn, white wooden steps led up to the porch and the front door. Inside, the living area centred on an open fireplace which contained the only bricks in the house. Scratched and faded orange laminex benches and cupboards, an old white stove and a rounded cream fridge with an over frosting freezer they had to chisel out every fortnight, made up the kitchen. Past the round dining table, worn armchairs hidden under brown and yellow blankets and a comfy green velour sofa gathered around the fireplace. Grandma's tall reading lamp stood in one of the corners. After Winter the rugs on the wooden floor were packed away in preparation for the tracks of fine sand that they brought in on their bare feet from the beach in the warmer seasons.

At the back of the house was a big open deck. On a warm blue Saturday morning one Spring, his Dad had bowed out of the chorus of droning lawnmowers and announced that he'd be putting in a new wooden deck. The old skinny landing and flight of rickety steps would be going. The old gum tree would stay. He'd be building round that he'd proudly said. Once his Dad had committed himself to something there was no turning back. But it was a bigger job than he had imagined and he was hammering and sawing and letting go the odd short word that the kids weren't supposed to hear all through the following Summer on his breaks before he and Mum had their first beers on it and gave the two bigger kids a sip. Billie helped him on the weekends, more enthusiastically when the sea breeze came in, fetching tools and nails and water and relaying messages.

Out the back, past the new deck and the outside dunny and the brick walled barbeque off to the side, where sausages were cooked on a rusty hot plate until they were crusted to charcoal and brittle and skinny as a twig and had just the faintest trace of pulped god knows what left in the centre, right at the end of the back lawn, next to the lemon tree, was his Dad's shed. It was out of bounds unless he was home. Billie knew where the key was though and stole in there when he could but he made sure no one saw him go inside and touch the furniture his Dad chiselled and turned during his breaks.

Next door were the Killyahs. The Killyah's were actually the Blaney's. The Saunders called them the Killyah's amongst themselves. From time to time there were nights at the Killyah's which put the surrounding neighbourhood on high alert as hefty, massive chested, bottle blond Sharyn Blaney tucked into the rum, beat the life out of the pots and pans in the kitchen and raged and ranted at rock concert volume against her lanky gaunt grey haired husband Terry and their two withdrawn girls and anything else in her line of sight. Her most common threat to the members of her family on those nights was 'I'm gunna farkin killyah'. Every now and then one of the girls would scream back a desperate pained response at a few decibels higher but there was nervous fear in their responses and Mrs Killyah seized on it and escalated her already irrational rampage into an intoxicated tirade and door slamming which shook the foundations of the little stilted weatherboard house they rented. Terry Blaney had learnt over the years that it was best to walk away but sometimes he couldn't help stepping in to try to set things straight and make her ease off the girls and his voice would bellow fleetingly over the top of hers. Now and again, the cops were called out by neighbours fearing an assault was about to happen or something worse. The girls suffered badly. They were cowering unhappy kids with a rich knowledge of expletives and a doubtful future.

*   *   *

To get to his new high school Billie snaked indirectly along backstreets up the steep hill on his bike and then fanged it down hill in a tight tuck without pedalling, to get home. He was proud of his bike. It was a lime green dragster with curved handlebars, white-rimmed tyres and a shiny backrest behind the long seat with an Australian flag. He'd got the bike for his last birthday. It wasn't new then but the paint glistened and his Dad said he'd got it from a proper bike shop and it was as good as new. The day he got it, he spent the whole day tearing around the neighbourhood, racing other kids who had bikes and dinking kids who didn't. His Dad also gave him a tyre repair kit and taught him how to fix holes with a bucket of water to look for the bubbles, giving the inner tube a scratch before gluing down the patch and putting a brick on it all to set. He became pretty adept at it from three corner jacks picked up in the nearby bushland.

Riley's house was higher up the hill. Most days they would ride their bikes there at the end of the school day and talk at the gate for a while before Billie coasted home down the hill. Riley's house was big. Modern. Two stories. Built out of brown bricks. They had nice stuff inside. Some days Riley's Mum opened the front door and called out to them to come inside for afternoon tea and he'd sit down at the table with Riley's older sister, to biscuits from the shop and soda stream fizzy drinks on tap.

Riley's Mum was smaller than Billie's. The top of Riley's head reached up to her brown eyes already. She had careful thin-stranded mouse brown hair, the bulk of which sat suspended at a distance away from her scalp in low crested waves, glistening and defying gravity under the hold of hairspray. She wore foundation patted down on her cheeks and lipstick and dressed in white blouses and plain skirts with block-heeled cream shoes.

Riley's Mum was pretty strict. Kids had to take their shoes off at the front door before they went inside. They weren't allowed in the good sitting room with the plush white carpet even though the arms of the new cream lounge were still wrapped in the delivery plastic. After afternoon tea, she kept a beady eye on them while they cleaned the kitchen bench and made sure their plates and cups were washed and put away. Up on the fridge under a small magnet, she had a neat table in big capital letters showing the chores the kids had to do each day before and after school during the week. Billie called her Mrs Riley.

Mrs Riley called Riley 'Digby'. Billie never called him Digby. No one did. A few of the gang saw what happened to Angus Finch one lunch time when he'd baited Riley about his first name for a few days and ignored the warnings. Word soon got around. Riley wasn't a bully but he hated his first name in those volatile early teenage years.

4.

At first light on a Sunday in March a few weeks into the first school term, Billie scampered across the front lawn and out the gate and scaled the tall pine tree on the grass verge three houses up. The branches wound around it closely together like a circular staircase. The first branch was high off the ground but if he took a run up he could jump and grab it with his hands and swing himself up. After that it was easy.

As he climbed that morning he could feel a cool wind coming from the direction of where the sun would rise. That was a good wind. It made the surface of the sea smooth and the faces of the waves clean. Two thirds of the way up the tree he got to the branch where he could see if the waves were any good. He'd been higher. He'd been to the very top but the branches became thinner and greener up there and even if he stood on them where they were strongest close to the trunk, it felt like he was asking for trouble. For Billie there was surf if he could see something, anything, breaking. It didn't matter whether it was small or if the waves were closing out in a long line of white water. It was always better out in the water than it looked from the tree.

In the early morning haze before the sunrise everything was still in shadow. A couple of sentries were standing on top of the dunes looking out at the slate green sea. It was hard to tell how big the waves were. Maybe waist high. That was pretty good for the end of Summer.

Billie slid down the tree and slipped back inside the house through the back door and changed out of his pyjamas into his boardies and a t-shirt. He walked softly into his Mum's bedroom and asked in an excited whisper if he could go to the beach. And then again when she didn't respond. She opened her eyes and blinked a few times and groggily asked: Who would you be going with Billie?
I'm gunna ride up the hill to see if Riley from school can come... I'll come back for my board. The waves aren't very big, he said.
Ok, have something to eat before you go, she said.

Billie shot off out of the room before any further directions could be given. She glanced at the clock and rolled over and smiled and closed her eyes. It was just past 5 o'clock.

Billie gulped down some cereal, clanged the bowl and spoon into the sink and shot out the door as Little Tom began to wail. He rode up to Riley's house. It was cool and quiet on the streets. He took the direct route up the steep hill to save time and when he got to Riley's house, he was hot and out of breath.

He tapped on Riley's window. After a few taps, Riley's anxious face peered out from a small gap where he had pulled the curtain aside and then became a broad grin as he recognized Billie. He lifted up the window and put his head out: Hi Billie. Want to come to the beach and go surfing? Billie whispered, I've looked, there's waves.

Yeah, I'll ask Mum… wait here for a bit, Riley whispered back excitedly.

After a little while Riley's Dad opened the front door dressed in long legged pyjamas. Wisps of thinning brown hair waved and circled around the top of his head in the easterly wind. He was tall but stooped with rounded shoulders on a lean frame. Blue eyes sparkled above his smile. He was always smiling. Riley said he even had a special angry smile in which his teeth pressed together tightly and his eyes narrowed in. Billie liked Mr Riley. He was never in a rush. He invited Billie in.

In the kitchen he asked the boys a thousand questions – most of which Billie had to answer. Riley ate breakfast, hunching down lower and lower over his plate hoping the interrogation would end. Riley's Mum drifted down the stairs in a dressing gown and many of the same questions started coming up again. Billie was beginning to shift in his seat uncomfortably and Riley was getting at his fingernails until Mr Riley explained what was happening and, with promises to be back by a certain time, they were finally on their way down the hill. Riley followed Billie, steering his bike with one hand, his blue and red surf mat squirming about under the other arm, the wind rushing against his face, revelling in his new found independence.

They let their bikes fall on their sides on the front lawn of Billie's house under the big Jacaranda tree and went inside. Billie's Mum was up making a cup of tea with one arm and cradling Little Tom in the other. She smiled as they came in: Hi Riley.

Hi Kath, Riley blushed. He always blushed near her. He'd never get used to using her first name like she made him.

Wanna put some air in your mat? Billie asked.

Yeah, Riley replied hastily and followed Billie to his room.

Billie kept his board in the corner of his bedroom. He could see it at night there.

Before they left, Billie's Mum cornered Billie and applied toxic smelling blockout which dried on contact with the skin with a sting and hurt like hell when it got in the eyes. She got hold of Riley as well and he stood there limply and embarrassed, not knowing where to look as she applied it to his reddening face and rubbed it on his shoulders and back.

They set off on foot with their surf gear under their arms and towels around their shoulders. Billie pointed out the pine tree lookout to Riley. On the front lawn of the house behind the tree, the Ellen sisters were already bouncing and tumbling around on the trampoline in their bikinis. They waved at the boys in mid air and giggled as they passed shyly by.

A few houses further down, a black dog with a wide-jawed head barked and growled menacingly on the other side of the high fence and worked itself into a leaping frenzy when Billie teased a stick at a run along the corrugated iron. On the next street, a short grey haired bloke with peppered whiskers wearing khaki stubbies and a taut white singlet pulled down as far as it could go half over his barrel belly, was bent over his overgrown front lawn. He slowly straightened up as the boys approached and, levering one hand on the knee of his scrawny leg, creaked stiffly up and greeted them with a wincing grin, brandishing the Sunday paper he'd unearthed from the shin high barley grass.

At the bottom of the hill they passed the last of the fibro shacks and entered the bush along a dusty limestone track which wound through the sand dunes in a low valley of gum trees, acacia, bottlebrush, grass trees and other bush. On the way two magpies called out to each other in a hollow melody and, as if in reply, a kookaburra laughed on its perch on a lone dead branch, silhouetted against the rising sun in the east. Dragonflies darted across the track, hovering in front of them from time to time in mid-air and then droning off into the bush. Cicadas screeched rhythmically with all they had. At the base of the dunes, the vegetation became rampant pig face, low tufted grasses and tea green coastal rosemary which clung bravely to the exposed sand, battered day in day out by the wind rushing in from the sea.

They ran up the dunes and paused at the top. The ocean stretched out immensely before them as far as they could see. The island sat low on the horizon out to the west. Barely visible. Waves rose up in the foreground and momentarily reflected the golden glow of the morning sun before breaking on the shallow sand banks. Away up the beach a surfer paddled and leapt to his feet in a fluid motion and glided across the face of a wave on his long board, drawing smooth lines. Then he stepped off in the shallows and paddled back out on his knees, bent over, his arms pulling the water beside the board in long easy double strokes. The boys looked at each other and tore down the dune and across the deep sand towards the water's edge, casting their towels, thongs and t-shirts off haphazardly on the way, barely breaking stride.

Riley glanced across at Billie's board resting on the sand while Billie was putting his leg-rope around his ankle. Then they walked out into the shallow water, their hands guiding their surf craft floating beside them, cringing and arching their backs as the cold spray from the first small passing wave was blown onto their bare skin in the strong offshore wind. When the water became deeper, Billie climbed onto his board and paddled out. Riley kicked along behind him on his mat.

Billie's board was much taller than him, even when he put his hands up above his head. It was a sun yellowed 7 foot 2 inch single fin with a big red lightning bolt on the deck. It was thick and tapered fairly sharply towards the tail and less so up at the nose. A proper fibreglass board. In pretty good nick except for a few old dings. One big one on the rail at the side Jack said had happened when another guy fell off his board as Jack was paddling out. Jack said that he didn't know how the board missed his head. He had fixed the ding so water didn't soak in.

Jack was one of Joe's old school friends. He was a wiry, bow legged bloke with long brown hair and a skinny moustache. Billie never knew when he was pulling his leg and when he was fair dinkum. He laid bricks and shook hands like he was going to break them.

When they were at the beach one day in the Summer before, Billie had seen Jack walk over to his Mum and Dad with a board under his arm after he'd been surfing and they had stood talking for ages while Billie was catching waves on his surf mat. When Billie finally went in later on, Jack had gone but the board was still there on the sand. His Dad said that Jack had left it there for him. He had looked at his Dad with disbelief, then looked at the board and back at his Dad and asked hesitantly if he could try it.

Billie had marched proudly to the water's edge, awkwardly clutching the board too far towards the front under his right arm, its nose pointing high to the sky and the tail dragging in the sand. He'd stumbled every now and then when his feet got caught up in the leg rope which he'd attached with the leash sticking out in front of his shin and on the wrong ankle. He had had to be waved in from the sea by his parents that day in the stiffening sea breeze. Jack had not asked for his board back since then but Billie lived in fear that he would.

That morning Billie and Riley found an uncrowded spot down the beach from The Point. The swell came in out of the deeper blue water and rose up, as the sand shallowed, into glistening turquoise peaks. Riley watched Billie paddle lightly onto waves with his chest raised off the board, then stand up and drop down the front of the wave and ride it into shore, with his arms spread out wide either side for balance. Sometimes he angled across and rode along the blue wall. Other times he went to shore with the whitewash. Riley followed his head from behind as he shot along, the rest of his body hidden by the wave.

They stayed out in the water for hours that morning. Riley flew into shore time and again on his mat, dropping suddenly down with the breaking wave at the last minute, hands gripping the handles at the front of the mat, and then bouncing along, buried in the whitewash, his face inches from the water, exhilarated by the rush.

After a while Billie caught a wave in to the beach on his stomach, holding the front of his board as he planed in. He walked robotically straight and stiff with cold up the beach and lay down on his towel with his face to the sun to warm up.

Riley joined him a bit later and sat down in the sand with his arms around his knees. They talked and watched the waves. People strolled along on the hard sand at the water's edge. Tennis balls skimmed across the water in the shallows beyond them. Up towards The Point in front of the lifesavers' clubhouse, whistles sent clubbies in budgie smugglers racing out to buoys on paddle boards and back. Junior clubbies lay on their stomachs and on the whistle, ran across the deep sand to dive for small sticks sitting upright in the sand. On the flat sand along the base of the dunes, a group of balding men were carrying a large roller with coiled rope, marching upright and in time in the deep sand, the red faced leader calling the shots. Everyone had brimless cloth hats clutching their heads in squares of red and yellow with white strings tied off under their chins.

All along the beach colourful beach umbrellas mushroomed up as the offshore wind dropped away to stillness in the late morning. Riley started to feel the sun burning his skin. He looked down at his chest, raw in places from riding his surf

mat and over at Billie: Wanna go for a body surf?
Yep.

They left their gear on the sand and found a spot away from the board riders further down the beach where the waves didn't peel as well. Out the back they tottered on tip toes on the deep sand bank, losing and then momentarily regaining their tenuous footholds, rising and falling as the swells passed through. When a bigger one loomed further out, it was a mad scramble to kick and swim to get in position to catch it or dive to the bottom and lie flat, fingers gripping into the sand down there until it had crashed and rumbled past, sometimes pulling them with it in a whirl of bubbles and swirling sand.

They competed to ride the waves the furthest, experimenting with different styles to plane in to shore. For one, they would have both arms out in front, their bodies one long plank, streaming along to shore, heads down, relying on one big breath at the start, buried in the wave and feeling the speed of the water on the palms of their outstretched hands. On another, both their arms would be tucked by their sides and heads would be up out of the water like surprised seals, chests reverberating as the water rushed against them. Kicking after the initial burst to catch the wave was cheating. After each wave in, they ran and leapt and dived over small waves and under the bigger ones and dolphin kicked underwater to get out the back again.

Better get back, Billie said rubbing his hair with a towel back on the beach.
Yeah... what time do yah reckon it is?

Dunno but I'm bloody starving, Billie said, eyes slitted and face screwed up tight against the blinding whiteness of the beach in the full sun.

Me too, Riley said.

Half way up the dune on the way back, the hot sand started to scorch the soles of their feet and they bolted up and over it in short rapid steps, pausing fleetingly at places where the sand was cooler from the shade of a low bush to catch their breath and cool their burning feet, before darting on. Then they skittered home along the hot pavement, prancing from shade to grass where they could.

Back at Billie's house, his Mum was swinging gently in a hammock in the shade on the porch. As they came across the grass to the front steps, she put her finger to her lips and pointed at Little Tom asleep on her chest, whispered that there was some lunch for them in the fridge and suggested to Riley to call home. Inside, the radio was on. An American was over energetically counting down the top 40 for the week and introduced 'Video Killed the Radio Star' by The Buggles. Riley put the phone to his ear and started to dial, pulling clockwise with his finger in the hole for the first number all the way up to the catch and then riding the hole in fast clicks back to the start ready to dial the next one.

Billie tugged open the fridge door and stood there surveying the shelves while the cool air wafted onto his hot skin and out past him, singing along to the radio. He sculled orange juice out of the bottle and wiped his mouth with his forearm, then sat down, elbows splayed on the table and took chunks out of the sandwiches, piping in mid mouthful for the part of the chorus he knew.

Riley had his head bowed during the call and didn't say anything except "mm" on a few occasions and "yes Mum" obediently at the end.

What'd she say? Billie asked when he got off the phone.
She said I was an hour late already. She sounds pretty mad.
Riley bit into a sandwich.
Better get going in a sec.
Yeah sure, Billie said getting up and opening the pantry door.
I'll probably have to do some chores this arvo but it was worth it, Riley grinned.
Do yah think you'll be able to go again? Billie asked looking out towards the front porch and then quickly tipping his head back and squirting a stream of Ice Magic into his mouth.
Yeah, I reckon, she gets a bit worked up sometimes but Dad usually calms her down after a while.

5.

The week at school had three distinct phases. On Monday the boys lived off the weekend as they daydreamed at their desks replaying the details, scraping sand out of their scalps and ears, faces shining from the sun and wind they'd copped. Their whole demeanour on the first day of the week radiated the weekend's freedoms. School drifted by in the background. After the first day of the week, the weekend faded and the routine of lessons and homework settled in from Tuesday to Thursday.

But Friday was hands down the best day of the school week. They had PE for a double lesson to start and went to school in sneakers and sports gear and, except when they had theory for part of the lesson which was greeted with muffled groans and endured with a steady patter of paper spit balls hitting the ceiling, spent the morning tearing around after balls on the school oval or inside in the gym swinging on roman rings and jumping over the vaulting box.

On Friday, Riley and some of the others in the gang ordered lunch from the tuck shop. For Billie and the others that didn't, tuck shop lunches were to be shared and they sea-gulled about, relentlessly squawking for handouts of twisties or chips, a bite of buttered finger bun or a pastried corner of meat pie, until the brown paper lunch bags were scrunched up into balls and chucked on the ground and it was time to belt about after a ball.

Friday was also the day that Billie and Riley hatched plans as they rode home and sat on their bikes outside Riley's house.

What are you gunna do for Easter? Riley asked one Friday, not long before the first school holidays for the year.
Dad said we're going Down South to the coast at the end of next week, I'm taking my board… wanna come? Billie asked.
Nah, can't… fogies are coming from Over East. Mum said I gotta be here.
Ok, Billie said and, after a pause: what are you doing this weekend?
Dunno… I've gotta do the paper run early tomorrow… maybe I'll ask if I can ride down to your house after that? Wanna come and look for a board?
What?
I been saving up, got some dosh.
How much?
Sixty seven bucks… plus the papers tomorrow.
Yeah, that should be enough for a good secondhandi… I know a shop we can check out… see yah tomorrow, Billie grinned.
He pushed off the ground and shot off down the hill without pedalling, grey school shirt billowing behind inflated with wind, arms outstretched to the sides.

* * *

He'd started saving ages before he met Billie. Getting a board was not on his list then. Despite his claims on that first day of school, Riley barely went out on his surf mat then. His Mum didn't much like sand. They weren't really beach people. Back then he was saving up for a few bike parts for his BMX or a music stereo with a double cassette player if he could wait long enough to afford it. But from the moment he saw Billie ride that first wave on their first trip to the beach soon after school had begun, everything changed. He didn't let his parents know though. He couldn't take the risk. They didn't have to know everything.

They rode down to the surf shop through the back streets. Riley's bulging coin laden pocket bounced against his leg. Inside the shop, photos of empty waves and girls in bikinis pulled out from magazines were sticky taped to the walls and promised good times. Billie led him down the back of the shop, past piles of boardies and t-shirts and stacks of new boards glistening under new resin with sprays and logos, to the second hand boards. They pulled some out and lay them down side by side and turned them over and cluelessly discussed them until the longhaired shop attendant scuffed over with a smile and helped them pick one out. It was a Cordingley single fin with green rails in pretty good nick. The bloke took a look at Riley's pocket: How much have you got in there?

Bout seventy bucks.

Wanna spend it all on a board?

Yep, Riley said confidently, looking over at Billie.

You're on then, you can have it for that, I'll chuck in a leggie and a block of wax and you're up and riding Tiger.

It was by far Riley's largest purchase in all of his thirteen years.

They put the boards side by side on the grass back at Billie's house and stood proudly looking over them. Riley's was a little smaller and thinner than Billie's.

You can keep it at my joint if you like, Billie said, save you riding up and down the hill with it under your arm.
Yeah or'right, Riley said after a while, still looking at his board.
Wanna go try it? Billie asked.
Yeah, ok, Riley grinned.

They looked out at the sea from the top of the dune like they always did. It was big. Long lines of swell marched into the beach and broke in explosions of whitewash rising up higher than the wave's crest had been. A handful of surfers stood next to their boards on the sand and watched the others out in the waves. One wetsuited bloke was riding half his board in on his belly towards the other half spinning around at the water's edge. Billie looked over at Riley: Carn let's give it a go... we don't have to go out the back.
Ok, Riley said.
Better see if you're a natural footer like me or a goofy, Billie said and ran down the dune and across the beach to the shore.

Riley followed. He had no idea what Billie meant but he felt pretty sure he didn't want to be a goofy footer. It sounded like he'd never be any good, like he'd always be a kook. Being a natural footer sounded like he'd be up and riding straight off the bat. He caught up to Billie and thought he'd try to nip it in the bud right away: I'm a natural footer.

How do you know?

Just am.

Yah don't even know what it is do yah, yah bloody twerp? Billie scoffed.

Do so, Riley lied.

What is it?

Riley looked back at him blankly, then down at the sand for a second and leapt into a low position with his arms out wide, legs apart and knees bent.

Nah that looks like you're squatting for a poo, you gotta turn side on and have one leg behind the other, Billie said.

Billie knelt down and started to draw an outline of a surfboard in the sand with his finger.

What's a twerp, Riley asked after a while, looking down at Billie.

Dunno, Billie said quickly, here lie down on the board and push up with your hands and jump to your feet.

Riley did.

Nah yah doing a poo again, get up side on to the board, so you've got one shoulder forward.

Riley lay down and jumped up.

Yep that's right. Do it again.

Riley did. His left leg went forward and his right leg back. He still had his arms stretched out wide beside him.

Ok, that's o'right. Now stand there for a sec with your legs together. I'm gunna push yah, it won't hurt.

Riley stood still as Billie came up to him and put both hands on his shoulders and pushed him back pretty hard. Riley's right leg shot out to stop him falling over.

What are yah bloody doing? Riley complained as he stumbled backwards.

Just stand still again, same as before. Don't be a girl.

Billie pushed him once more and Riley's right leg shot out behind him again.

Ok, yep you're a natural footer.

Told you, Riley said grinning from ear to ear.

Here's the leggie… you put it on your right ankle, on your back leg, that way it won't get tangled in your feet when you stand up. Got it?

Yep.

Riley put the leg rope on and picked up his board and strutted down to the water with the tail of the board dragging in the sand behind him. The leg rope snapped and flicked around his feet threateningly. He was as pleased with himself as he'd ever been. He waded out until it got deep and climbed on the board and, as the cool sea washed over him, it sank in that he had a surfboard, that he was a surfer, like Billie.

He started off lying down way too far back and floundered along with his head on the side resting against the surface of the board, arms flapping either side and half of his torso dragging in the water foaming behind him from his wild ineffectual kicking. The board protruded sharply out of the sea and pointed up towards the sky at a good 45 degrees off planing position like an aeroplane just after take off and moved forward barely at snail's pace. After he'd brought the board down closer to horizontal from its launching position under Billie's guidance, he tried to get the hang of staying on it lying down whilst paddling, snatching at the rails as it slipped out to the side from under him with no warning like it had a mind of its own.

For the most part they were buffeted about like flotsam in the heaving whitewash and driven into shore time and again. Riley spent most of his time upended or riding backwards on his stomach holding onto the front of the board. The sets came and picked him up, undid the ground he had made towards getting out and drove him back to the beach or flung him off the side.

On one wave he managed to stay holding on as the board swung backwards through a turn. He found himself pointing to shore on the flat sea, shooting along with the whitewash. He scrambled first to his knees and then wobbled miraculously to his feet and stood up tall and straight, with his arms by his sides and his legs close together facing the front, taking it all in wide eyed for just a second. Then he fell off the board backwards with one leg straight out in front and the other pointing at the sky perpendicular to it in perfect, horizontal, marching position while the board spat off out in front from under him like a darting tadpole. When he surfaced with the board pulling at his leg under the strain of the elongated leg rope, he was beaming. Billie had seen the whole thing and was leaping about in hysterics.

Riley's best wave that day came unexpectedly. It was huge. It had already broken a long way out the back beyond where he and Billie were. Out of fear he turned away from the towering wall of churning water coming at him and held on. It picked him up as it steamed past. He held on as he thumped along lying down, buried in the whitewash and sucking in drafts of foamy air. All of a sudden he shot forward out of it, rushing across the surface of the water and in a few moments he had a leg up in front of him and his hands were gripping the rails trying to find his balance. His other leg was bent behind him, knee still on the deck. He steadied himself and then slowly stood up and let go of the rails and extended his arms out by his sides, watching the front of his board. He kept going. For the first time he felt balanced on his feet. He was riding. He dared to look over at Billie shooting along next to him with his arms raised in the air cheering and they rode the wave together all the way in until their single fins bit into the sand and tossed them off onto the beach.

6.

In Winter when it rained, the rain fell hard. In big ripe drops. Furiously. As if letting out all of the frustrations of the barren Summer and Autumn months. It rattled so loudly on their tin roof at times that they could barely hear each other speak. The water rushed down their street into the drains and worked its way down to pour out of the storm water pipes onto the beach in thick torrents, cutting a deep channel into the sand to the water's edge.

In breaks between the downpours, Billie and his sister Emma grabbed their raincoats off the hook by the front door and disappeared into the bushland to watch the water running down the creeks, dam them up with mud and rocks and drag long branches across as bridges.

Sometimes, when the wind was roaring through the trees and they could hear the crash and rumble of the sea borne on the westerly wind, Billie's family would rug up and go down to the beach. They'd lean into the wind with their arms out and let it whip their coats and jumpers, sting their faces and layer fine grains of sand through their hair and ears and become part of the elements, alive and exuberant. They'd watch the stormy surf roll in through narrow slits and jump at the seagulls hovering into the wind low off the ground and patrol the high tide line for presents from the sea. Foraging amongst the tufts of seaweed flung onto the beach by the storm, they'd amass in their pockets and upturned jumper hems, floats and driftwood sticks weathered white, spiral cone shells, fragile purple urchins and smooth bits of broken green glass. Every now and then a good length of rope would show up. Billie would disentangle it and cut off the hard crusted barnacles with his pocketknife and walk home at a fast step with it coiled over his shoulder to show his father when he returned from Up North.

Some days Billie climbed the lookout tree to watch the storms roll past and feel it swaying in the strong wind, fluting through the pine needles. He had to pick his moment carefully though. If he was caught out there'd be hell to pay.

Surfing was put on hold when Winter set in. Neither of the boys had a wetsuit and the water was flat out too cold without one. They tried once in long sleeved woollen footy jumpers but barely made it out the back before their limbs became numb and useless and it was all they could do to belly board back to shore, shiver their way up the beach to wrestle off the soggy jumpers and fumble about their dry clothes with uncooperative fingers stiff with cold, mumbling incomprehensibly out of frozen faces. Besides, the swell was often pretty big in Winter as the cold fronts came through and blasted the coast with northwesterly squalls and the churning sea lashed and ate away the sand, violently pulling the beach into the water in hungry bites.

*   *   *

Winter was the footy season. Aussie Rules was footy. Footy was everywhere.

In the lead up to the big game on Saturday, there would be dobs on the oval at lunchtime between two packs a good kick's distance apart. Each pack would leap and clamber over each other as the ball sailed through the air – the bigger boys competing to catch the ball outright, arms extended above their heads and the smaller boys roving around the base of the surging pack to scramble for it if it went to ground. On Tuesdays and Thursdays there was after school training. Rain or shine, they'd tie up the laces of their boots, push their socks down to their ankles and scuttle out of the change room in the colours of their favourite club teams. Sometimes at the end they'd have a scratch match. That made the rest of the training all worthwhile. The coach ran them hard. Bent over, hands on hips, they'd suck sharp shallow breaths in the cold air of the fading day, steam rising off hot skin.

Outside of training there were random rendezvous at the local park and a thriving footy card economy. Cards showing club players in action, sold in packets with a stick of leathery chewing gum at the local deli in exchange for hard earned pocket money, were tenaciously bartered.

Sons usually barracked for the same club as their fathers out of blind filial solidarity or because the father had made it abundantly clear that none of his offspring would be supporting a rival club as long as they lived under his roof.

The Under 14's game on Saturday morning was man-to-man time between father and son. Sons sat next to their fathers in the front of the car in tracksuits and playing gear on the way to the game and were served with a raft of tips on the upcoming game punctuated by stories of the many and varied on field successes and moments of glory of their fathers in their earlier days. Sons were old enough to understand that adults didn't always speak the truth and still young enough not to follow suit.

A row of fathers lined the side lines for the game and proudly watched their sons run out of the change room under a chatter of sprigs and participated in their son's triumphs and failures to varying degrees. Some stood quietly by with an arm bent across a rounded belly and watched each and every second of their son's involvement in the game. Others tapped into some latent primordial instinct and paced up and down the side line bellowing instructions. Referees copped it and the occasional unpleasant relay of insults between parents of opposite teams on a shared side line bubbled and burst. Each time his son did something good out on the field, the father pushed his chest out a little and felt fit and lithe on the side line and attributed it to genetics enhanced through the one-on-one tuition he'd given him over the years. The father would grin proudly around and nod if he caught an eye.

Simon Morten's Mum never missed a game. Simon's Dad lived overseas. Something had happened but Simon didn't let on. Billie got a lift with Simon and Mrs Morten sometimes when his Dad was Up North. Kill 'em boys, she always said as they pulled up at the game.

She was a rotund lady with curly brown hair, a chubby flat face with a thin shadow of dark hair above her upper lip and a few lonely twisting whiskers sprouting in and around the mole on her fleshy chin. Simon would shoot out of the car before it had come to a standstill and belt across the field at an embarrassed gallop and Billie would follow suit while she worked her bulk slowly out of the car. She'd pull her striped deck chair out of the boot and waddle across the oval in a grey coat to set up on the side line and there she'd sit throughout the game, clutching a bottle of coke with a fag drooping out of the side of her mouth and let rip a series of screeches at a raucous grating pitch revealing a competent, albeit biased, grasp of the game: "put yer glasses on ref" or "who's payin yah", "in the back yer wanker", "holding the ball", "free fuckin kick", "bin 'im" and others and all the while leaning back in her creaking overloaded chair with her short stubby legs out in front, crossed at the ankles, petite desert boots hovering just above the grass. She was loud and gruff and the boys tried to keep their distance.

During the intervals, fathers formed an outer ring around the huddle of boys tucking into cut up oranges and listening with bowed heads to one of the fathers passionately detail the pros and cons of their game to date and map out the way forward for the next quarter with his clipboard folder tucked deep and authoritatively into his armpit.

Riley and Billie's team came away more battered and bruised than usual from the games against teams from the schools on the other side of the city. They were made up of 13 and 14 year old men with dark facial re-growth who had completed their development into thickset torsos and hairy legs to become indistinguishable in size from their fathers on the side line and called out to each other on the field in intimidating unfaltering baritones. Riley and Billie's team – with their spotty faces, sprouting errant whiskers, untrustworthy voice boxes and lean frames with years of fleshing out to come, filed anxiously past them to shake hands before the start of play and were physically overpowered in every aspect of the game.

On wet windy days, the leather ball became sodden and heavy minutes after the start of play and would twist and shinny across the wet grass in front of the pack of lunging boys like a slippery eel. The meagre number of goals kicked by Riley and Billie's team were mostly scored from lucky grubbers sliding through the posts at ground height. Their dripping coach tore his hair out at the near complete absence of footy as it should be played with its flowing hand passes and players running into open spaces to cleanly mark nicely weighted kicks. The boys finished those matches cold and muddy with stubbed fingers and corked thighs and hobbled about on Sundays as the bruising settled in.

7.

The end of the footy season coincided with the return of warmer water at the beach. The furious southerly storms eased off. The Spring days became longer, sunnier, sweeter. Raincoats and beanies were put away. Grey school trousers were mothballed until the following year when cuffs and waists would be got at with quick unpicks and sewing machines to extract another year's wear.

Spring meant athletics. At the start of third term a rectangle of straight lanes was marked out on the oval in white paint for the 100m and a track with circular lanes wound around the oval for the longer distances. A stack of hurdles with white and black wooden bars and rusted green metal legs grazed off to one side and a truck brought a pile of fresh yellow sand for the long-jump pit. In the afternoon after classes, kids ran around on the grass and larked about and practised for the big school sports day. Some sneezed and sniffed back trickling mucous and rubbed itchy eyes bloodshot red with their fists, tickled crazy by hay fever from the cut grass and the Jacaranda trees and most pretended for as long as possible not to see parents waiting in cars.

The last school term was an inevitable slide towards the Christmas holidays. There was nothing that even came close to the excitement of those endlessly long hot Summer days.

First term was hard going because it signalled the end of those barefoot carefree days. In second term they were way too far away to be worth thinking about. But by third term they were real. The only bumps on the way to the holidays were school lessons and the end of year tests. Billie and Riley got by around the middle of the pack. Riley got a hard time sometimes from his parents about his grades and from time to time when they sat in the sofa after dinner, he overheard them talking together in low voices about getting him some extra tuition in later years if things didn't improve.

Billie and Riley copied things down off the blackboard in their exercise books like everyone else but their minds were often elsewhere and especially so on the days when they had got up at dawn to go surfing before school. They would try to get tables by the window where they could look outside and feel if the wind still had some east in it and maybe catch a sniff of the sea if it was blowing the other way.

Those were also the days when a gush of salt water would run out of their noses without warning. Riley was a bit embarrassed when it happened to him but Billie didn't care and laughed and bent over and let it run and then put a finger to each of his nostrils one after the other and blew them clear and admired the wet patch below. Nose drips were a reminder of the sunrise and the clear ridged sand below the blue water and the waves they had ridden early that morning while most of the city slept. It reminded them that they and the small pack of other surfers who had gravitated towards each other in the schoolyard over the year did something exhilarating that most of the other kids didn't.

* * *

The Christmas holidays at the end of that first high school year were by far the best holidays Riley had ever had. There were many firsts those holidays. They were the holidays when he and Billie surfed their first real reef. They had ridden their bikes up past The Point and paddled out a few times but they weren't real reef breaks like the ones Down South.

In the lead up to asking his parents if he could go with Billie and his family, Riley's behaviour was exemplary. Even Riley's Mum, who exacted high standards as a matter of course, became a little uneasy wondering what was coming. He spoke to his Dad about the trip first and looked away when he thought he saw a slight hint of hurt in his smiling eyes.

In the end it really wasn't a struggle at all and the only thing was that he had to be back for their family holiday to The Island. He did wonder whether he might have got away with less ground work but as he sat next to Billie, the backs of his legs sticking to the vinyl, bouncing and squeaking down the highway on a hot blue day in January with Joe Saunders' big hands on the wheel of the white Kingswood station wagon and the rest of Billie's family spread out across the car, their boards and bikes tied down in the low metal cage on the roof and the boot jammed with stuff all the way to the ceiling, he knew he'd have done a lot more if he'd had to.

Billie got his first surfing magazine for Christmas. Over the two weeks Down South, he and Riley pored over it back at the caravan park, reading and rereading it until they knew its tattered pages off by heart. They lay about in the shade of a peppermint tree and tried to hold the pages down against the wind and ran after the occasional fold that worked its way loose from the staples in the spine. They'd stare at the photos of waves, pinching the size of the surfer between their forefinger and thumb and measuring him against size of the wave and try to get their heads around the tube riding sequences. Getting inside the barrel of the wave was, at that time, even for Billie, unfathomable, unattainable, something they didn't even think about when they were out in the water let alone consider attempting. In later reads they soaked up the advertising for clothing and wetsuits, wax and leg ropes and turned over the pages with shapely girls barely in their bikinis less and less quickly. They learned that there were competitions in which people won money for going surfing.

But it was the travel articles that they drooled over. They came to know them word-by-word and still read and reread them. They discovered, with a ballooning excitement, that not only were there waves Down South but there were waves beyond Down South. There were waves to surf in a place called Noosa which was apparently Over East and even people surfing in other countries. The magazine showed black and white pictures of waves breaking in cold water alongside the desert in Mexico wherever that was and islands somewhere where empty waves peeled behind brown skinned local people squatting on the ground with no clothes and broken stained teeth smiles. The articles hinted at the endless discoveries of new surfing breaks still to be made even in the places they described. For Billie and Riley the complex and confusing world made up of countless countries and cultures and languages which they had struggled to comprehend in Social Studies and Geography classes, was suddenly unified by the millions of kilometres of coastline which it comprised. There were bays, peninsulas, points and river mouths and everything in between and the possibilities were endless.

From then Billie and Riley started to dream of exploring for surf on the coasts of the world and stepped up for action straight away by pioneering the rocky shores around the popular bay Down South.

The caravan park gave access a short distance down a dirt road to a large sweeping bay which horseshoed around from one point to the other and, in between them, housed a sprinkling of fibro fishing shacks nestled low in amongst the trees and bushes. The northern point was a headland made up of huge granite rocks which tumbled down to the water's edge. Tucked inside the headland, falling into the sea, was a wall of red rocks stacked on each other and on some afternoons, when they glowed red from the falling sun, the Saunders and Riley picked their way over to them with rods and buckets to have a go at reeling in herring. The point on the southern side of the Bay reached a long white limestone arm further out into the ocean and ended in a jumble of giant granite boulders strewn about off its western tip constantly under siege from the thumping swell marching in.

In the mornings if it was too early for the family, the boys pedalled their way from the caravan park and discovered the predictability of reef breaks. Their surfing leapt forward. Billie coached Riley into almost doing a cutback. They watched older surfers glide along the bigger waves out at the limestone point as they sat on their boards waiting for the waves to roll further inside The Bay to their reef. No one attempted the waves off the point on the north side.

On flat days Billie's Dad headed out with a screwdriver and a mask for abalone. The boys had to keep them in the shade in a bucket of salt water and clean them back at the caravan park. There were black periwinkles and cone shaped shellfish to prize off the rocks and poke at, a calm beach in the middle of The Bay for swimming and combing. A trickling creek wound its way inland through the peppermint trees to a stack of boulders piled forty feet high for climbing. Beyond the points the possibilities were endless and the days passed in a whir of activity before the family gathered around the kerosene lamp at night, swatted at bugs intrigued by the light and ate a big dinner to make up for the light pecking they got in during the day.

After dinner the boys and Billie's sister Emma fell in with the other kids circling the caravan park. They buzzed around from place to place until dark – on foot, on bikes, up trees, under bushes, amid squeals and protests and flying dust.

On the last night of the holiday Billie had his first kiss and feel. He wasn't IT to begin with but one of the mullet haired older Gibson twins who was had found him pretty early on hiding up a peppermint tree and told him, looking up from the base of the tree, that he'd found him and if he came down he wouldn't thump him but if he didn't, he bloody well would. Billie stayed where he was until the Gibson brother had got a fair way up the tree and then launched himself off the branch onto the ground and got chased down fifty metres down the track with a hefty thump on the arm. They split up and Billie shot off down to the bush end of the caravan park to catch some others.

Bernadette Shaw was the same age as Billie but a whole lot more enlightened physically. When they stood back to back early on in the holidays she was two inches taller than him, whether or not he tilted his head. Her dark brown hair was almost permanently bunched up in a ponytail. It bounced as she ran. Her skin was fair and lightly freckled. She was one of the dominating members of the pack at the caravan park. She snorted when she laughed. Everyone called her Boonie.

When Billie found her at dusk on that last day of the holidays she'd burrowed deep into a thick bush and lay there curled up in a ball on her side amongst the fallen leaves.

Got yah, Billie said.
She sat up and parted the foliage in front of her face: No you haven't, gotta come and get me.
He crawled through on his hands and knees and brushed aside low branches and, as he neared her, she squirmed around to

the other side of the trunk of the bush. When he got close to the trunk, she smiled coyly and asked him: Do you like me? Get out of it, he said shrugging it off and kept worming his way in.

D'yah wanna kiss me? She asked sliding back a bit across the dry leaves on her backside with her legs, covered in dirt and scratches, out in front as he came towards her.

Na'ahh... you gotta be kidding, he said, rounding the trunk on his knees.

Can't catch me, she said pushing herself into a more open area at the other edge of the bush.

Yep I can, he said sliding over and lunging for her to get it all over and done with.

As he reached out she grabbed his arm and dragged him to her across the dirt and the next thing he knew he was twisted low on his side below her and her face was plummeting down towards him, growing larger and larger, lips quivering open, flecks of food caught in her bracered teeth. Taken by surprise and in unfamiliar territory he froze and, all of a sudden, she had planted her face down onto his through the branches with a giggle and his lips became wet from her mouth and pretty soon her tongue was thrashing and flapping about wildly inside his mouth like a freshly caught fish on a dry deck, hunting around for something in there and her braces were biting and grating his lips as an entanglement of branches and leaves poked into his ear and cheek. Then she had one hand planted behind his head forcing it towards her while the other grabbed his wrist and pulled his hand up onto her hormonally charged chest. She shoved it under her t-shirt onto her bare skin and Billie's resisting palm felt a mound of clammy soft skin with a hard tweaked peak. With his mouth sealed off by her manic pashing, his whole head being devoured, snatching at thin strips of cold air through blocked nostrils snotty from a fading cold, all he did down there in that bush with Boonie Shaw was try to survive.

8.

The Summer holidays finally ended. The first day of Year 9 hit throat-lumpingly hard. Feet, wide and tough from months of shoelessness, cramped awkwardly again into black leather Clarkes and bodies into ill fitting grey uniforms. Structured classes and breaks timed to the minute by the bell replaced the spontaneous free-wheeling days.

* * *

How they came to be holed up in the dunes at the local beach one Saturday night a few weeks into first term, each propped up on an elbow lying on towels in the sand talking across a low open fire, was more taking advantage of an unexpected situation than a premeditated effort to deceive their parents, although they did have to pull the wool over their eyes a bit.

In the morning Billie and Riley had knocked about taking turns on Billie's skateboard in the cul de sac down the street. They had talked about staying over the night at one of their places and going surfing the next day. Later in the day Riley rode down the hill and skidded into the driveway at Billie's house.

I talked to Mum… you can stay at my house tonight if you want, Riley said happily as he sat down next to Billie.
Yeah, me too… you can stay here as well, Billie said.
Cool. Billie thought for a while.
Know what I'm thinking? He grinned.
Riley looked at Billie and was quiet for a few moments. It would be by miles the biggest swifty that he'd ever pulled and he had no idea what the consequences of being found out would be except that they'd be painful and probably pretty long lasting. But he didn't want to pike on his best friend. He looked at Billie sitting in the grass chewing a twig between his teeth with an expectant grin lighting up his face and said more confidently than he'd expected: Yep.

The corner deli had thick white walls pasted with posters advertising beaming people drinking cans of Coke beneath coconut palm trees in an idyllic tropical setting and a square jawed cowboy on horse back in Cuban boots, tan chaps and blue jeans, leaning his head towards his cupped hand as he lit up a cigarette out on the prairie in the late afternoon. Bleached and tattered flyers for upcoming and past rock concerts flapped here and there and, lower down towards the back near the bins, the walls were covered in graffiti, blazing with the colourful swirls and pictures of the tags of the various artists. A few hastily scrawled messages had also been left: "Jeff was 'ere", "Daza 4 Kylie 4 eva", "ACDC rules" and "Mitch is a nob". A rainbow of faded plastic tassels hung down across the entrance to the shop and rustled in the opening under the light breeze.

Inside it was cool and dark and dusty like a cellar. Wide floorboards were worn smooth from decades of traffic. They creaked and bowed into deeper undulating grooves inside the doorway and in front of the high wooden counter. On the floor next to the counter were piles of daily newspapers and on the wall behind, rows of shiny cigarette boxes beckoned. High shelving ran down the middle of the shop forming two aisles for day to day essentials. A wall of fridges squatted squarely at the back with milk and ice cream, fruit juices and frozen peas. Overhead a fan turned slowly from the gentle push of the breeze through old frosted louvres rusted permanently open high up near the ceiling.

A low table ran along one wall just inside the doorway in full view. Day in day out wide-eyed drooling kids shifted on their feet procrastinating with tingling cheeks in front of jars and jars of lollies cloudy and smudged from heavy pawing. Mint leaves, cobbers, fads, metro gums, snakes, redskins, raspberries, pastel coloured musk sticks, milk bottles and licorice bullets priced between 1 and 5 cents stood side by side. At the end of the table was a big basket of mixed lollies bulging in small white paper bags sealed off with twisted corners going for 35 cents each.

For as long as most people could remember Mr Thomas had presided over the small shop from behind the cash register on the counter in his self-prescribed uniform of white shirt and khaki shorts with long white socks pulled taut and folded down high on his calves. He was bald and peered at his customers with a stern smile through the smeared lenses of his round spectacles set permanently on the bridge of his bulbous nose. He never missed a trick. From time to time a new kid in the neighbourhood would try to smuggle something out under his shirt. Mr Thomas would lean down and pull a long whip out from under the counter and walk slowly out and whistle at the kid scurrying off down the street. The kid would skulk back and the stolen item or the money for it would be tossed at Mr Thomas' feet from a safe distance away and that'd be the last time the kid ever tried it on.

Billie was standing out the front in the shade with a green canvas bag slung on his shoulder and their two surfboards propped up against the wall next to him, hunting around with a finger in his nostril when Riley showed up.

Geez, been waiting for a while, he said pulling his finger out of his nose and grinning.
Yeah I know… Mum made me stay at the house for ages to wait for her cake to come out of the oven to give to your Mum for having me over. It's in my bag.
What is it?
Banana cake… it's huge, weighs a ton.
We'll have to keep it with us, we can't go back to my place now… I've already said I was going to yours.
Yeah I know.
Can you wait here with the boards while I go inside and get a few other things?
Yeah no worries.
Got 'ny dosh? Billie asked.
Yeah, a bit… here, Riley said as he dug into his jeans pocket and handed over three dollars twenty.
Thanks, I've got three bucks as well… that'll be heaps.

While Billie went in, Riley hovered outside by the boards, shifting from leg to leg, hoping that he didn't see anyone that he knew. Two bent old ladies dressed in spanking white teetered towards him along the footpath pulling their two-wheeled trolleys on their way from the local bowling green. They broke their loud conversation about people they knew to cast a sharp look from under blue ribboned white hats at Riley and the surfboards and issue a few tisk tisks that made him feel that he was not good for much. They shuffled past and settled back into their lively gossip. Three younger kids came out of the shop with bowed heads, intently studying their bags of mixed lollies. Catching sight of Riley, one of them asked how the surf was. Riley told him too hurriedly that it had been ok.

Thanks Mr Thomas, Billie said as he walked out cradling their supplies.
What'd yah get?
Meat pies, a box of Coco Pops for brekky, lemonade... and mixed lollies. Here's some change.
Thanks... should we get milk for the Coco Pops?
Nah, we haven't got 'ny bowls, we'll just eat 'em dry.
Ok.
Carn, let's go, the sun's almost down.

Riley got on his bike and Billie tucked a board under each arm and walked alongside. They pulled their hats down low and took a different route to the beach in the diminishing light. When they reached the top of the sand dunes, the sea shimmered in greys and silvers. A wide bank of low clouds merged with the horizon. Aside from a few fishermen just visible on the reef to the north, immersed in the water up to their thighs, patiently holding their rods like flag bearers at the head of a march, the beach was deserted.

They debated whether to base themselves up in the dunes or down on the beach and in the end chose an elevated hollow in a dune at the edge of the beach away from the track and settled down with their gear. With the coming of darkness, as they sat with their arms around their legs looking out into the blackness and watching the lights come to life around the sweep of the coast far off to the south, they each had a few moments of silent misgiving. Neither of them let on.

Billie flicked on his torch and shone it into Riley's face: Carn let's look for some sticks for a fire.
Yeah good idea, Riley replied with his hand up to the light and then dug around in his bag for his torch.

They found bits of stray driftwood on the beach and dragged ragged branches from the dunes back to their hollow and piled them up. After a few unsuccessful attempts, Riley took the inside packet out of the Coco Pops box, tore the cardboard into strips and piled leaves and dry twigs on it and eventually they got a fire going. It cast a comforting glow on their sandy hollow. They put their lukewarm pies on a piece of flat driftwood near the flames and hooked into Riley's Mum's banana cake. The pies were only slightly warmer on one side when they picked them up after making a good dent in the cake but they tasted good anyway. Out to sea, the lighthouse on the island flashed rhythmically. They made out the lights of a tanker and watched it heading out to the open ocean bound for somewhere. They stared at the flames and talked across the fire, dipping into bags of mixed lollies.

When the fire had died down and their backs felt cold and damp from the creeping dew borne on the light wind off the land, they hunted for more wood under torchlight and piled it on the fire. They spread their towels out on the sand close by and lay down. The reinvigorated flames flicked and swayed. The sky above was mostly clear now. As they lay on their backs looking up, Billie pointed out where the Southern Cross was and explained how to find south by using the long axis of the cross and an imaginary line between the pointers like he had learnt from his Dad camping in the forests in the south.

Sometime into the night, Billie felt a weight on his legs and shifted them unconsciously in his sleep to get comfortable. The weight stayed. He became aware of a sensation of movement. He opened his eyes and blinked for a few seconds, then lifted his head and, in the dim glow of the remains of the fire, saw the thick muscular brown length sliding and swerving slowly and deliberately up and over his legs, its small sinister head propping and swaying eerily from side to side in the semi darkness.

It was probably exactly what he should not have done in that situation. He should have just stayed still and quiet and held his breath without moving. Waited for the snake to slip away over the sand and back into the bush. Instead Billie sat up and let out a blood curdling high-pitched scream and then madly started to back peddle across the sand sliding on his backside in a state of terrified panic. With the sudden movement the brown snake stopped slithering, raised its head and turned towards Billie, flicking its tongue and looking through him with beady eyes as old and as dark as the holes in the night sky overhead. Billie froze and felt a sense of inversion as all his blood rushed to his tingling head and tumbled into an all consuming powerless dread.

What... what is it Billie? Riley said and sat up and looked over bleary eyed. As he took in the scene unfolding across the fire's glow, said quietly: Oh shit!
Billie's whole body had seized up and was shaking feverously, his terrified eyes fixed on the thick brown snake, paralysed save for his trembling lips. Barely audibly he gasped: oh no... oh no.
In a flash of movement too fast to see, the snake swung back and struck at Billie's foot. Billie felt the impact and yelled and snapped out of his stupor and, as the snake recoiled, he kicked out madly and flung it onto the sand, scrambled free and shot down the dune to the beach in a stumbling whir without looking back.

Down near the water's edge, Billie crumpled into a ball in the darkness, whimpering. When Riley caught up, he leant over him and asked: Shit, you oright?... Did it get you?
Yeah... got me on the boot, I felt it snap... I'm gunna die aren't I? I'm gunna bloody die, Billie blubbered looking up at Riley, tears running down his cheeks.
Riley looked at his friend nervously: Nah you'll be right.
How do yah know?
Maybe let's check your shoe.
Billie felt his shoe and then took it off and inspected it more

closely with his fingers to see if he could make out any holes.
Take your sock off and we'll look at your foot, Riley said.
Billie, still shaking, clumsily took his sock off and lifted his foot up towards his face with both his hands.
Can't see a bloody thing, he sniffed and put it down.
Riley knelt down and peered at it: It's too dark to tell... do you feel ok?
Dunno.
I'll go back and get a torch, Riley said.
Back up there in the dark? You gotta be kidding.
Yeah but if it bit you we gotta go quick, brown snakes are deadly... hang on a sec, I've still got the matches in my pocket.

Riley pulled the box out and struck a match into Billie's hands cupped over his foot and peered down. They did it many times until the box was empty. After the last match in the box had gone out Billie fell back hard onto the sand and lay there still with his arms by his sides.

Billie... Billie?
Nothing. Riley became more animated, Shit... Billie... can you hear me?
Billie! Riley yelled and shook him.
Sshh, I'm trying to get some sleep here, Billie said softly and opened one eye and grinned.
Yah bastard, had me going there, Riley thumped him on the arm and sat down on the sand.
Bloody hell that was full on eh, Billie said propping himself up on his elbows.
That snake was huge... it was way longer than you.
I know, it was pretty heavy on my legs, that's what woke me

up… man I was scared… freaked out a bit didn't I?
Yeah a bit… I would've too, Riley said.
Shoulda stayed still and quiet… d'yah reckon it could follow us down here?
Dunno, geez… maybe.

They were both quiet for a few moments, thinking about calling it quits and taking the punishment but they kept quiet, neither of them wanting to be the first to suggest it.

Maybe we should dig a moat in the sand around us? Billie suggested.

On their knees they scooped out handfuls of sand as deep as their outstretched arms in a circle around them in the cold damp sand just back from the water's edge. It took them ages but it was good to have something to take their minds off the snake and the exercise kept the cool of the night at bay. When they had finished digging, they sat listening to the crack and wash of the waves, making out the whitewash rolling in amid the blackness of the ocean. Every now and then one of them would turn and peer behind. There was no way they were going to fall back to sleep.

They stayed like that on their waterless moated mound until the sky began to lighten. The darkness gave way, at first almost imperceptibly and then steadily, to ever lighter greys until soft pastels heralded the rising sun. Soon the ocean mirrored the morning sky. Small swell lines pushed in over the deeper water to break on the shallow sand banks. Hard damp low tide sand stretched down from their refuge to the water's edge where a couple of seagulls hovered on single legs and preened and screeched at each other with their wings fanned out.

Looks pretty fun out there, Riley said.
Yeah, I know... our stuff's still up on the dune... d'yah reckon the snake's gone?
Dunno... probly. Let's go look.

They ran across the beach and stopped at the base of the dune cautiously and then trudged slowly up through the deep sand. Where the fire had been there was a pool of ash and bits of charcoaled wood scattered here and there. Their things were as they had hastily abandoned them the night before. Riley's bag lay open in the sand. He picked his way over to it tentatively and, in a single movement grabbed the tip of one corner of the bag and flung it away. He flung it by the corner two more times before he was satisfied that all was clear and shouldered it. They kicked sand over the remains of the fire, grabbed their boards and other things and walked back down.

The beach was still empty. Billie pulled the Coco Pops out of his bag and they face planted into cupped handfuls while the sun slowly appeared over the top of the hills behind them in the east. When it had brought the last part of the ocean, where the water met the shore, out of the shadows and into its soft clear light, they waded out side by side into the sea.

9.

By late March, news starved papers had endlessly harped on about the late heat wave and the cyclone. They had written about broken records and pressure cookers and jigged and re-jigged the statistics until they'd exhausted all the angles.

It had been over forty degrees for a week by Saturday. On the first day Billie's family's thin walled house had heated up uncomfortably and with each subsequent day the temperature inside had steadily climbed. Inside the air was thick and hot. Usually they'd open all of the doors and windows in the late morning to allow the cool sea breeze to march in and blast the hot air away but for the last week the breeze hadn't shown up at all. Instead a gusty easterly rushed the heat all the way from the inland desert furnace. It was sweltering in the daytime and not much different at night. They barely slept and tossed and turned in bed, kicking off hot clinging sheets to lie spread eagled on their backs with sweat pooling in the hollows of their throats and in the undulations of their torsos.

Sleep deprived tempers were frayed and flared up with little urging in the heat. They stayed indoors out of the sun and the kids snipped and snapped at each other all morning until a fight broke out between Billie and his usually passive sister concerning the last Anzac biscuit which disintegrated in the struggle. Warned, they lay down on their backs on the wooden floor in the living room with books, heads on pillows and the old ceiling fan ticking overhead. They dragged damp face washers over their stomachs and faces and sucked on homemade lemon icy poles while fat blowflies zigzagged around the room and collided with the windowpanes.

Outside, the birds were silent and still and dogs lay low, sprawled out on their flanks panting on porches, under houses, wherever they could find shade. Small black cicadas still flitted about but even their screech lacked conviction. Saturday papers stayed where they'd been flung by the paper man at the crack of dawn. Dry tree branches and lifeless bushes hung defeated, buffeted about by the hot wind, breaking off now and again, adding more fuel to the growing pyre of dead leaves and twigs and brittle yellowed grass. The sun-scorched land baked and cracked and died.

It was still hot later in the afternoon when Riley turned up on his bike dripping with sweat just as Billie's family were getting ready to head off to the beach. He dropped his bike on the front lawn and he and Billie set off ahead of the others, carrying their boards down the street and along the bush track to the beach.

They paused at the top of the dunes. Out to sea, a straight-topped wall of dark cloud hovered low in the sky just above the horizon. The water was full of people all the way down the sweep of the beach to the south and up to The Point in the other direction. Escaping the heat. With periodic regularity long lines of shoulder high swell were coming through. They looked somehow different. Longer. More powerful. Swinging down the beach from the north. Billie and Riley dashed across the hot sand and waded out into the water. Billie stopped and lay on his back in the shallows for a while to let the cool salt water wash over him.

Out the back a small pack of surfers waited. Two old guys with deep creased faces were looking out to sea to the west, squinting into the glare, sitting astride their big Malibu boards, bobbing in the ocean waiting for the next set: First swell from the nor'west for as long as I can remember.
Must be coming from that cyclone Up North.
Swell's got some push for its size.
Yeah... Point looks good on the tide.
There's a few... pretty packed up there but... here's a good one, wanna go?
Or'right.

The boys watched as one of the old guys slid down in sitting position towards the bottom of his board. As the board protruded further out of the water with his shift in weight, he reached up and grabbed the rail towards the front and, paddling his legs under water, swung the board around to face the shore. He lay down as the wave loomed up behind him and, after a few easy paddles, stood up and set his course along the face, putting his arm out down the line to touch the steep wall next to him. His fingers left a light trail of white across the translucent greens and golds of the wave as it curled just behind him, illuminated from behind by the afternoon sun.

The other old guy with the dark moustache took the next one in the set and quickly danced up to the front of his board where he stayed for the whole ride – upright, knees bent forward, toes hanging over the front of the board and his arms splayed wide beside him like a tightrope walker, the rest of his long board biting into the face of the wave behind him and balanced in an unlikely equilibrium. Hoots of encouragement came from the small pack as he slid along and a small chipped smile broke out from underneath the bushy hedging above his top lip.

Billie and Riley sat inside the pack closer to shore. Far enough out to be able to get out of the way of people riding the bigger waves and close enough in to paddle onto the smaller ones the pack was mostly letting go. They caught waves into shore, sometimes ending up near Billie's family playing in the shallow water in close. Billie's Dad held Little Tom by outstretched arms. He looked down in wonder at the sea swirling up around his little legs and giggled as he was lifted up above the water in the bigger surges washing up the beach.

As the sun drifted down towards the sea in the later afternoon, a cloud haze advanced from the west and settled over it like a sheer curtain, robbing it of its glare and sting, bathing the sky and the ocean in a wash of milky pinks and oranges as if it was the tropics. The low dark band of cloud was still visible just above the horizon away off in the distance. Billie was sitting on his board out the back with one of the two old guys and two other blokes on smaller boards, tired and thirsty from the hours in the water. He hadn't had a ride for a while. The old guy with the moustache like Dennis Lillee's turned to him: What's yer name son?

Billie Saunders, Billie replied nervously.

You from round 'ere?

Yeah, my house is behind the dunes, Billie told him.

Who's yah mate?

That's Riley.

You's are good kids in the water, 'spectful an everythin.

After a pause he added: Jim and I been surfin for 20 years now... there was barely anyone out 'ere... used to surf The Point at this time of year by ourselves all the time... water's a bit busier now... but we reck'n it's better for making new mates, he smiled.

Everyone calls me 'Bomber', he said holding his hand out to Billie. Billie reached out and shook it firmly like his Dad had told him, trying not to topple off his board and got a good close up of his blue eyes and nicotine stained front teeth.

From the northwest a line of swell appeared, visible in the near distance from its crest which was higher and darker than the ocean before and after it. As it bent in towards them, it looked like it was another one of those long ones that started peeling further up on the sand bank which the good guys waited for. Bomber grinned and said: How 'bout showing us all how to ride this little one, son?

Really? Billie asked.

Yeah, go... better not miss it or it'll be the last wave I eva give yer.

Billie paddled out towards it and then turned around and stroked hard to pick up the wave's momentum, just managing to scramble onto it. He pushed up with his hands to get to his feet and dropped down the face, his toes just making contact with the board underneath. At the bottom he turned his board out of the wave's hollow trough to ride the wall bending around towards him, green and groomed by the light wind off the land and as tall as the top of his head. He rollered down the line, board shorts flapping on his skinny thighs and when the wave finally petered out, he fell off backwards and lay on his back in the water. The ride was a slow motion blur of intensity, the details of which he could not really recall except seeing Riley kicking to get out of his way and grinning at him from the top of the wave as he flew past below. It was his best ride ever.

Riley caught a small wave on his belly and washed in next to Billie: That was a good one.
Thanks, Billie grinned.
Shit a brick what's that? Riley exclaimed, looking past Billie.
What?
That, Riley said pointing at a spiral of smoke billowing up into the sky behind the dunes.
Bloody hell, Billie cried and looked over towards his family.

They were staring up at it and in a matter of seconds the whole beach had turned to look at it, transfixed by its exponentially increasing size and, for a suspended moment, all was quiet and motionless except for the ebb and flow of the sea. Then there was a flurry of activity as wild armed parents rounded up offspring and stuffed towels, beach umbrellas, balls, surf craft, buckets and spades under their arms; young couples pulled apart and bikinis were quickly retied and straightened; and most of the people on the beach beat a hasty retreat. A bunch of the surfers scattered up and down the beach stayed where they were alternating between looking out to sea for an approaching set and back over the dunes to where the bush fire was escalating.

The boys went in and ran across the beach.

I'll check things out, see what I can do and come back with the car, Joe said.
It's already out of control Joe, we should all just stay here where it's safe, Kath said.
It'll be ok.
Look at it, it's not worth it.
Nothing's covered, we'll have to start all over again if it gets our place, right from scratch, he said quietly.
Doesn't matter.
Yeah it does, he said and hugged her and walked away.

Billie watched his Dad's long sure strides across the beach amongst the tide of other people leaving. He looked over at his mother and she shook her head.

They sat on the beach for a while in a close pack as the daylight continued to fade, belittled by the smoke towering overhead. Tight-chested and coughing. Towels and t-shirts held over their mouths and noses. Other families were huddled together on the beach. Pushed by the offshore wind, the fire's smoke now reached all the way out over the sea towards the horizon and painted the skyline in mushrooming swirls of ash grey with strokes of flame and dirty yellow and all of the colours in between as the bush and anything in the fire's path was torched. The wash of the rising ocean was overlaid by the crackling, hissing, exploding fire, calls and cries of people trying to help or run, dogs howling, cars screeching away to safety and the urgent sirens of fire trucks rushing forward to fight.

After a while, Billie's Mum held out a few crumpled dollar notes to Billie: I'll wait here with Little Tom and Emma, can you and Riley go up to the kiosk and bring us back some things to eat and drink... don't be long... come back along the water's edge.
Billie stood up and took the notes. As they started to walk off, she called out: Get some milk for Little Tom... Riley I think there is a phone box up there where you can try to call your parents. Use the change. Tell them you're with me and we're all safe on the beach.

When the boys returned, they put the hot chips down on the sand and ripped at the small hole in the newspaper they'd already scratched out on the way back. They talked quietly for a bit in the darkness, picking at the chips. Little Tom was tired and insisted on holding the cardboard milk box himself and some went down the spout into his mouth but most ended up rushing off down his chin. He rubbed his eyes and moaned and cried for a while. Billie's Mum rocked him to sleep in her arms under a towel and he'd not really had much fight left in him after his big afternoon stumbling through the deep footsteps in the soft sand at a toddling run and swinging from his parents' arms in the water. In time the others also drifted off to sleep on their sides wrapped in towels against the smoke and ash. Billie's Mum stayed sitting up against a rest she had carved out of the deeper damp sand, holding Little Tom.

At dawn Billie woke. He peered through the grey light. The other kids were strewn about still asleep on the beach. He blinked and looked over at his mother still sitting up holding Little Tom tightly. He raised his head slightly off the beach. She was gently shuddering and staring out to sea. There were tears on her worn face. He'd never seen her cry. Petrified and hollow, he knew the world was about to end.

* * *

The funeral was black and sombre and the sky poured down hard on the roof of the church. Billie couldn't talk or think or hear what anyone said. He wept and raged inside as the wet earth piled up and buried the shiny wood in mud and fled from the shovel when it was his turn and didn't stop running in the pouring rain until he got to the sea. His Dad had lost his shed and his life fighting for it. He hadn't just gone away Up North again. He'd gone for good and was never coming back and what the hell was he gunna do without him.

The days and weeks after were a blur. The weight slid off his Mum's already slim body and Emma wouldn't leave her room. Their faces were swollen and creased with sleeplessness and their eyes red from a sadness that reached all the way to the centre of the blackened earth. Little Tom cried all the time but was too small to understand why and that was harder still.

Billie moved in a hopeless stupor. His orphaned chest burned with pain and confusion and a hurt that he wanted to pin down on someone so badly that he almost started to believe in god so he could. Walking along the track to the beach through the charred bush was like walking through another world. Everything was burnt to powdery ash. The earth was stark, lunar, attended only by desolate charcoal trunked sentries. It smelt of soot and death. Lifeless and laid bare and eerily silent without the call of birds. It was as Billie felt.

Now when he looked out his window, he envied the Killyah kids next door. Least they were a proper family. Least they had a father.

Part II

10.

They rattled along the highway through the Nullabor in the far south of the continent. The land was immense and old and unchanged since the beginning of time. Here and there along the way signs with Aboriginal names promised places they couldn't see. Small green markers with white figures showing the diminishing distance to the next town bobbed up on the side of the road every so often, reassuring travellers out there in the middle of nowhere that their journey over the unchanging vastness was real and progressing. They'd driven for days and passed hundreds of the markers on the trip so far. A while after the straight road finally bent around towards the southeast, fences started to appear but there was no sign of any stock on the barren wasteland.

A pair of crows, glinting ink in the afternoon sun and pecking and tugging voraciously at the remains of some flat unrecognisable carcass splattered on the road, looked up as they approached and hopped aside at the last moment, annoyed at the inconvenience of the interruption. Then flapped back into the middle of the road after they had passed.

That day alone they'd passed a dozen kangaroos lying stiff and crumpled by the side of the road with their legs in the air and heads twisted back or missing. They were tragic casualties of the road which brought a little edible vegetation along its flanks from whatever dew or rain runoff was around and at the same time, high speed multi tonne missiles with schedules to meet. Like everyone else in the country, Will and Riley had grown up seeing kangaroos and wallabies dead on the side of roads and drifted past them more or less with passive immunity except when the pungent odour of decay from a decomposing carcass was sucked in through open windows as they passed.

All around the desolate land waited patiently. It would go on as it was and despite anything they or anyone else did and long after everyone had finished skittering across it.

How the hell could anyone live out here... you'd be so cracked and crusty and lonely... nearest neighbour would probly be a plane ride away, Riley said.
Yeah, it'd be tough... take a special kinda person... even if you could hack it... be hard to find a girl to stay with you out here. Riley took a swig from the water bottle: You know we were together for nearly five years, thought she was the one mate.
Yeah I know... you never told me what happened... k'ive the water, Will replied.
Riley handed the bottle over: Thomo saw her all over a guy at the races while I was Down South after Christmas... she

denied it at the start and wouldn't look me in the eye for a few weeks... then she said she'd just drunk a lot that day and it didn't mean anything... a few days later she said she wanted to split up.

To be with the other guy?

Nah, I heard she didn't get together with him, just wanted some time.

What did you say? Will asked returning the water.

Not much. Spose I couldn't believe it was happening... everything felt kinda upside down and I couldn't really talk. Thought I knew her. We'd been friends for ages at school even before we started going out.

Yeah I know what you mean... You know mate, she's pretty young... we're pretty young... twenty-five is pretty early to settle down... maybe she just needs to explore before things get too serious, Will said.

Yeah maybe... when things are good why look for change... there's plenty of people that stay together who don't have even half what we had.

Yeah dunno, Will said, guess people are all different... people also change... maybe some people have gotta just see what is out there, experience other things. It's a big world...

I dunno 'bout that mate, I get what you're saying but that sounds like just theory, like a good excuse for someone to have lots of sex, Riley laughed and said: not that there's anything wrong with that.

You'll meet someone mate, there's plenty of fish in the sea.

Don't like my chances much out here, Riley grinned.

Riley looked out his side window for a while and then said: It's good to be on this trip mate... we haven't done one for a while.

Yeah I know, it's good to be getting away... on the road... glad you called. I need to finish cleaning up my act... you know, get off the gear once and for all... get away from the scene. It's pretty bad up on the mines. It's rife. Guys've got nothing to do outside working and the work is pretty numbing. You're on the piss and mull every night and, before you know it, you've tried heavier stuff when you're already off your face and then you're trapped in the cycle. You need the work up there for the big bucks to support the cost of the gear and when you're up there the gear is everywhere and you can't get away from the bloody stuff.

Riley looked over at his friend. He was heavier and paler than he'd ever seen him. His belly was heavy with rings of folds. He was on the way to having man boobs like tubby little Anthony Barnes had had at school. The skin below his eyelids sagged in bruised bags and his eyes were hollow and drawn. He looked old and tired and pretty unwell.

What happened with you? Riley asked.
Will sighed and paused. Yeah... got caught up like the others in some heavy stuff. Haven't told many people... Life's really good when you're on it and pretty bad when you're not. Then it wasn't just when I was Up North, I started doing it back at home, got caught up in the scene with a couple of blokes from work. Some girls were into it... had some wild nights. Then back at work one week, got random drug tested on site and the bastards fired me same day. Said I was a good worker an' all but they had to let me go. Said if anything happened to me on site and they had those results from before and didn't do anything, they'd be screwed. That was a couple of months

ago now, before Chrissie. Didn't think so at the time but it was probly the best thing that could've happened to me really. It was only gunna be a matter of time before things went really pear-shaped somehow.

Shit I had no idea mate, you should've called, come Down South for a bit, Riley said.

Yeah I know. Tell you the truth, I was really tired for ages there and pretty ashamed of what I'd become.

What've you been doing since? Riley asked.

Not much, just hanging out at home. Sleeping a lot. Getting out for a surf every now and then. Trying bloody hard to stay clean. Was gunna start looking for work. After you called and I said I was in, I decided that I'd use this trip to fully clean myself up, you know, get right back into surfing, swap it for the bad stuff.

They drove along for a while in silence, looking out the windows at the desert.

Hey mate, it's cool if you're low on funds, I can cover us for a fair while, Riley offered.

Thanks, it's ok, still got some savings, mines pay pretty well… but 'preciate the offer.

More markers flashed by and the sun started its descent in earnest towards the horizon. The land was still unchanged since they'd started travelling at dawn.

Eventually they reached the sign for the small town where the turn off to The Point was supposed to be. Rusted windmills were scattered on the dust blown tawny plains and turned lazily under the breeze. There was no sign of any crop out there and it seemed that, no matter how many times the wheels of the windmills turned and how hard the farmers toiled and prayed, the land would never produce a grain of anything.

They entered town. A few buildings stood next to each other on one side of the road. Walls and roofs were covered in flax coloured dust. Aside from a truck which passed through from the other direction heading into the wide emptiness from where they'd come and a mangy black dog with white paws and exposed ribs skulking haggardly down the side of a building with its tongue hanging down, hot and thirsty and almost finished, they saw no one and nothing moved.

They turned slowly off the highway and pulled into the only petrol station in town. A huge burgundy semi trailer with dozens of tyres lay off to the side in the car park. "Horny" was displayed in big black letters across the white bug guard spanning the front of the bonnet and there were two stickers of curvy girls with long legs and stilettoed heels looking back over their shoulders in alluring positions on the front window.

As they came to a stop at the bowser, a wide bloke bursting out of a blue t-shirt with thinning dark hair and sweat beading on his wobbling pock-marked face scuffed slowly over, coughing the wheezing cough of a long time smoker. He unhitched the nozzle from the side of the bowser and gruffly asked: Fill 'er up?
Yeah thanks, Will said getting down and shutting the door.
The big bloke jigged the nozzle into the opening at the side of the car and pulled the trigger and looked over at Will: Hot 'nuff for youse today?

Yeah, it's been a long day on the road... It was hotter than hell out there in the middle of the day... bit cooler now, Will said stretching his back with his hands on his hips, stiff from sitting for hours.

The big bloke nodded at the boards stacked on the roof: Headin to The Point?

Yeah... whereabouts is the turn off?

The big bloke pointed: Take that track over there and just follow your nose to the sea. You'll go across some salt lakes and you can't miss the dunes.

Thanks... far?

Nah... about 20 k's.

Ok, thanks... we'll grab a few bags of ice with the fuel as well... hey Riley?

Yep, Riley said looking up from fossicking around at the back of the car.

I'm gunna go for a piss, wanna get something to eat from here before we go?

Sure.

The only customer in the dining section was a thin man sitting alone at one of the tables dressed in blue King Gee shorts and a matching short-sleeved shirt. His long tattooed arms were elbowed to the table, working hard on trying to keep a burger with the lot together as he gnawed chunks out of it, hovering over the plate, leaking tomato sauce.

As Will and Riley entered he turned his white whiskered face towards them and regarded them for a few moments with circumspection, chewing his mouthful all the while. But the brief lapse in concentration proved costly as a good sized bit of tinned beetroot with a bite out of it slid out of his burger and dove for the remaining hot chips on the plate and set in motion a series of other losses from inside the burger which caught him off guard and sent him into urgent damage control and, as he put the remainder of the dilapidated burger down on the plate to regroup, he angrily spat out "Fuck it" and a few flecks of burger.

Will and Riley made their way over to the line of display cabinets assembled side by side along one wall, patrolled by a hefty girl in an apron with a smooth fleshy face and bobby pins pasting her oily hair down hard and close to her scalp. Steam dripped down the inside of the glass panes of the cabinets and back into the stainless steel tubs which contained a greasy assortment of pre made toasted ham and cheese sandwiches wrapped in white paper, chubby sausages unsettlingly pink, more sausages in yellow batter on a stick, fat grey ones the colour of death wrapped in a shawl of fatty bacon, limp chunky hot chips adjacent to a stack of small buckets, fried chicken drumsticks, pies and sausage rolls, fried rice and other items all sweating inside the cabinets. Burgers and fish and chips and steak sandwiches and a number of other options could be made up fresh on request according to the coloured chalk scratched on the blackboard on the wall above her head.

Will and Riley placed their orders. The girl screeched them through to the kitchen behind without moving save for a slight turn of her head and then smiled sweetly at them with bulging rose cheeks and told them that it wouldn't be long.

After a while, with a sideways glance at each other, they moved away from the food counter where the eyes and smile of the plump girl in a small town in the middle of nowhere had become unnervingly fixed and slouched down at a table and waited. A couple of other customers drifted in and paid for their fuel at another counter. The truckie nailed the rest of his burger, pushed his plate to the side and leant back with a pair of hiccup burps. He slowly plucked a pack of Winnie Reds out of the top pocket of his blue shirt, lit up a cigarette and heaved a draw on it deep into the recesses of his skinny chest, sucking the creased sallow skin taut over his cheekbones with his eyelids closed and his face blissfully inclined in supplication for the sacrament it wasn't.

Let's fill up our water containers and pick up a couple of cartons... I saw a pub on a corner on the way in, Riley said on the way back to the car.
Yeah, good idea... I'm drier than a Nun's nasty, Will said.

They made room in the back for the beer they'd picked up from the pub. Riley tore into one of the boxes and pulled out two roadies each for the drive down to The Point and climbed in.

Will pointed the car south. They left the highway behind and drove along the dirt road in the red skied glow of the sunset, swigging on their cold longnecks and singing along with the Triffids about the wide open road, loud and hard with veins sticking out on their necks and all the windows down blasting the warm desert air and a faint hint of the sea across their faces and chests, running free in front of the long parachute of dust billowing behind them, obscuring where they'd come from, burying the notion of time.

In time the road bent and cut a narrow slightly elevated track for a distance through still sheen salt lakes – one in dirty jade green, another puce, a third had a hard-crusted milky mirror cracking and splitting all over. Black and white banded stilts stood on pencil legs in the shallows in front of the rolls of froth around the edges of the lakes.

Further down the way, huge white sand dunes with sharp ridges sculpted by the wind rose up out of the earth and piled upon each other high up into the skyline like mountains under snow. Their peaks were painted with the softening colours of the sky in the dwindling daylight. They trundled along through the shadows of the towering dunes and rumbled over the corrugations in the road towards The Point, drinking from time to time, now silenced by the mysticism of the place.

Dusk was well advanced when they turned off the dirt road at a sign for the campground painted on a bit of driftwood hanging from a fence. They navigated their way through a maze of smaller dirt roads that cut through the low salty bush to the coast. When they could go no further, they pulled up. Will yanked the hand brake on. They could smell the sea. Leaving the doors wide open, they hurried up the low dusty rise to check out the coastline and the waves that they'd driven half way across the country to ride.

In the last moments of day, the sea was the colour of steel and quilted in glistening small pools and bumps which swirled and formed and reformed and reached out to meet the sky a few shades lighter at the horizon in an imperfect hand-drawn edge. The breeze had gone and it was still and quiet save for the wash of the ocean. The smell of stale urine wafted up from the ground where they stood. In front of them a set broke and peeled down the reef. Around to the left a wall of jagged limestone cliffs plunged into the sea, belted by whitewash surging below. There was more whitewash to their right and, a lot further on still, another faintly discernible headland in the distance. Down the beach nearby there was a glow from a fire and a huddle of silhouetted figures and the sounds of a guitar and singing drifted in and out.

After a while Riley looked over at Will standing with one foot resting on a broken post, arms crossed against the cooler air: Looks like a good set up... how big do you reckon it is? Pretty hard to tell with no one out... doesn't look that big, probly a bit over head high... it looks fun, Will replied.
Yeah, there's definitely a lefthander in front here.
Looks like there's a wave over there as well, Will said pointing over towards the limestone cliffs.
Mmm yeah... where d'yah reckon the righthander is? Riley asked.
Think the book said it was over that way, Will said gesturing towards the headland away off to the right, can't really see too much now... wanna go and find a place to camp and set things up? I'm pretty rooted.
Yeah, sure.

They poked around along the tracks looking for a place to set up. A few other campers scattered here and there shuffled back and forth between their campfires and tents, going about their dinner preparations under the light of torches and kerosene lamps.

They ended up not far from where they'd first parked. There was a fireplace with white limestone rocks stacked upon each other in a circle and a heavy rotating iron hot plate on a pole. What clinched the spot was the pile of wood next to it. The ground was hard. Where it was flattest they cleared away the loose rocks under the light of the car's headlights and lay their tents down. They hammered pegs and bent them and swore and straightened them out, shifted the position of the tents a bit and did it all again until finally they got the pegs in good enough in crevices and the tents went up on their pole frames and they established home for the foreseeable future.

11.

In the morning, before sunrise, when it was light enough to see, Will got up out of one of the deck chairs and walked down the short dirt track to the lookout. The breeze had picked up in the night and blew cool from the desert and offshore out to sea in gusts. A hooded shape was already hunched over leaning on a railing and looking out to sea. A dog sat loyally by his legs.

He turned as Will scuffed over and smiled out from beneath a mass of dreadlock stranded hair filling his grey hood and nodded at Will: Mornin.

Gday, Will replied and stopped nearby and looked out at the surf.

Looks pretty good... 'bout same as yesterday... you come in last night?

Yeah, me and me mate... got in at dusk... been here for a while?

Yep... not sure how long zactly... 'roun four or five months. Drove over from Vicco... headin to West Oz but haven't got there yet... get there some day.

We've just come from the west, Will said.

Righto... How was the trip across?

Pretty bloody long but we took it easy... went via the South Coast and got a few waves there on the way.

Some beachies down there aren't there?

Yeah.

How long are you guys gunna stay here for?

Dunno... we'll check it out... probly a while, Will replied.

It's a pretty easy place to hang out, there's waves and the fishing's good... Gotta keep an eye out for noahs and locals in the water though.

Where've you been fishing?

Anywhere you can throw a line in round here mate. It's plentiful. There's a beach over the headland there as well, he said nodding in the direction of the cliffs nearby, there's also waves there when it's smaller... and a jetty on the other side... name's Randall by the way.

Will shook his hand: Will.

Good meetin you Will.

What's yah dog's name?

Pepper.

Border Collie?

Yeah... she's a bit of a mix... I shaved her cos of the heat.

Belly looks pretty big.

I know... she must've hooked up with one of the other dogs round here.

They watched the ocean for a while.

Hey think I'm gunna get some brekkie and head out while it's offshore... see you in a bit, Randall said as he started to wander off.

Ok, no worries, Will said.

Randall stopped after a few steps and said: Hey Will.

Will turned and put his hand up to his face to shield against the rising sun. Randall was pointing at a burnt orange VW combi covered in dirt parked with its roof raised up on an angle, I'm camped over there... that's my bus... drop in anytime.

Sure, thanks... we're just there, Will said pointing at the tents and the four wheel drive nearby, might see you in the water in a bit.

Yeah, cool, we're neighbours then, Randall said and turned and took slow lanky strides down the track with his hands balled in the pockets of his hoodie and his dog trotting along beside.

Will stayed looking out at the ocean. It was ruffled on the surface from the offshore wind and in the sunlight, now cobalt blue. Lines of evenly spaced swell were stacked way out into the sea to the southwest and marched in parallel with increasing speed towards the shore where they broke and rolled, frothing white chasing down walls of blue. When those lines had finished their long journey from a low somewhere far away in the Southern Ocean and expired on the beach, more marched in to take their place. Will hopped up and balanced on the broken post to get a bit more height, looked down the coast at the low cliffed brown headland about a kilometre to his right and watched the spray fanning high off the back of the waves breaking out beyond the headland. He thought he could make out a couple of black dots in the ocean already out there. Behind the headland, the dunes that they'd seen from the road yesterday reared up majestically and, off their blindingly white peaks, fine sand whipped by the strong northeasterly wind streamed out in smoking plumes in the direction of the sea.

Hey Riley, wake up, it's offshore... it's going off, Will said giving Riley's tent a gentle shake.

After a delay, Riley groaned sleepily from inside the tent: yep... be up in a sec, and stretched... geez I slept like a bloody log. How big is it?

It looks a bit overhead on the sets, Will said pulling the esky out from under the car and getting some things out of the back of the car for breakfast.

How long have you been up for? Riley asked from inside his tent after a while.

Got up just before it was light... couldn't sleep any more. Did some stretches... are you getting up?

Yep.

A few moments later the zip slid down the front of Riley's old khaki canvas family sized tent and Riley stepped out in shiny trackies and an old white t-shirt. They had breakfast in the deck chairs with the sun on their backs and looked at their surrounds. Scattered here and there through the terrain were other camps and a few people moving about in the dirt in the early morning, squatting to blow life back into fires from the night before and wandering unhurriedly along tracks to the beach.

Where do you wanna go out? Riley asked.

Maybe we could try the left out in front... there was no one out when I checked it, looked clean and fun, Will replied.

Ok, Riley said and chucked his banana peel into the fireplace a few metres away, could you see the righthander?

Yeah, kind of from behind... it's a fair way down the beach... in front of that headland we could just see last night so it was

hard to tell what it is like, there are a couple of guys out already. Maybe we could check it out later on this arvo.
Yeah, sure.

They unstrapped their boards from the top of the car and picked out one each and put the other boards inside Riley's tent. After digging around in the back of the truck for a few minutes, wetsuits were tossed out the back door onto the dirt and leg ropes followed and Will clambered back out. They struggled with their dry shrunken wetsuits for a while and eventually got them on up to their waists and leant down and grabbed their boards and leg ropes and, after rubbing a bit of wax over the existing covering, trotted down the track to the beach.

They stood on the beach looking at the wave for a few minutes while they pulled up the rest of their wetsuits. They swore as they stepped into the water, surprised by the cold in stark contrast to the heat of the desert. They paddled out, feeling the cold biting into their hands, keeping their heads above the whitewash rolling in, trying to put the first duck dive off for as long as possible.

They surfed for most of the morning out there. It was a good wave for turns and cut backs and as one of them paddled back out after a wave he watched the other riding and hooted and grinned as he swooped past. They were alone for the first while. Then a wiry guy with fair freckled skin and a flop of sandy hair and a beautiful dark haired girl joined them. A few other people also drifted out as the morning progressed and the strong offshore wind lightened off. They all took it more or less in turns and in breaks between waves, bobbed about in a small pack, sitting astride their boards with their legs dangling in the dark ocean below and talked about where they were from and The Point and where they were headed.

When Riley wandered back to camp around midday, Will had already lit the fire and dragged the card table and a chair over and was busy piling cheese and tomato and onion in between pieces of buttered bread in the jaffle iron, shaking his head and blowing over his lips and snorting to get some brief peace from the flies picking and sticking in the corners of his eyes and around his mouth and nostrils.

Smells good mate, Riley said putting his board down.
Yeah... I was starving, had to come in... did it stay good out there?
For a bit after you left it stayed good... glassy, no wind... then the sea breeze started to waft in. It's come in now and the waves are a bit crumbly but the wind isn't too strong at the moment... not like back home... the Frenchies are still out there, Riley said as he pulled his wetsuit down to his waist.
Here wrap your laughing gear round this, Will said handing a toasted sandwich to Riley and taking a swipe at the flies near his face.

Riley put a towel around his shoulders against the burning sun and they sat in their deck chairs by the smoking fire with the breeze blowing in across the low dune and ate a pile of toasted sandwiches using up the best part of a loaf of bread between them, swishing away at flies with bits of broken bush.

Think I'm gunna get out of the sun and the flies and have a kip for a bit, Will said getting up out of his chair.

No worries, I'll probably do the same... wanna still check out the right later on if the breeze isn't too strong?

Yeah, ok.

There were no trees tall enough to give any shade anywhere. Their tents baked in the dirt under the hot sun of the middle of the day. Loose bits of canvas flapped about without rhythm in the sea breeze. They lay splayed out on their mats and sweltered groggily through the heat of the day.

In the afternoon, a truck pulled up and an ill-fitting door creaked open and slammed shut: Anyone 'ere?

Will unzipped his tent and squinted into the glare through puffy eyes at a bloke in khaki overalls standing with his back to him looking down at the thin trail of smoke rising up from the remnants of their lunch time fire. A skinny black and tan dog was sniffing busily around with its nose to the ground weaving across the dirt on the trail of something. It paused at their car to lift its leg on one of the back tyres. It looked up with its leg in the air, panting hard, as Will climbed out of his tent. Will walked over towards the campfire and said: G'day.

The bloke turned around. He had bleached straw like hair which fell straight down either side of his face and chopped off horizontally across his forehead. The skin on his face was tanned and cracked and tough like a beaten up boot left for years out in the elements. The creases on his face deepened as he smiled and put his hand out to Will: G'day... sorry if I woke y'up.

No worries, time I got up anyway... I'm Will, Will said shaking his hand.

I'm the caretaker here... you guys just get in?

Yeah, last night.

Gunna stay for a while?

Yeah probly a few months, maybe longer.

Ok... it's bloody hot during the day at the moment 'cos it's Summer but cools down at night... Autumn is the best time of the year if you're still here then.

Probly will be... at least for some of it.

Here's an info sheet on the place... it's a bit dog-eared but it's got a mud map of where's where and info on what's bloody what. We get the wood for you... I come round once a week or so to collect the week's camping fees.

Ok, Will nodded.

How many of you are there?

Two, mate 'n me.

Righto... there's a dunny and a shower over near the washing up shed over there... can't drink the water... it's bore water.

Ok, thanks... how long have you been here for? Will asked.

A bloody long time mate. He waved his arm to the south: My place is over the hill. There's a shop there but we don't have too much stuff in it usually... unless we do a trip to the big smoke... got some fishing gear if you need any and some drinks and a bit of other stuff.

Ok, we'll come and check it out later on.

I'd better be off... waves are looking good for a few days... see yah round, he said as he turned and walked over towards his dusty truck.

Yep no worries... see yah.

He whistled for his dog and patted the tray at the back of the truck as it trotted over towards him and said: Git up.

*   *   *

Around the campfire at Randall's place later that night, after the daylight had faded and the night desert sky had started to blaze magically overhead, the flames of the fire lit up the faces of the small gang gathered around it with a gentle glow and they shone deep with colour from the sun. It was an unlikely bunch having a drink out in the desert, keeping warm from the cool night, brought together by surfing. Everyone had about them an earthy dishevelled crustiness from living in the dust and salt water. Clothes had taken on the colours of the desert and hung down stiffly on frames faded and skinnied from long days in the water and the heat.

The gang was listening to Randall talking and staring at the flames when Will and Riley wandered over, each with a beer in one hand and a chair in the other. He stopped: Hi guys, pull up a pew… everyone this is Will and Riley from West Oz… got in yesterday, introduce yourselves.

Will and Riley said G'day and recognised the Frenchies who smiled and nodded and said they were Didier and Sabine. The others said their names as they reached over to shake hands: Ferret, Dingo, Tammy, Scott.

Ferret got up off the esky and got some beers out. He was a small lean guy with dark hair sticking out on all sides like a trimmed echidna, patchy facial growth and a roasted peeling forehead. He grinned almost permanently. Next to Ferret,

Dingo was a big bloke, wide shouldered, still wearing a straw hat. Tammy was sitting side on across Dingo's legs with her arm around his shoulders. She had freckled skin and wavy strawberry blond hair.

Ferret sat back down and leaned forward looking at Randall:
Yeah... so what happened?
Right... yeah... well as I was saying I was talking to this local bloke in the car park at the right hander after a surf this morning and he was saying how his mate... another local, Lucky they're calling 'im now... had been out at the break across the deep channel from the right a couple of days ago... the other guy out there with him had just caught a wave and Lucky was sitting on his board waiting for one when he saw a dark shape moving in the water below him off to one side... said he watched it move around in front of him still a couple of metres below... reckons it was so massive he could've counted a few seconds to himself while it swam slowly past. Then it disappeared for a few seconds... went deeper or further away or something for a bit... bloke said his mate was so frigging terrified he couldn't move, said he was just sitting there, frozen stiff, waiting to be attacked... bloody hell imagine that... and then he saw its dorsal fin break through the top of the water a little way away in front of him and then grow as it glided up closer to the surface, said his mate reckons in the end the fin was higher than his bloody shoulder when he was sitting on his board... Said it swam straight towards him... but slowly slowly... when it got to only a few metres away, pushing water in front and its fin huge and gashed in places, it turned a bit to one side and rolled and he saw its dark eye looking straight at him above the surface of the water

and rows of exposed teeth and gums and then part of its white underbelly as it drifted alongside and then past him. Said the thing looked so vicious… massive… and wide and thick… as big as some of the ones in the photos down on the walls in the pub down the coast at The Bay, like a bloody sub… Reckons he could smell it… seaweed and fish, strong, all the way from the bottom of the ocean… Said it all happened in slow motion… it started to swim down after it went past him and then he lost sight of it in the darker deeper water and then, while he was looking everywhere below him, shifting around on his board with his feet up on the deck not knowing what to do – whether to stay there and hope like hell it went away or lie down on his board and start paddling but that'd mean his arms would be in the water and his head'd be down low – a set suddenly loomed up and he paddled like a maniac for it and kicked like a bastard and misjudged it and got too far in front and the lip of the wave landed on him and drilled him but there was no way in hell he was letting go of his board and so he bounced and wrestled his board in the whitewash and got in a fair way… then the whitewash of the next wave in the set picked him up and took him all the way into shore on his stomach. Bloke said Lucky started bawling when he got to the beach and limped up the sand with his board dragging on the ground behind him and didn't stop bawling for hours after. The other bloke out there who had just had a wave also went in straight away. Said he knew something major must've been up as Lucky never bellied in. They packed him a cone in the car park and that calmed him down a bit… he hasn't stopped pulling cones since… practically hasn't moved from the couch in his shack.

The campfire was quiet and still.

Struth… that's heavy, Dingo said finally.

Yeah, makes you think twice about going out in the water over 'ere, Ferret said. We've got a few sharks back home but nothing like the sound of that.

Where's home for you guys? Riley asked.

Me 'n Dingo 'n Tammy are from Ballina… s'in northern New South Wales… just a bit down the coast from Byron.

You got some good surf up there?

Yeah it's a good place for surf… water's warm and there's some good point breaks – heard of Lennox Head or Broken Head?

Heard of Lennox.

It's gettin' pretty busy up there now though these days… a bit touristy and all the banana benders flock down on the weekends and in the holidays. There's quite good beachies around though so if you know where to go you can get some less crowded days.

When did you say this happen? Didier asked Randall.

What?

The shark.

Coupla days ago, Randall said.

Non… I mean to say… was it early morning or in late afternoon?

Nah… think he said it was mid morning sometime. It was a sunny day… I remember that.

They all stared down into the fire.

Sorry boys, Randall said looking at Will and Riley, pretty full on story for your first day here eh?

Yeah, bloody oath, Will said.

But like I said to you this morning, you gotta keep an eye out for the noahs, they're definitely out there. But ya know that's the first shark sighting I've heard of while I've been here so it's not like it happens every day.

They're out there... like back home... like a lot of places... just gotta hope there's enough fish for 'em, Will said.

Riley looked up and across the campfire and noticed Sabine reach for Didier's hand. Didier jerked it out of her reach in a slight movement and folded his arms and stared at the fire with a fixed expression on his face.

Dingo got up and still holding his beer in one hand, shoved the ends of a few branches into the flames with his thong and picked an armful up from the pile on the ground behind the circle and threw them on the fire. Riley tilted his head back and took a sip from his beer and glanced at Sabine.

Randall picked up his guitar from beside his chair and strummed it and said: What about some music?

Yeah, for sure, Ferret said cracking open another can.

The older quiet guy in a blue jumper, with curly greying hair and bushy dark eyebrows, sitting a little apart, skulled the rest of his drink and picked up his empty cans from the dewy dirt. He tucked his chair under his arm and said 'Goodnight all' and slipped out of the dim light of the fire and into the darkness. They were the only words he'd said.

They played music and sang along with the flames flickering and shadowing across their faces and coughed and ducked for cover from time to time when the light wind blew the smoke into their eyes. One of the girls clicked spoons, Ferret thumped the esky and Will eeked out some sounds from his harmonica and they all bumbled along through the lyrics with Randall on the guitar. They passed a spliff from hand to hand, some pausing to smoke it and others moving it right along, and another one followed it around when it had became a tiny soggy butt too small to hold and put to the lips for a puff.

They talked about The Point and about other travels. Randall talked about going to Indonesia after West Australia. He said that new waves were being discovered in the islands up there all the time. He asked Will and Riley about West Australia and Will told him a little about some of the waves in the south west, the small towns and caves and trees down there and the cray fishing fibro shack towns along the coast to the north and talked about the city and the winding river and the islands off the coast. He told him about the red inland and blokes who worked rotations on the mines out there like him. While Will was talking, Riley noticed Didier and Sabine start having a side discussion in strained whispers in French which seemed to be going awkwardly and after it finished, Sabine got up and left. Didier stayed slumped down in his chair and looked glumly down at the fire. Riley watched her step into the blackness outside the circle and looked over now and then to follow the light of her torch jumping over the ground until he could no longer see it. Dingo got up as well and told them he'd be back.

It's time I christened this little pipe, he said sitting back down. Got it from a souvenir shop at a roadhouse on the way over. He rested one end on the dirt between his knees and held the other end close to his face.

Never played one before so hold your applause until the end, he grinned.

He gripped it with his big hands and put his lips down to the end and spluttered and blew and spat into it and got pretty red faced and sweaty while Ferret rolled around in the dust laughing his head off and the others chuckled along, handing around the number. Eventually he conjured up a reverberating deep guttural hum. The sound grew and tingled their skin. As it went on it seemed to bring together the earth's hot core and all the layers up to its dry desert crust and the blazing milky way overhead and all of the blackness around it, the cool wind off the land and the salt and dirt on their skin and the camp fire's warmth, into a unique unbroken sound which filled the silent night and echoed around The Point until he ran out of breath and gasped for air. He looked up and cracked a wide grin under his straw hat and they all packed up again and a few kept going for a long time, tears streaming down aching spliffed cheeks, locked into laughing.

12.

Hey mate!... Mate! Oi!

Riley looked around. A surly bloke with a close shaven head and a thick stubbled goatee was looking at him menacingly, sitting high in the water on a thick board in an old black wetsuit at the deepest position inside the small pack.

Yeah I'm talking to you pretty boy... piss orf, he snarled.

What? Riley said.

Piss orf... you're not welcome... we've had enough of you holiday poofters for one Summer. He was glaring hard at Riley, dark eyebrows pushed down low and close together over his eyes.

Riley glanced at the rest of the pack. They sat astride their boards with their arms crossed tightly over their chests, hands fisted deep into their armpits trying to preserve some warmth against the early morning offshore wind, chilling as it whipped across their wetsuits. They all stared blankly out to sea as if nothing was happening. Staying neutral. Uninvolved. Out of it. It was not their problem. Each silently thankful that it wasn't them that he'd picked on. Riley was quiet for a moment. Weighing up his options – whether to say something or paddle in or just ignore him.

They had settled into an easy pattern of getting up and shuffling over to the lookout to wake up, working out what the conditions were doing. Then heading straight for the waves or having some breakfast beforehand and staying out in the water all morning. Things rolled along. An afternoon nap in the heat of the day after lunch and then there would be another surf if the conditions were good and sometimes even if they weren't or fishing or hanging out with other travellers on the beach. The Point was not the place to be in the water at dusk unless the waves were flawless. It was sharky out there off the end of the low headland, feet hanging in the water above the reef, the deep shelf drop off just a few tail flicks away. At the end of the day they prepared dinner and rinsed off the day with a beer and from time to time gathered at night with others around a campfire to talk and play some music.

The days were more or less synchronized with the rising and setting of the sun. Going to bed more than a couple of hours after dark was a late night. They hadn't come across any locals in the water yet. So far they'd surfed other breaks when, through the binoculars, they could make out the locals' beaten up vehicles perched on the edge of the cliff over at the right pointing out to sea.

He looked back to shore and saw Will and Randall standing in knee deep water on the reef, holding their boards in their hands, about to launch themselves into the water.

Are you still here? In you go, quick sticks, he growled.

Listen mate, I'm gunna wait my turn and catch a couple of waves. I've driven a long way to surf here like everyone has... like you would have, Riley said.

There's other breaks... go surf 'em. Not here. So get the...

He stopped mid sentence as the pack started to paddle hard out to sea to meet a good sized set looming up out the back and focused on getting into position for the first wave. He paddled out to sea, then hurriedly stopped and sat up on his board to spin it around as the wall reared up hard above him. He took a few strokes to pick up its momentum, got to his feet and disappeared down the other side of the wave as it roared past.

There were more waves in the set behind the first one and when a guy on his inside, closer to the place at which the wave would first start to break, pulled out from taking the third one, Riley paddled hard for it at the last minute and, blinded by the white spray fanning off the top under the offshore wind, picked up the momentum of the wave. He dropped down late with it into the bowl, shook his head and blinked at the bottom to rid his eyes of salt water and sized up the long wall of water bending in towards him. Then he lent forward into a bottom turn propelling a jet of water out the side as he carved a deep track through the trough of the wave and drove his board up high into the rearing blue pocket and snapped it back down to the next bowl with the wave curling and crashing behind him and then did it again and again before sliding off the back of the wave where it ended inside the low headland.

That's your first and last wave out 'ere, the guy with the bald head said paddling back out after his wave, having watched most of Riley's.

Mornin' Nugget... he's with me... he's ok, knows the rules... that was a nice one you got, Randall said to him.

Nugget looked at Randall and grinned for a second and then frowned and looked at Riley and then at Will also paddling out and swore and muttered something under his breath about the place not being like it used to be.

Well you butt plugs better wait your bloody turn and stay out of my way and show some bloody respect... if I see you drop in on anybody... ever... you're dead men. Got it?

Will and Riley exchanged quick glances as they all continued to paddle back out and Randall said: It's cool.

Nugget paddled back out ahead of them on his bigger board, grumbling. He slid straight past the two remaining members of the small pack waiting at the peak and sat up on his board just inside them and looked out to sea. It was his turn again next and it always would be his turn when he was ready and it didn't matter how many others were out there and the only time it would was when another local bloke was out there and he'd been around for a good honest time and had earned his place in the line up and was not just one of those blow ins, one of those bloody overnighters that only stayed around for a few years and thought that made them a bloody local.

After Nugget caught his last one, rocketing along half way up the face of the wave on his big board and gesturing wildly with his arms at a bloke paddling back out, miles away from crossing the safe straight line Nugget was taking and yelling: "Get out of the bloody way yah faggot", things relaxed considerably and the rest of the pack got on with sharing waves and talking between sets. They stayed out in the water all morning through the lightening offshore and then the wafting windless period.

It's a good wave, Riley said paddling up alongside Will.
Yep, Will said, it's fun out here 'cept keep thinking about noahs... been holding onto a piss for bloody ages... bladder's the size of a footy... good to have a few extra numbers out in the water, drop the odds down a bit.
Yeah... trying not to think about 'em. Getting pretty peckish myself though.
I know, I'm friggin famished.

They sat up on their boards when they arrived out the back.

Might start off with a few chicken crimpies to keep the wolf from the door, Riley said.
Salami, Will added.
Roasted over the fire.
Yeah, for horses douvers.
Toasted sambos?
Yep... cheese, maybe throw in some onion.
Spread some of that pasta sauce we had last night on the bread.
Maybe... what'd you do with it?
Nothing... should still be in the pot.
Didn't yah wash it?
Nah, I shoved it in the esky.
The whole pot?

Yeah.

Fair enough.

A while later, they each caught a last one in as the breeze strengthened and the waves began to crumble. After picking their way across the reef, they walked slowly up along the beach in the hot sun with their boards under their arms, black neoprene arms flapping against their legs, tight and tired in the arms from the hours of paddling, hollow with hunger all over and swollen salt mouthed from thirst, bearing armies of flies on their backs.

After rescuing and operating on the block of cheese which they found floating waterlogged and mushy white around the edges in the esky they'd left out in the sun all morning, they dragged their chairs in under the shade of Riley's tent awning and ate their lunch with the flies. Riley lost a game of paper/rock/scissors and got up out of his chair, went inside his tent to the plastic food box which they called the pantry and got the fruitcake. He looked over for a second at the knife on the table near the fire place in the full sun and broke hunks off for each of them with his hands instead. It was supermarket brand but it tasted good. Everything did when you were hungry enough.

Not long after, they gave in to afternoon naps, heavy from eating a lot at fast pace, groggy from the heat of the glaring midday sun radiating off the fine sandy dirt and worn out from the dawn rise and the long morning's exertions.

In the mid afternoon, the onshore breeze was still blowing. Riley stirred from his tent. He put two beers in a bucket with a thawed small bag of bait and his orange tackle box and shoved the esky back under the car with his foot, grabbed his fishing rod and scuffed off to the beach. At the beach he studied the coastline for a while and headed off to the south. He walked up part of a white dune blazing in the glare, sand whipping at his ankles and shins. He followed a track worn into the limestone rock along a cliff edge which ran out to the south west, falling in jagged spires into the ocean belting at it below.

He stopped at the tip of the headland, rigged up his line and threw out into the water and settled in to wait, fishing rod in his hands, high above the water on limestone cliffs in the middle of nowhere, not a soul in sight. Damp salt spray showered lightly over him, carried on the wind from the waves hitting the cliffs below. Clouds raced across the hazy afternoon sky and the green ocean, crested in white peaks, stretched out endlessly. With nothing between him and the frozen South Pole, he stood on the southern tip of the country, at the very edge of the earth and the whole of the huge continental mass waited silently and patiently behind him.

By the time the sun started to soften, he had one good-sized salmon in the bucket and had had quite a few strong tugs on his line. One fish that he thought he had in the bag he had lost together with his hook and bait amid thrashing whitewash below and there wasn't much doubt about what had taken it.

Away in the distance in the late afternoon someone was slowly picking their way around the headland from the other direction and gradually getting closer, stopping every now and then to look out at the sea, white shirt billowing lightly. In the other direction to his right he made out a few figures in black wetsuits sitting on their boards down at the left hander. Another was heading out, leaning on his board with both hands as he walked gingerly across the reef. The onshore wind had gradually dropped during the afternoon and had just started to blow off the land again. As the walker came nearer, he made out her dark hair flowing out from under a red and white checked bandana tied like a scarf on her head and olive skin coppered from the sun and recast his line into the sea.

Hi, she said coming up alongside him.
Bonjour Sabine, ca va? Riley said and grinned.

She smiled. She had topaz coloured eyes and a small black freckle above her lip to the side. One tooth turned out a little and added a cheeky twist to her face.

Tu parles français?
Pardon?
You speak a little French?
No... that's all I know, he laughed, did you have a good walk?
Yes, I went all along the beach and out onto a big rock over there at the very end and back this way... was very nice... no person anywhere. Little bit hot at the beginning but now nice.
That's a pretty long way.
Yes... scuze me, Riley do you have any water?
No sorry, I've only got a beer... it's probably a bit warm now but you are welcome to have it.
Thank you... maybe I will have a sip... I am very thirsty.
No worries, here hold this for a sec, Riley gave her the fishing

rod while he took the top off the bottle and handed it to her and reclaimed the rod.

She drank and said: Ave you caught many fishes?

I've caught one salmon... it's in the bucket over there... hoping for one more for dinner.

He felt something on his line and pulled his fishing rod up and started reeling it in quickly and then stopped: False alarm... did you surf this morning?

Yes, we went out at the left. It was so fun, very clean... would you like some of your beer? She said holding the bottle out to him.

Yeah, ok... it's thirsty work up here... after all a man's not a camel, he said taking it from her and drinking.

What did you say?

He handed the bottle back: a man is not a camel... it's a saying... you know, a camel can go for a long time without drinking because it can store water... people can't.

Ah... yes, that's funny, she said.

Are you having a good time in Australia?

Australie, I like... Sydney was nice city and then we drive up the coast to Noosa and then we are coming all the way back down again along the coast to Melbourne and along the bottom to Adelaide. We are stopping all along the way... many places – Byron Bay, Crescent Heads, Ulladulla and Bell Beach, Lorne, Johanna Beaches... many places. We are driving since nearly nine months.

Yeah, it's a big country isn't it... how much longer will you be here for do you think? Riley asked.

She took another drink from the bottle and handed it to him: I'm not sure... Didier he is wanting to go back to France soon... he worry about his money... me I like Australie and it is very far from France so I want to stay as long as possible and probably I can find work in Margaret River for some money... so we will see.

Is Didier out surfing at the moment? He asked.

She looked out at the setting sun and back at Riley uncertainly. After a while she said: He is smoking some marijuana when I left... I tell him maybe he smoke too much here and he is becoming not the same person any more and maybe he should smoke little bit less but he get angry with me so I go for my walk.

Riley stayed looking out to sea: Yeah you have to watch out for it... it can creep up on you... how long have you been here for now?

Here at the Point? She asked.

He nodded.

Yes, not quite one month now... I like it here. It is like nowhere I have ever been before.

You would be pretty popular round here... even with the crusty locals in the surf, he laughed and realized he still had the bottle and handed it back to her.

She blushed and laughed: yes maybe, and put the bottle to her lips and tilted her head back a little to drink.

It's finished, she said and handed it back to him.

You can keep the bottle, he said, it's a present.

Oh... ok, she said hesitantly.

Just kidding, here give it here, he said and put it in his bucket.

Riley watched a surfer walk back across the shallow reef to the beach, lean down and undo his leg rope and said: Maybe it's time to head back.

Yes, I should be getting back also.

He wound in his line and put the other empty bottle and his fishing tackle box in the bucket with the fish and followed Sabine as they walked back along the cliff edge. At one point, she caught her thong on a low rock and stumbled for a few steps until she put her arms out to the side and regained her footing. She swept her hair back with her hand and looked over her shoulder and said: That was little bit close.

Maybe walk a little further in from the edge, you don't want to be swimming with the sharks at this time of the day: Riley said.

She moved a little further away from the edge and as she walked in front of him, he watched her feet and calves, initially protectively in case she should trip again and looked up her brown legs to her hips moving in her tiny denim cut off shorts. Each time she stepped forward, the bare brown skin of the lower curve of her buttocks was fleetingly visible from under the frayed edges of her shorts. As she walked along in front of him, one of her arms swung to the side a little more than the other. He shook his head lightly and looked out to the ocean. They reached the end of the cliff and walked down the sand dune to the beach. She turned and said: Thank you for the beer, see you later Riley. No worries, thanks for the company, see you round.

She walked on. He watched for a moment as she continued along the beach and then walked towards the campsite in the fading day.

How did you go? Will asked hanging his wetsuit on the fence as Riley neared.

Riley looked up: Good thanks mate, and grinned.

Did you catch any fish?

Sorry yeah, a salmon… here it's in the bucket… have a squiz… if we make some rice or boil some potatoes or something it'll be enough for us.

Will came over and peered into the bucket: yeah, good work… it's a good size… I'll start the fire.

Ok, I'll go over and clean and scale it… did you go for another surf?

Yeah, just out at the left in front… it was fun, wind dropped out and then it went offshore late, just a couple of us out, no locals.

Yeah I noticed the wind change from the headland.

That was you up there was it… there was someone else up there with you wasn't there for a bit?

Yeah, Sabine came past on her way back from walking around the coast, he tried not to for a moment and then grinned.

What are you so happy about?

Nothing, he said and leant his fishing rod against the car and put his bucket down next to it. He picked the fish out of it and headed off to clean it.

*   *   *

Randall tapped the long stick he'd been holding in the flames against a branch shoved into the fire and let loose a shower of sparks. His dog got up from lying at his feet, looked up with concern and resettled around the back of his chair with her head down on her black and white paws stretched out in front of her like a sphinx.

It was lucky that it was only Nugget out there this morning... if some of the other boys were out there and Nugget had marked you like he did, you would've had to go in, Randall said to Riley.

Yeah he was pretty full on... I wouldn't be too worried about him by himself... but I thought if I'd confronted him, it could've got ugly later on when word got out to his mates... thanks for helping out, Riley said.

No worries... I can kind of understand Nugget and the other guys though... they live out here in the middle of nowhere and put up with the solitude and harsh living conditions for the surf, for that right hander really, and feel pretty protective about it... thing is... out here there are no real locals... no one that surfs here was born and grew up here... everyone is from somewhere else, from miles away... so no one really has the right to control the spot.

Is that what you reckon makes you a local – being born at a place? Riley asked.

Yep, Randall said.

No matter how long you live there for, even twenty years or more, in your book if you weren't born there you can't be a local?

Yep, it's not in your blood if you're not born there, Randall said.

Localism is no good, not here, not back at home, not anywhere... doesn't matter whether you were born there or not, Will said.

Randall looked over at Will sharpening a stick with a pocketknife and looked down at the fire.

Surfing is getting pretty popular... there's lids everywhere... if there's not some kind of control places will be chocker block full of chaos... even now let alone down the track when it gets even busier... Take Torquay. I was born there and grew up riding my bike to the beach to surf when it was mostly just beach shacks. After a while, I don't know exactly when but a while ago now, all these people from Melbourne started coming down on the weekends and staying overnight and then they started to move down and some started to buy land and build houses and the land got exxy and breaks started to get busy and overrun with out o' towners. Now you see local blokes who had surfed there all their lives just sitting there on the shore watching. It's sad.

Torquay also got busy 'cos of the Bell's comp, Riley said.

Yeah sure that put it more on the map and it's so packed at Easter time, it's the last place you want to be even though the surf's firing then usually so you kinda do wanna be there... but I'm talking about normal days... when there's waves... people still flock down from all over and it's crowded in the water and people get frustrated.

A bloke that was born at a spot has no more rights than some one who wasn't. The ocean belongs to everyone... the sea is constantly moving, waves start from a long way away, thousands of ks away. It's not right for one bloke to say that those waves belong to him just 'cos they happen to break just offshore from where he lives, Will said.

When the wave becomes rideable... in its last few seconds as it breaks near the shore... that's when there need to be controls, not out to sea where the wave starts and rolls on in wide open space, Randall explained.

Will looked up from sharpening his stick: Localism is ugly mate... people sitting out in the ocean barking at other people to go in 'cos they weren't born there and getting all agro is not what it's about... never will be.

114

People don't have to get agro about it... just explain to blokes out in the water not to come with lots of their mates... if it's too busy they should wait or find another break. It's about having some respect.

Riley laughed: I don't reckon that's gunna do it mate... if a bloke wants to surf at a spot he'll only listen if he's threatened and gunna get beaten up.

Yeah that's right, so that's what it comes down to mostly... but that's not the fault of the local blokes who've tried to reason with him... hey, feel that, the wind's just changed, that's a nor'wester... about due for a change to come through... been over a week.

Yeah, the smoke's changed direction, Will said. You know, I reckon it all sorts itself out in the water... each spot can only handle so many surfers... each spot is a bit different but each has its limit... guys who know a place well will always get more waves 'cos they're more in tune with the spot... less experienced guys will get less waves... can't take a wave and paddle back inside everyone after it though... if a bloke is not getting as many waves as he wants, he can always go somewhere else... maybe it's not as good a wave, maybe it's a bit marginal but that's up to him, people don't have to get territorial about surf... Australia has a huge coastline, Will said and leaned back in his chair and stretched his arms up above his head and his legs out in front of him.

Yeah and that's part of what's driving people to explore for waves, Riley said.

That's my plan, Randall said, get to West Oz and surf there for a while and then head up to Indo for as long as my money lasts. A buck goes a long way up there... the water's warm and there are empty waves everywhere... new ones still being found all the time.

You been there before? Will asked.

Nah not yet, guys I know have been up there, a few went to west Java last year.

That's west of Bali isn't it?

Yeah, surfed a long hollow left, really shallow and sharp... reckon next time they'd take thin wetties with them to lose less skin.

It'd be pretty amazing to discover a place and be the first person to surf it, Will said quietly feeling the point of his sharpened stick with his finger.

D'yah reckon you'd keep the spot to yourself if you did? Randall asked.

Will thought for a while and stared into the fire and yawned and smiled: I dunno... that's a tough one... think I might sleep on it, I'm gunna hit the hay guys.

13.

Morning.
Morning.

Riley stretched standing up under the awning in front of the doorway of the tent. Behind him its khaki walls were pushing and pulling in the wind like there was a live animal belting around inside. He looked up at the clouds marching across the sky and back at Will sitting in his chair reading, dust whipping all around him.

What's happening?
Not much… swell's come up a fair bit but it's onshore… dead seal washed up on the beach over the back near the jetty with a big bite out of it, you can see the shark's teeth marks in the flesh.
Shit, really?
Yeah. The seal must've made it to the beach still alive and then died, otherwise there would have been less of it left.
Riley scuffed over and pulled up a chair. He sat down and blinked and squinted in the glare.

Must've slept in… you got up early, that's a fair walk isn't it?
Yeah, woke up at dawn and did some stretches and thought
I'd go for a walk… ended up over there.
It feels like it's a bit cooler today… good to have a break from
the heat… what do you wanna get up to if it's onshore?
I was thinking maybe a drive into town to get some ice and
a few supplies and see what happens this arvo with the wind.
Sure… do you know what day it is today?
Nope.

They drove through the campground on their way to town,
weaving slowly around the narrow dirt roads. Randall was up
and bent over a small table writing. Pepper was lying in the
shade under his bus on her side, burdened with her unborn
puppies. They stopped and leant out the windows and talked
with him about the wind and swell and said they were heading
into town and asked him if he needed anything. He wrote a
couple of things down in the back of his journal and ripped
the page out and handed it to them.

A bit further on they drove past a couple of blokes who must
have just arrived. Their boards were still strapped on the roof of
the green Panel Van. All the doors were open and their stuff lay
scattered on the ground. On one of the windows was a large
yellow 'Moana Boardriders' sticker. One of the blokes, with short
hair cropped all over save for a long rat's tail platted in a skinny
rope from the top of his neck down to below his shoulders, was
wrestling the wind for his tent. The sun reflected off the orange
lenses of his sunglasses. The other was sitting in the driver's seat
with his feet up on the open door tossing his head around to
Iron Maiden thumping out of the car.

Further on Will and Riley stopped to talk with Ferret, Dingo and Tammy. It turned out that they were thinking of going into town themselves so they put the back seat back up and Ferret jumped in with Will and Riley. As they were leaving, Dingo strolled over to the car and leant in on the driver's windowsill and told them not to dilly-dally as there was a cricket match scheduled for the afternoon. Ferret told Dingo to make sure he got the numbers for the match and to invite the Frenchies even though they probably would never have played before. He said to send Tammy out recruiting if numbers were looking shaky and Tammy put the rest of her piece of toast in her mouth, shook her blond hair, pointed her knee and tilted her head seductively with her hands on her hips and they laughed.

On the way back from town, skimming and chapping over the corrugations, they talked above the sound of the wind rushing in through the windows and the cricket commentators droning on dryly about the third day of the test match in breaks between the static.

What was the name of that quiet older bloke who was at the campfire a while back... on our first night here I think it was... you know the guy with curly hair and a big forehead? Riley asked after a while.
Not sure, Will said.
Do you mean Scott? Ferret asked.
Yeah... what happened to him... haven't seen him for a while? Riley asked.
He left a while ago, Ferret said, didn't stay too long... didn't say goodbye to anyone... was a bit of a strange bloke... came round one night, before you guys arrived... seemed like he'd had a lot

to drink and was pretty hammered, just came round and sat down in the dirt by the fire with his bottle of Jim Beam without saying G'day or anything... and after we'd all sat about in silence for a while and it was getting a bit weird, he started to tell us about how he had to get out of Tasmania. He'd put his car on the ferry to Melbourne and then driven all the way here and was heading to the south coast of WA to try to find a place to live somewhere down there and start up again... said he used to run a backpackers in Tassie and one of his cousins came out from Ireland to see Australia and stayed with him for a while. He showed her round a bit and then one morning he found her cut up in pieces on the front lawn of the hostel... said the cops kept coming round day after day to talk to him and check the place out... said he didn't know anything... and he felt the whole town staring at him like he'd done it and steering clear of him... he said after a while he couldn't handle it anymore and so he just packed a bag and drove off and left everything as it was... didn't seem like he was on the run but he was a pretty strange bloke... all quiet and a long way away with his thoughts and everything. Me and Dingo had a talk about it after and there was definitely something not right with him... probly never know whether he did it or whether it was the shock of the murder and discovering her all cut up on his front lawn that caused it... if he did it and was on the run it was funny that he came and told us about it... but then he was pretty drunk when he did... so yeah me and Dingo and Tammy, we don't know what to think but guess we're glad that he headed off... You get all sorts out here.

They creaked along the dirt track. Down the road, where the salt lakes started and the sand dunes rose high off to the west, an old white Falcon station wagon was pulled off the side. A man in a faded blue t-shirt and an old pair of board shorts was bent over the engine of the car under the bonnet propped up with a piece of wood. He emerged as they slowed down and squinted at them through deep-set narrow slits with his bristled face creased and crunched up tight against the sun's glare.

Will pulled over and turned off the cricket and leant his arm on the window sill: Need a hand mate?
Yeah probly, me fan belt's busted.
Will got out of the car and bent under the bonnet: Yeah hopefully that's all it is... got another one?
Nah don't think so but one of the other boys probly does.
Where are they?
Back at The Point.
Wanna lift, we're headed that way?
Too right I do, tah, and he grabbed his surfboard and wetsuit out of his car and walked over and put them inside the back of Riley's car.
Hop in... don't you wanna grab your other stuff?
Nah she's right, there's bugger all in there and no one's gunna steal it anyway... everyone round 'ere knows it's my car, he said climbing up in the back seat with Ferret, name's Squid by the way.

They introduced themselves as Will started up the car and trundled along the dirt road splitting the blinding salt lakes. Will turned the radio back on.

What's the score? Squid asked.
It's pretty even... Windies are still batting, need another

eighty odd to get to Australia's first innings score… they've only got a coupla wickets left, Will answered looking up into the rear vision mirror.

They drove along listening to the cricket, getting drowsy with the monotone commentary and the motion of the car in the midday warmth.

Where are you camped Squid? Will asked.

Nah I live 'ere mate… there's a turn off a bit before the camping area… I'll show you, it's just up ahead.

Ok no worries… how long have you lived here for?

Long time mate… long time, Squid answered guardedly.

Pretty mild change today, Will said.

Yeah, just enough to stuff up the surf and not enough for any rain… not that we ever count on that out 'ere but evry now and then we get a few drops… 'ere it is 'ere… if you stop 'ere I'll walk the rest and get one of the boys to take me back.

We can drop you in if you like, Will said.

Nah mate, boys'd kill me if I brought you in 'ere, and he pointed at the signs hanging on posts at the cross road written in faded blue paint on scrap pieces of timber weathered grey by the elements. One said "PRIVATE PROPERTY KEEP OUT" and the sign writer had picked up one of his spelling mistakes on the other and it read "TRESPASØERS WILL BE SHOT".

Thanks fellas, Squid said as he got out of the car and grabbed his things from the back.

No worries… let us know if you need a hand later on, Will said.

Squid nodded and turned and slung his wetsuit over his shoulder and put his board on top of his head for shade and walked off down a tyre groove in the sandy track which stretched out long and straight ahead of him to nowhere, flanked on both sides by the remains of a rusted wire fence and low saltbush.

In the afternoon the onshore wind continued to blow. Grey cumulous clouds bunched and spread across the sky and rolled into each other and away off to the north. There was a good turn out for Dingo's cricket match. Even the Frenchies turned up. Riley watched them coming down the dusty track together, each drinking a long neck and busied himself with setting up a bench of beer filled eskies in a line side by side on the ground just inside an old fence line. A flattish dusty carparking area without a single blade of grass was the field. The eskies made up the grandstand and marked the boundary of part of the field. The rest of the boundary was loosely defined by scrub, a bit more fence line, a parked car and, where the dusty plain stretched out to the north, by the general feel of what was a fair distance.

At the start of play Tammy waited front on with the bat in her hand. She was tapping its bottom corner in the dirt before three rough sticks for stumps in the middle of the field while the mulletted Panel Vaner strutted in in a singlet at the rubbish bin end to bowl with a unique flourish, crossing and unwinding and re-crossing his arms like a Turkish belly dancer, before he finally released the ball to loop towards her.

They played all afternoon. Tip and go. If you hit the ball with the bat you had to run. There were no fours or sixes. Every one got a bat and a bowl, the girls got two lives and no one could get out first ball or lbw.

When it was Dingo's turn he swung the bat around, drawing big circles in the air, alternating arms and did a few back twists and other warm ups as he strode out to centre pitch. He put the weathered wooden bat to the ground and tilted it vertically . He looked up at Will umpiring at the other end and asked for middle and off. He marked it out with his thong turned on its side and saw the ball well off Didier's first ever attempt at bowling, sending the dogs scurrying off in a burst of dust, sniffing and yelping deep into the scrubby desert outfield for the ball. He panted and sweated out the runs before Ferret took the ball and came in off the long run and banged down a delivery which must have hit a rock in the pitch and took off sharply and he was caught at short cover under protest that Ferret had overrun the bowling crease by a hell of a distance which was not far from the truth but it was time Dingo was out anyway.

Riley was behind the stumps keeping when it was Sabine's go. When he saw her perched off to the side of the pitch with all three stumps exposed and the bat around the wrong way, he put his hand up to stop Randall coming in to bowl and walked over to her. He showed her where to stand side on in front of the stumps and, as he positioned himself just behind her to show her how to hold the bat, he noticed bruising on the side of her face. He held her hands to help her take a few stiff awkward practice swings and saw more bruising on her wrists.

He left her and walked backwards behind the stumps while Randall was heading back to the start of his run up. He saw her look over at Didier who was concentrating on rolling another joint at mid-wicket. Then she quickly looked behind with a flick of her hair.

She missed a couple to begin with, then connected with one that went over the bowler's head and, as she stood there in surprise, everyone yelled at her to run and she made it up and back and her score went to two. The next ball hit the top edge of the bat and she skied it. One moment Ferret was under it ready to take the catch as she ran up the pitch towards the bin end and the next moment it had found its way over to the esky boundary along the ground with a flick of the wrist and Ferret nodded at Dingo and announced that it was time to break for afternoon tea.

They walked off the field and sat down on the sandy dirt in the shade cast by the low bush up on the dune in the later afternoon, some with their backs leaning against the eskies and others spread out in front and they sipped on beers and handed around a box of barbeque shapes and a packet of chips and talked and Ferret and Dingo kept them entertained. They didn't make it back out onto the field.

The sun slipped away below the horizon unnoticed, concealed by the thick clouds and a misty haze settled in, softening the harsh surrounds. Randall said he'd had a pretty good morning fishing and invited everyone to his place to share the fish he'd caught. One of the Panel Vaners said they'd rustle up a fuckin good damper and the others all pitched in with offers of rice and a big pot of vegetable curry. Sabine went to find Didier who had left after close of play at the cricket and they all wandered off back to their campsites, carrying eskies between them.

That was pretty hilarious, Riley said as they walked back. Yeah I know, Will laughed.

It's good to be hanging out again mate... you're looking much healthier, Riley said looking off towards the sea.

Feeling a lot better... Geez it was hard the other night to pass the weed on but I'm not gunna touch it... good to be a long way away from the city... surfing and eating fish and stuff, just living day to day, it's good for the soul... and playing cricket in a dust bowl in the desert with strangers, he grinned.

They all picked up where they'd left off back at Randalls' place and ate together sitting around the campfire with the world beyond blacked out by nightfall and the almost starless cloud covered sky.

Randall asked The Panel Vaners where they were from and they told them all about the Mid Coast and, as they spoke ,their singletted chests grew and they talked with a great deal of pride about the waves there and in hushed tones about a place they'd recently been surfing at the base of some cliffs. They said they had only started surfing a few years ago. They'd worked on a house with another apprentice who was always running off at lunchtime to go for a fuckin surf when there were waves. He took them along a few times and they borrowed old single fins and got hooked. They were young, straight up and down blokes, emblemmed with tattoos, who managed to find a place for fuck or one of its grammatical forms almost every time they spoke.

Randall picked up his guitar and strummed a few chords lazily while they all talked and watched the fire and stoked it from time to time with more kindling. Ferret asked Sabine where Didier was and she said that he wasn't feeling very well and she looked down and then flashed her eyes quickly around hesitantly at the gang. Dingo pounced on a scorpion scuttling away from the heat towards Tammy's feet and trapped it in a glass jar. He handed it around the circle and they each turned the jar around away from the apricot jam label and stared at the scorpion scrabbling around in the inside of the slippery glass with its pincers raised and tail curled, alarmed and ready to fight for its feisty little life.

After a while they all felt the wind die down. Overhead the clouds had mostly cleared away and the brilliant sky show blazed above again.

Might be pretty big tomorrow, had a look at the ocean after the cricket, swell looked like it had built, Randall said.
How big? Riley asked.
Hard to tell with no one out and the waves junky from the wind, least eight foot.
Reckon the wind'll swing by tomorrow?
If we're lucky... probably still have some south in it.
One of The Panel Vaners, breaking a fire staring pause, asked:
Anyone caught any fuckin squid or what around here?
Not yet, Ferret replied.
You could give the jetty on the other side of the peninsula a go if you want... probably best to drive there if you want to go tonight... it's a bit of a hike, Randall said.
The Panel Vaners nodded at each other and the one with the skinny rat tail skulled the remains of his can and crushed it against his forehead: Righto, see youse later... cheers for the fish and everything, it was fuckin beautiful mate.
Might turn in and get some rest in case the surf is on in the morning, Will said as he got up.

Night all, I'm going to head off as well and check the waves… owe you some fish mate, Riley said looking at Randall, won't keep you waiting long.

Back at their campsite Riley started to wander off to the lookout and stopped: Wake me in the morning if the surf is good, doesn't matter how early it is.
Righto, Will said.

Riley walked off towards the beach in the dark.

He paused at the lookout listening to the unbroken rumble of the waves and then strolled down onto the beach with his hands stuffed into the pockets of his jeans against the cool desert night. He peered out at the sea with the light wind on his face. The moon was pale, washed clean by the passing storm, lighting up the rows of whitewash rolling in below. Out beyond the breakers, it laid an ever-changing shimmering track on the top of the charged black ocean. He kicked off his thongs, sat down and dug his toes into the cool coarse sand, closed his eyes and breathed deeply, filling and refilling his chest with damp salty air.

He caught the soft scrape of her footstep in the sand just a moment before she put her hands gently over his eyes from behind and touched her cool cheek lightly against his.

Guess who? She whispered.

He paused for a moment and breathed in with her hands still over his eyes. A faint scent rose up from beneath the smell of wood fire smoke. Lime. A hint of honey. He reached up and took her hands, pulled her around to him and she was looking at him and then her lips touched his and they were full and hesitant and salty. They leaned in closer and allowed their lips to part and she pulled her hands gently away from his to put her arms around his neck to get closer still. The moon lit up their foreheads as they kissed and a tear slipped unnoticed down her swollen cheek. They broke away to breathe and looked at each other with glistening eyes, laughed and leaned in to kiss again. The sea pushed untamed over the reef and up onto the beach and retreated and washed in again. The sea would do that forever. That was something that would always be, that no one could ever take away.

14.

Hey Riley?... Riley? Will said urgently.
Riley jerked awake, lifted his head off the pillow and blinked at Will standing in the doorway of his tent in the dim dawn light: What?
There's trouble over at the Frenchies, we'd better go over.
Shit, let's go, Riley said and got up.

They took fast long strides over the dirt tracks, following the sound of the trouble.

Nous partons ensemble maintenant... il faut que tu viens avec moi, Didier yelled at her as he pulled a bag and some bedding out of the tent and shoved them roughly into the back of the dusty van and went back to the tent for more gear.
Non, je peux pas, Sabine cried back at him, her face wet and bloated and streaked with strands of matted hair.

She tried to wrestle her things away from him as he brought them out of the tent. They tussled for a moment before he flung her away. She stumbled and lost her balance and fell down on her hands and knees in the dirt and stayed there bent over for a moment looking down, crying. He threw the things into the back of the van, stomped over and grabbed her roughly by the arm. He hoisted her up and marched her towards the open door of the front of the van while she cried and struggled in his grip and blubbered: Je ne peux pas... je ne peux pas.

He stopped at the door of the van and pulled her roughly around to face him and shook her by both her arms and put his hot ruddy face twisted with anger, close to hers and screamed: Pourquoi Sabine? Pourquoi?

And she shook her head, tears streaming down her face and shaking with fear and held so hard and tight and high by her arms that her torso was all caved in and her grubby toes only barely touched the ground, and saying all the while: Je ne peux pas... je ne peux pas.

He shook her again and screamed in her cowering face: Tu étais ou hier soir?... Tu étais avec qui?... C'était qui? C'était Riley?

She whimpered and struggled in his grip and said crying: Non, c'est pas ca... c'est toi... tu as beaucoup changé... tu me frappe maintenant... je ne peux pas rester avec toi... J'ai peur.

Tu vas venir avec moi, he yelled at her and tears started to well in his eyes and he forced her against the side of the van and started to lift her up into it with one arm under her leg and the other pushing her shoulder in through the doorway while she gripped the edge of the van with both hands and tried to resist, crying: Je ne peux pas... Didier, laisse moi.

Oi mate... mate... leave her alone, Riley yelled rounding the bend and running hard across the dirt with Will coming up behind him.

Didier looked around and saw Riley and Will and let Sabine go and stamped across the ground towards them with wild eyes and a blustering face.

What are you doing with my girlfriend? He yelled as he came near to Riley.
Listen mate, she's bloody scared of you... you hit her... I saw the bruises yesterday. Leave her alone now, Riley said calmly.

Didier ran at him with arms swinging. Crazed. Riley held his arms outstretched trying to keep him away. He landed a blow on the side of Riley's head. Riley shook his head and kept his arms out in front of him trying to fend off Didier's manic attack.

Easy mate, you're going to get yourself in real strife if you don't calm down, Riley said.

Didier renewed his swinging with increased fervour and thrust aside Riley's arms suddenly with one hand and belted him hard in the chest with his other and cursed and swore at him in French. Riley stumbled back and regained his footing and sized up Didier for a few moments. He looked at Will and Will shook his head and they moved in together on Didier and between the two of them they managed to wrestle him to the ground.

They wore a few blows in the process but they eventually pinned him down without laying into him. Will grabbed a strap lying on the ground near the van and tied Didier's hands up behind his back and told him that he'd better calm down or it'd be a long time before they let him go, that there'd be more than enough time for them to go and get the cops and then he'd be thrown in the slammer for assaulting his girlfriend and them as well for that matter and he'd have to scavenge in a dirty hot rat infested cell in a small town out in the desert where the cops might just forget all about him.

Didier sat slumped in the dirt with his hands tied hard behind him and continued to swear at them in French. Riley went and got a chair and they each reached under his shoulders and helped him up into the chair with his tied hands pushing out through the gap at the back. He stayed there for a moment and then got up and kicked over the chair. He glared at Riley, walked away to a rocky area on a rise nearby, sat down and looked out to sea, fuming.

Tammy had come over and was hurriedly helping Sabine collect her things and they piled her bag of clothes, surfboard and wetsuit, a fold up chair and a few other things in one area on the ground. Sabine went through the car for other belongings and put them in her backpack. Will and Riley pulled the tent down and repacked Didier's van and slid his boards in last on top of the mattress. When they had finished and Sabine had said she had gathered all the things she wanted, Will and Riley walked up the low rise to where Didier was sitting. Will held the keys to the van in his hand and said to Didier:
Listen mate, we've packed everything up for you. It's best for everyone and for you if you get going now. Sabine is gunna stay here. We're gunna untie you now and give you the keys but we don't want any more trouble. Any more trouble and

we'll block the road out o' here and then I'm gunna drive like the clappers and get the cops and they'll be mighty excited about you 'cos not much happens round here by the looks. Do we have a deal?

Didier sat there and stayed looking out to sea for a few moments and looked at Will and then at Riley and watched Sabine and Tammy walking down the track in the distance carrying her things away from him. He put his head down on his knees and stayed there for a while and then banged his forehead against his knees half a dozen times and shook his head and looked down again and back up at Will and Riley and nodded.

Will squatted down and asked him to stay still and as he was untying his hands he said: You know you gotta stay away from the weed mate. It does different things to different people. It's no good for you. It was no good for me either believe me. Stuffed me right up for a while.

Will finished untying him and put the strap in his pocket. Didier rubbed his hands and wrists. Will stood up slowly and held out his hand to Didier. He pushed it aside and got up off the ground.

The three of them walked back down to the van in silence. Will gave him the keys and Didier got in and put his sunglasses on and started the van up. He looked over at Will and Riley standing off to the side and asked them to tell her he was sorry. They nodded. Dingo and Ferret had gathered on the track higher up and stood with their arms crossed watching him go, bodies ringed with platinum halos in front of the rising sun like characters in a Western. Riley and Will raised their hands as the van moved off. Didier looked straight ahead and drove the van slowly out along the track, alone in the middle of nowhere in a foreign land. Sad. Twisted. Beaten.

Thanks mate, Riley said as they walked back to camp.

No worries, we had to do something or god knows what he might've done to Sabine... how's your head?

Riley felt his cheek with his fingers. The skin was split and he scratched at a bit of congealed blood. It'll be fine... he got a good one in on my chest though that I'll feel for a few days I reckon... geez it was hard not to have a crack at him... Did he lay any on you?

Nah nothing much, clipped me on the arm... he was more after you, Will laughed.

They kept walking and Will looked over at Riley and asked with a smile: Reckon she's worth it?

Riley grinned: yep, dunno, think so... what are the chances out here?

When they neared their camp, Sabine ran down the track and hugged Riley around the middle with her head against his chest and broke off and did the same to Will and went back to Riley and wrapped her arms around him again: I'm sorry... thank you, I never see him so crazy before.

Will walked off and Riley held her for a time and then he helped her put her things inside his tent. He walked over to the fire and dug around in the ash with a long stick until he unearthed some coals and threw a few handfuls of broken twigs in on top of a bit of screwed up paper. He picked the dented kettle up off the ground and filled it with water from the container in the back of the car and when the twigs caught alight, sat it in amongst them.

Will came back and told them that he was starving after his morning gym session with his French instructor and they laughed and Riley asked him if he'd been to check the surf.

Yeah… not so good here… out of control for the waves out the front… Randall reckons the wind's got a bit too much south in it still for the right and it'd be too big for it as well, reckons there must be another front to the south that's sending up this swell… said there's a long left hander down the coast that'll be firing today.
Yeah , really… whereabouts? Riley asked.
Coupla hours south… wanna go have a look? Probably need our bigger boards… Randall's keen.
Yeah, for sure, Riley turned to Sabine: want to come along?
Ok, that would be fun, she smiled.

*　　*　　*

They drove out along the dirt road to town and filled up with petrol. No one said anything about Didier. They were hoping not to see him. Out on the highway, with the boards on the roof, Riley lucky dipped into the tape box and they listened to Midnight Oil and the steady buzz of the straps tying the boards down as they drove through dry farming land and past tall cylindrical grain silos and a few small towns.

A few hours later they pulled up at a dusty dirt car park high up on a hill overlooking the ocean near a brown station wagon and a rusted white ute with an old silver board bag lying empty in the tray at the back. Randall leaned forward from the back seat and rested his arms on the top of the seat in front and they studied the ocean for a minute. Then they all got out and stood on the hilltop looking out. Pepper sniffed car tyres and squatted for a wee and came back and sat at Randall's feet.

The sparse sandy cliff line stretched away in front of them to the south west and continued in the other direction to the northeast. A haze of wheat coloured dust blew across its top and around them in the car park, whipped out towards the sea by the stiff south-easterly. Along the base of the cliffs next to the ocean, huge granite rocks and slabs lay at rest, some warming in the sun and others glistening wet under the ebb and flow of the ocean which had washed over them for millions of years. Away in the distance out to sea, two black figures were sitting on their boards a lot further out than the trail of whitewash from the waves that had just broken. Another surfer was sliding fast down the crumbling dune with a big board under his arm, his wetsuit half pulled on and flapping about with the hasty descent.

Will glanced over at Randall who was looking further up the coast and they watched a big set push in up there and break and peel, unridden, down the boulder-lined point. They followed those same lines of swell as they rolled across the ocean to where the surfers were sitting. There the waves rose up tall and majestic on the shallowing reef and then broke one after the other and peeled down the point away from them to the right, white foam exploding and chasing the long walls of blue brushed smooth by the southeast wind and glistening under the midday sun.

One of the surfers paddled onto the third wave in the set and dropped down the face with his back to the wave – a black stick figure away off in the distance. It loomed several times his size as he bottom turned, running before the crashing whitewash and then rode back up in the clean blue water and down again and repeatedly, in long drawn out turns, fleetingly carving his own unique mark in a white trail on the wave before the lip crashed down and erased it forever.

They glanced around at each other and laughed nervously. Will said it looked pretty big and Randall said it was better than the last time he'd come and Riley glanced over at Sabine who raised her eyebrows and looked a little nervous.

They climbed up onto the side of the car, undid the old straps and got their boards out of their covers and lay them on the dirt. They each took turns rubbing on wax in circles while others inspected their leg ropes and smeared sun cream on their faces and nearly rubbed it in. They shook their wetsuits and dusted sand off the insides, shoved an arm in each of the arms and legs to turn them back from inside out and balanced on one leg and hopped around a bit to regain balance while they pulled them on under towels tied around their waists for cover because there was a lady present. Will hid the keys in one of the back wheels like he always did and he and Randall shot down the hillside first, bits of broken limestone tumbling down with them.

It was warm and protected from the wind at the base of the high hill. Riley and Sabine stopped at a small beach flanked on either side by smooth slabs of granite rock. Sheltered between them was a calm pool of water which became a deep channel leading out to sea and gave access to the area where the waves started to rear and break. Will and Randall were already picking their way across the rocks. They were small against the size of the waves looming and crashing and rolling off down the point out beyond them.

Riley helped Sabine zip up her wetsuit and kissed her on the nape of her neck and while she bent down to attach her leg rope to her ankle, he turned his face to the sun for a moment. He patted Pepper on the head and they walked down to the water and waded out up to their thighs and climbed onto their boards. As they slowly paddled out past the pool together and started to climb the undulations of the galloping ocean and see it from the sobering reality of absolute sea level, Riley said that she didn't have to catch any waves if she didn't want to and maybe she could sit wide and watch and wait until she felt comfortable. She nodded and smiled and kept paddling alongside him.

As they headed more to the north around out the back of the reef into deep water towards the line up, paddling over larger and larger walls of water swinging in to end their long journey, Sabine's paddling slowed down. Riley looked over and her eyes were wide and her face furrowed and filled with fear and as a bigger set appeared in the distance and marched in towards them, she stopped and changed direction and said hurriedly: Is much too big for me Riley, you keep going out but I going back in.

Without waiting for Riley to say something she started to paddle back in, looking over her right shoulder watching the big set coming closer. Riley stopped and looked at the approaching set and back at Sabine. It wasn't going to break on them. She'd be fine. For a few seconds, he wrestled with his excitement at getting out to the line up to join the others, looking at the waves booming down the reef and back at Sabine paddling away. He turned his big board and caught up to her and she smiled at him and he paddled back in with her for a little while until she got near to the pool. He stopped and told her he'd see her in a little while and she nodded and he headed back out.

How is it? Riley asked when he got out the back.
Pretty good... triple overhead, not hollow but long workable walls... a bigger set just came through a little while ago, Will said.
Yeah... I saw it, Riley said and looked around and nodded and said G'day to a blond haired guy with blue eyes and a ship captain's beard obscuring most of his face sitting on a big red board deeper on the peak. He nodded back. Behind them away off in the distance a surfer rose over a swell line, paddling back out next to the trail of whitewash of the last set and disappeared down the other side. Randall and the other couple of blokes must have been back down there somewhere also.

They stayed out there for hours. Huge buildings towered towards them from out to sea with long walls and unsteady teetering rooflines, too tall in the deep to be straight topped until they hurried in and gathered height and speed over the shallow reef and the offshore breeze groomed their walls and ruler edged their tops.

Some they let go, some the decision was made for them and others they sized up and scrambled to get into position to catch. As they turned their backs to the wave growing and rushing at them ready or not and peered back over their shoulders at it arcing up behind them, they were held hostage to hesitation and fear for a few heart pounding moments before throwing themselves with gritted teeth and fast, furious strokes and kicks into catching it on a surge of adrenalin. Picking up momentum they rose up onto their feet and leant forward over the spraying edge, open mouthed, to drop down into the boiling depths on the other side, toes barely gripping the deck and boards pointing down, almost vertical, chattering with speed as they levelled out at the bottom, backs to the wave, poised in a low trapeze armed crouch through the bottom turn, waiting for the moment to glide back up the face and into the pocket of the wave to turn and then re-live it all again.

Every now and then someone would spot a bigger set approaching and let out a whistle and the small pack sitting out the back on constant alert would hastily drop down onto their stomachs and paddle and kick with urgency, hoping to rise up and over its crest from where they could look back down with whooping awe at the trough, dark from the reef a long way below. If they didn't make it far enough out, they'd have to take a deep breath and push and kick their boards through the wide wall as it was breaking and keep pushing and kicking as they were pulled up and through the wave, desperately trying to avoid not making it all the way through for that meant getting sucked up into the rearing lip and driven backwards, head first, over the falls all the way down with it, immersed in it, to thump into the flat surface of the sea below with an unpredictable fibreglass weapon on the loose, and writhe and tumble uncontrollably at the mercy of the ocean and end up deep inside with more waves in the set bearing down and the rocks patiently waiting to strike.

From time to time other cars pulled up at the car park in a cloud of dust and people got out and stood on the hill and looked out for a while, hands held above over their eyes as visors against the sun. Some climbed on top of car bonnets and leaned against the windscreens and stayed to watch. A few more surfers paddled out. Others retreated to the safety of a cool beer or slipped back to their fishing or tractors or went to fiddle busily on a long outstanding job in a shed somewhere muttering something about the wrong swell direction or tide.

There was not much opportunity to talk out in the water between riding waves, paddling back out against the current running down the point and dodging the huge sneaker sets. They spoke to each other from a distance in loud whoops and warning whistles, yells and cries. The raw ocean levelled and sobered and demanded the truth and their unchecked elation and apprehension and exertion were painted on their faces and spoke a thousand words and not much else was needed.

Will had already seen the big set coming and had started to paddle further out when the warning whistles started. He struck out hard and climbed up and over the preceding swell lines until there was only a wide stretch of flat blue water between him and the first wave of the set. Wide. Thick. Massive. For a fleeting second or two, as it rose towards him, drawing up water from the flats in front, building on its already huge stature, he thought seriously about changing his mind and heading for the safety of the shoulder like they'd all been doing so far when the huge sets came in. His board started to point that way as he paddled. Until something switched. Some deep-rooted instinct took over which set him into a state of focused determination.

Then he no longer heard the whistling and yelling from the water. Or the horns being thumped and sat on up in the car park. He wasn't aware of Randall paddling hard off to the side to get out of the wave's path. As he ploughed deep strokes in the water with his arms and kicked hard and powered towards the growing peak, everything else was shut out. With the wave rising up over him and casting him into its towering shadow, he stopped paddling and quickly sat up on his board. He turned it around to face the shore in one fluid movement and then started to take strong urgent strokes and kick hard as he was being rapidly drawn up the face of the wave. His chin was held down low almost touching the board, spray flaring and darting at his eyes. Blinded, immune to sound, his board snaking forward side to side with his exertion, picking up forward momentum, he pushed up to his feet. He stood in a low crouch at the apex of the mountain, tilting his weight forward. He teetered up there for a couple of seconds, trying to launch over the edge, then for a few more, held in the rearing peak by the wind whipping up the huge face and under the front of his board, the lip growing thicker and whiter.

Suddenly, inevitably, it threw out and all he knew was that he was no longer connected to his board and he was in mid air falling towards the ocean. Then he was rotating so his back was underneath him and he was still falling and he kept turning, out of control. Then his feet started to come around again and he was still falling and he had time to think that he was still falling and he gathered into a partial tuck a split second before he slammed down onto the hard flat water. The lip brought down with it the whole heaving weight of the wall which exploded on him and pushed him down. Then he was drawn back up into the wave as it continued to break, pulling water off the reef and anything that was in the water, before he was driven back down with it again and this time deep into the swirling, tumultuous depths where he was tossed around in the dark like a ragdoll, arms and legs pulled and torn at and flailing wildly, holding his breath. He covered his head with his hands and pulled his legs up into a tuck to ride it out and conserve air while his balled frame was shoved, flipped and turned.

He lost his bearings. He no longer knew which way was up as the onslaught continued. After a time, his chest started to tighten with the stale air he was holding onto and a sickly feeling crept in. He let some air go and opened his eyes, looked into the churning blackness and saw nothing. Pinned down under the constant turbulence, air starved and panicking in the dark, he broke his tuck and desperately thrashed about trying to free himself from the tumbling. He reached down to his ankle and found his leg rope and grabbed it and started to haul himself up. Bubbling out the last dregs of the toxic air in his lungs, he followed its extended stretch. Out of air he let go close to the surface and frantically struck out with his arms and kicked and burst through the surface of the water. He took a huge gasp of air and frothy salty suds and coughed and wheezed as he sucked them into his lungs. He just had time to splutter to clear them and take a clean breath and look behind him before the thundering whitewash of the next wave in the set ploughed into him and it all started again.

The second wave got hold of his board and dragged him along by his leg rope underwater, tugging hard on his outstretched leg until the pressure suddenly released and, as he tumbled around underwater holding his breath and trying to go with it, he knew his leg rope had snapped and his board would now be sliding and bouncing towards the rocks and he'd have to swim in.

An age later he came to the surface in the foam with his lungs screaming for air and took another big breath. He looked around treading water, weak, helpless against the surge ushering him along. The back of the second wave was steaming its way towards shore. He watched it suddenly kick up hard as it smashed onto the rocks. As the water recoiled it revealed granite ledges covered in barnacles a throw away and the sea thrashed and whirlpooled below them. He swore and starting to cramp, turned his head to look behind him and saw the whitewash from the third wave in the set bearing down on him already and he swore again, filled with dread. He didn't have the energy to try to dive down deep and hope the wave would not thrust him onto the rocks underwater and there'd be another wave after this one and probably another and another and he thought that he really was stuffed this time, that he really was going to bloody die.

He stayed treading water, clumsy with fatigue and fear and, as the mountain of whitewash rumbled towards him, took several deep breaths and looked to the sky and knew that whatever it was that he'd never believed in would see straight through him anyway, see him as a fraud leaving it to the last bloody second. He gave a few big kicks and pushed himself up with his arms to get as high as he could just as the wave hit him like a battering ram. As he became consumed, he tucked into a ball again for the third time and put his hands over his head and held his breath and closed his eyes and went with it. He counted six bounces before his knee belted a rock and then he was weightless again. He stayed in his tuck, bits of him catching on barnacles and sliding on over the slippery surface of the rock until his momentum finally slowed.

He opened his eyes and grabbed at a tall barnacle with his left hand and stuck the fingers of the other into a crevice and puffed his cold cheeks in and out with short deep breaths and held on, his whole terrified cramping body pressed down hard against the rock as the whitewash surged back out to sea over him, pulling, tearing, ripping at him. He hung on until it had retreated and then scrambled on his hands and knees across the black rock as slippery as ice and barely made it to a dry area before the next wave ran up and over the ledge and spread out over the wet rock looking for him.

He dragged himself up and leant his back against a low rock and sat there breathing hard. He closed his eyes and lowered his head and breathed slowly and deeply and shook for a very long time as the rest of the endless set boomed down and bulldozed in to shore. When the pain of the gashes became stronger he opened his eyes and inspected the tear on the palm of his left hand from where he'd held the jagged barnacle and tilted himself to the side and looked at the blood dripping out through cuts in his wetsuit on his upper arm and legs. He looked down at the cord of his broken leg rope still tied around his ankle and remembered his board and stood up slowly. Pain shot through him and he sat down again and looked at his sliced bleeding foot. He got up slowly and limped over the rocks to higher ground.

Out to sea black shapes were bobbing on their boards a long way out the back. Others were paddling back out through the trail of whitewash of the big set. He couldn't see his board from where he stood. He looked up at the steep hillside and slowly limped towards a goat track bending up it, coarse sand grating into the cuts in his feet and congealing with the blood.

Hey mate!

Will stopped and turned and saw two guys picking their way hastily below him along a sand track between the base of the hillside and the rocks. One of them put his hand up as Will looked over. Sabine was hurrying along behind them. Will shifted his weight off his cut foot and waited.

When they got close to him, the bigger guy with sandy hair and a skin full of freckles said: Need a hand mate?
Nah, she's right, Will said, I'll just take it easy. He looked over at Sabine as she caught up.
The bigger guy looked at the sand bloody from his foot and the drips from his open wounds. Carn mate… I'll give you a hand, it's no worries, he said stepping up the rise to Will,

here... chuck your arm over here, he said as he leant down and got his shoulder under Will's armpit. He stood up and pulled Will's arm around his neck and shoulders and they started off up the sandy track.

After a few steps Will leant down and undid the broken leg rope from his ankle and put his arm back over the other guy's shoulder and they started off again. Sabine followed.

Thanks mate, Will said and after a pause, you guys didn't see my board come in did you?
Yeah, we saw it all from the car park... reckon it washed in over the rocks a fair bit further down... probably copped a bit of a beating like you, he laughed, Sean's gone to have a squiz. Will looked over his shoulder down the rise and saw the other guy heading down along the rocks and said: Thanks a lot mate.

Part way up the hill, Will slumped off and sat down and put his head between his knees for a while. Sabine gave him some water and he drank the whole bottle dry and waited for a bit and they set off again.

That was a pretty heavy wipe out.
Yeah I know, Will said.
Reckon that was the set of the day.
Maybe... there were a couple of waves earlier that were pretty big.
Looked like there was a strong gust of wind as you paddled into it and it held you up in the lip.
Yeah, I got held up but dunno what happened, it's all a bit of a blur, couldn't see a thing.
Can't believe you didn't get totalled on the rocks.

Nah I know, I thought I was a goner... honestly thought that was it when I saw the dry ledge and the whitewash from the third one coming at me.

Reckon you were pretty lucky mate.

Yeah I know... still can't really believe I'm out of it.

Where you guys from?

My mate and I are from WA and, he turned his head and nodded back towards Sabine, Sabine's from France... camping up at The Point... just came down for the day... you from round here?

Yeah, me and my brother work on the land a bit further south, family farm, surf here a bit... reckon it's a bit better when it's a bit smaller... there's lots of waves round here, gotta know where to look but.

They kept trudging up the hill.

You right now? He asked as they reached the top of the hill and let Will go.

Yeah, thanks a lot... better get some stuff for these cuts, Will said and headed slowly over to his car.

No worries.

Sabine opened up the car and helped Will take his wetsuit off his shoulders and then she dug around in the back of the car for the small black bag with medical stuff he'd asked her to try and find while he got out of his wetsuit. He poured water on his head and cuts, dried off and climbed up slowly onto the side step of the car and sat down on the front seat. He dressed a few of the deeper wounds. Sabine slid in beside him and they watched the guys out in the surf for a while.

The younger brother appeared at the top of the hill carrying Will's big board with yellow rails under his arm.

Found it, Sean grinned as he neared Will's car.
You're a legend mate, Will said and shuffled out of the car and stood down gingerly, how is it?

Sean reached up and wiggled the nose of the board back and forth as he walked over, you've got some work to do up there on the nose mate but least you've still got it… rails are pretty dinged up but should be pretty easy to fix… still got all your fins, there's a few other dings on the bottom, he said as he turned the board over and showed Will and then handed him the board.

Thanks, Will said looking down turning the board over in his hands, you going out?
Yeah, in a bit, wind should back off pretty soon, he said and they looked out at the ocean… see ya round mate, he said and scuffed off.
Yeah, thanks again.

Will and Sabine talked and swatted at flies and had something to eat and pulled the visors down against the sun. After a while, Sabine headed off down the hill for a walk and a swim. Will draped a towel across the front windscreen, jammed its corners in the closed doors against the heat of the sun and opened the windows. Then he lay down across the bench seat with his t-shirt over his head against the flies and dozed off.

He woke to the sounds of the others returning and talking excitedly about the surf session. He yawned and stretched and sat up and opened the door and put his head out.

Hi Will, Riley said drying his hair with his towel, bloody hell mate, that was a hell of a wipe out... saw the whole thing as I was paddling back out... the wave was on you quick.

Yeah, I know... thought I had it but I guess I needed time for a few more strokes to get a bit more momentum, Will said.

Randall had come around the back of the car and was pulling his wetsuit off.

What happened on the inside? He asked when Will had finished, we looked back from the top of the waves from the same set but we couldn't see you... thought you must've got washed down the point with the set... after it passed, we started to paddle around past the peak to come back in through the pool to see if you were alright when we saw you heading up the hill.

I got drilled, like a bad wipe out Down South when it's big, 'cept the water's colder here... what was worse was the exposed rock ledge with the waves belting into it, Will said and told them what had happened.

When he'd finished Riley shook his head: sounds pretty serious mate.

Yeah, I know... looked like you guys got a few good ones after? Yeah, it was still good out there... wind dropped a little and there weren't as many of those massive sneaker sets, Riley said putting his hat and sunglasses on.

A set rolled through. They watched the gliding riders, miniscule on the open faces of the waves.

On the dirt road heading back towards The Bay, Riley steered the car through a bend and looked over at Will and then up at Randall and Sabine in the rear vision mirror and asked if anyone could go a beer at the pub.

They walked up the crumbling concrete steps to the glass front door. The brick walled pub looked down over trees and grass to the calm bay. Randall tied Pepper to the railing and gave her some water. Inside two guys were cracking pool balls around the table at the far end of the room. Three older white haired blokes in shorts and flannelette shirts rolled up at the elbow were seated on stools topped with cracked red vinyl at the bar. They all had the same rounded hunch and leaned on their elbows, holding onto their pint glasses with their backs bent away from the view. One tapped a cigarette into an ashtray.

Will, Riley and Sabine padded across the worn carpet. Their feet stuck to it at the bar. Randall ordered drinks. The three blokes turned in unison to look at them with weary disinterest. They picked up their glasses and took a sobering walk around the walls of the pub staring at the gallery of framed photographs of dark submarine sized sharks roped up by their tails and hanging from huge pulleys on jetties and lying on their sides on the decks of fishing boats, with their proud assassins leering wildly, minute alongside the massive sharks, small kids poking through the crowd at hip level and other people looking on with fascinated horror. The date and weight and length and other details were hand marked in ink on the photographs for posterity.

Outside the windows of the pub, dusk came and coated the bay with a light lilac haze. They ordered counter meals. The men sawed at gristly huge T-bone steaks hanging off the edge of the plate and saved a few bits for Pepper. Sabine found the stretch of veal, tenderised to leather belt thickness and not much easier to chew, below a sweating lava of cheddar cheese and red sauce. They ate and talked and laughed about the day and Will said he'd probably preferred the fight with the Frenchman than the one with the ocean.

The old blokes at the bar took good sized pulls on their beers now and again, opening their mouths and pouring the liquid down. They idly drew lines in the condensation on the glass with a finger, moved coins around on the bar and flattened out the bar towel. Every now and then one of them mumbled something which the others acknowledged in a single syllable reply or nodded in silence. When it was time for another, they held up their empty glass and made eye contact with the bar tender who stopped towelling glasses and carefully pulled from the tap, placed it down on the coaster and selected from the coins on the bar in a wordless exchange.

*　　*　　*

The camp was still and quiet when they drove back through it. One domed tent glowed amber above the moonscape terrain. Riley parked the car back at their place and Randall said he'd get his board off the roof in the morning and shuffled off with his wetsuit slung over his arm and Pepper beside him. Will hung the other wetsuits on the wire fence in the usual spot, unzipped his tent and turned in.

Riley was looking up at the clear night sky and shadowing shapes against the tent with his hands in the moonlight when she came back from the washroom. As she timidly approached, he bent down and lifted her off her feet, cradling her in his arms. She put her arm around his shoulders and kicked her thongs off into the dirt and he carried her giggling across the threshold of the tent, putting her down to unpick a strand of her hair which got caught in the zip on the way in.

He went over and rolled up the flap of one of the windows and let the moonlight in and a gentle breeze from the east came in with it. He turned and watched her unravel her hair and then gently shake it. She looked up and caught him watching her. She smiled shyly and looked back down at her hands and stood there inside the tent playing with the brown hair band in her fingers. He came over and she reached out to him and pulled him close. He undressed her while they kissed and her clothes slipped down and she lifted her feet out of them and his clothes settled on top of hers and the curves of her olive skin glimmered and shivered as he followed the little bumps down her arms and onto her thighs with his fingers and touched the soft smooth parts of her he'd seen under her shorts on the cliff top.

She settled down on the bedding. Sitting with her legs bent and a little open, she reached up and pulled him down on top of her. Their bare skin touched as they lay back on uneven blow up mattresses side by side in the old tent in the desert, surfboards and boxes of food and bags of other stuff strewn about, sheets gritty with sand, no jobs, no plans, taking each day as it came, immersed in the dust and the sea and the sun. He slid his arms under her and hugged her tight and then rolled over fast onto his back and pulled her on top of him and she laughed and they kissed and she bit his tongue gently and pushed suddenly up with her hands on his chest to straddle him. She found him and their bodies moved together and she held his wrists in her hands and as they moved she threw her shoulders and head back and her nails dug deeper into his wrists. She arched her chest and between her breasts the skin glistened with perspiration in the moonlight and her knees gripped so hard they would never let go and, as she started to breathe heavily, he put one hand to her mouth and she bit the edge of his palm in her teeth and they moved together, eyes locked and glinting urgently. He shuddered and they kept moving, wildly, like they had harnessed the source of the hot lawless desert and the heaving ocean and found the souls of the ancient savage creatures that inhabited them.

And afterwards she lay down beside him and the sides of their bodies touched and she put her cheek and the palm of her hand on his chest and he stroked her hair. She hooked her smaller foot with his and gradually their breathing slowed and deepened.

15.

Summer rolled on. Each day came and went more or less like the one before it. Scorchingly hot in the daytime. Cold ocean reprieves. Starlit nights. Flickering campfires. Sleeping bodies contoured to the undulations of the rocky ground.

Leathery heels, already hard and flaking, wrinkled into meandering crevices and then cracked painfully open, canyoning deep into dirty, tough, sun and salt dried hide. Needlingly sharp to walk on and biting even in sleep. Splitting wider and wider. Drawing blood. Bodies were browned and dried and whittled down to their lean muscled essentials on meagre budgets and excessive exercise. Hair grew long, first as a recognisable extension of the original shape and then splayed and tangled into dusty disregarded jumbles.

The skin on Riley's face gradually disappeared under a mask of dark hair encroaching from all sides like a polar explorer and eventually only the rusted skin of his cheekbones and nose and around his eyes remained visible. Wispy bleached twists shot unconvincingly out from Will's chin here and there with a smattering of fluff on the sides above his jawbone and a bit more above his lip. The skin on his nose was in a constant state of shardy peel. His hair had become impossibly matted and resumed the bleached colour of his boyhood. Sabine's olive skin grew darker and her arms showed muscular rises and falls.

The wind usually blew offshore in the mornings. In the afternoons the sea breeze raced in. Every now and then a change fronted up. A day or two before, it would be unbearably hot. A gusty northeast wind would bluster in off the desert and lash and tear at the white peaks of the mountainous dunes under a blue sky. On those days, often the wind would gradually fall away to nothing in the late morning, then a light sea breeze would waft in half-heartedly for a few hours and fade away again to nothing in the late afternoon. The ocean would become a mirror and oily smooth and the waves would be good. The northwest wind would follow that night or during the next day and the change's stern wall of grey clouds would ride in hard to pull at tents and knock over chairs and whip dust about all over the place. As the wind swung to the west and then through to the southwest they would sit it out and enjoy the cooler days, put a bit more wood on the fire at night and wait for the return of the east wind.

The days revolved around the wind. Wind and swell. Will went to the lookout at first light most days and moved his face around to feel the direction of the wind until he felt it blowing evenly over both his ears and knew he was pointing into it. Randall was often there then as well and they'd stand out there and patiently watch the sea and pick up its rhythm. Back at camp, Will would call out to wake Riley and Sabine if the conditions were right. Other times he let them wake up when they did.

Will and Randall gravitated towards each other. Riley fell hard. He always fell hard. Last time he'd been so consumed by his girl there was not much room left for his mates. Will and the other blokes had tried for a while. He always had something he had to do with her friends or her family. It was only when she went away to see her sister or a friend Over East that he would suddenly call and they'd catch up. Will didn't say anything.

Most of the time they stayed at The Point. The waves were good at the campsite and there was a beach over the back from the shop when it was small and other breaks further on the other way. The locals got used to them at the right. Tolerated them. Even nodded at Will and Riley in the water every now and then. Until Kurt's drop in. Then they were off all tourists again for a good while and a thick band of tension hovered over the surface of the water.

Sabine helped bridge the gap a bit. They watched her curves as she paddled out ahead of them and grinned leeringly hard at her as they stroked up alongside. They were sex-starved bachelors living off poster girls pinned up on the driftwood posts of their shacks and the odd trip into town or further down the coast. Permanently dry, cracked, salty, reptilian, disconnected from society by choice or need, eating canned food and rinsing the dust off with the freezing salty water of the Bight or under the briny water of a trickling bore. Their faces and hands were roasted by sun and their minds by weed and they had no idea how to talk to a girl like Sabine. Attempts were made. In a toneless drawl, she was told that it was a fuckin sensational day and if it didn't put a smile on your dial nothing would and wasn't that right or that she'd be bloody fine out there as he'd asked the bloody sharks to leave her alone today. The expletives were blustered out with manly pride and burst up out of the flat monotone muttering like a firecracker. They seemed to help steady their nerves a bit, give them a bit of bravado. Sabine had trouble making out what they were saying but noticed them stealing glimpses at the outline of her body in her wetsuit.

Out at the peak it was a different story. It was serious business out there and the locals sat sternly and silently astride their boards inside the pack and dominantly seethed waiting for the next set. The out o' towners didn't exist out there and there was no way in hell they'd cut one any slack. A pretty girl was no exception. Probably worse in actual fact. It was fine for her to be in the water and especially if she stayed a little down the line and watched them take off on their waves. But there was no place for her out at the peak. They'd be the laughing stock of The Whole Bloody Point if they gave her one out there. They'd never hear the bloody end of it.

When the surf was no good or their bodies were stiff, taut and tired from too much of it, they caught fish or lay about reading books swapped with other travellers. Every couple of weeks they took a trip into town to get supplies. Besides the major repair to Will's big board, there were small dings to fix from where they'd hit the reef or a rock. They'd line up all of the boards with cracks and holes facing the sun to make sure they dried and cut fibreglass cloth to the size of the dings and mix resin and hardener. They'd work quickly to get it onto the dings before it went rubbery and then set rock hard. It dried quickly in the heat out there. The sanding was the time consuming part. When the waves were good, the boards were ridden with the hard raised lumps of fibreglass for a while before they got around to sanding.

In the evenings, the three of them pitched in to prepare the fire and dinner. They took their time. There was time. They were rich in it and fish and rice and waves and not much else. The quality of the evening meal went up a few notches with Sabine's involvement. There had always been lots of fish but otherwise there would be bread with canned baked beans or hot water added to packets of ready-made pasta and their sachets of powder sauce but not a great deal else. The focus was on volume. Since Sabine had joined the camp there'd been fish stews and green curries, rice and vegetable dishes and pasta with Bolognese sauce and even grated cheese. They ate slowly and savoured each mouthful. Nothing was left in the pot.

After dinner one of them piled up the pots and pans and took them down to the water's edge. There they'd dip them in the sea, grab a handful of wet coarse sand and scrub at their black crusted bases and then leave them to soak overnight above the high tide mark on the beach. Sometimes in the evenings they'd head off to another campsite or people would find their way to theirs.

Dingo and Ferret were born entertainers and fed off each other. Their real inventive flair came late in their stay in early March with the arrival of an army of starving mice. Summer was scheduled to have ended but there was no sign of the heat letting up and, if anything, it had got hotter during the day as the sea breeze eased off and sometimes didn't show up at all anymore. Across the campground, mice chewed through cardboard boxes and got at rice and biscuits and cereal packets and everything else they came across. For most out there living on welfare or a travelling budget which had to extend to covering beer and other essentials, the loss of food was a very serious matter. Each morning new stories would be exchanged about the increasingly extreme mice invasions. Even food hidden in closed glove boxes of shut cars disappeared, only shreds of the nibbled wrapper left as calling cards. As the days continued the plague swelled and became more and more desperate.

At night they'd feel prickly little claws skipping across their heads with a tickling tail while sleeping. A flurry of flinging arms and swearing would be followed by an outraged hunt for the little blighter. Holes chewn down low in tent walls and corners were taped and endlessly retaped. On trips to town, the upholstery would bulge and move as the car travelled along and a few would alight onto the ground from under the car when it stopped and scramble over each other in different directions. Will, Riley and Sabine had their fair share of raids like everyone else but their food was kept in a big plastic tub with a lid that snapped closed and there were easier targets.

Like Ferret, Dingo and Tammy's camp. Dingo declared war early on in the piece. For Dingo and Ferret though it was as much to do with the sport of it in idle moments as it was for preserving food. Like everything, they applied themselves to picking off mice with enthusiasm. At times it was about numbers and at other times it was about technique. Traditional mice traps had their place but they lacked style. They made themselves bows and arrows and sat off in the dark nearby waiting with strings pulled while mice cautiously sniffed their way over towards the plate of tit bits sitting on the ground in low kerosene lamp light. They coated a glass bottle in cooking oil and draped the neck with a cheese string necklace and suspended it above a bucket of salt water on more string accessible from the limb of a bush. Another favourite was walking the plank. A small light piece of wood would overhang and rest lightly on the rim of a bucket of water with an irresistible blob of peanut butter on its end. They spent countless hours planning their next method of attack, diagrams were sketched with fingers in the dust and each day they notched the new numbers into a good sized branch stripped of its bark after the ritual morning bucket inspection.

Riley and Sabine often went for a walk down to the beach before going to bed. Sometimes they didn't make it back to the tent and rinsed off in a shallow rock pool and dashed back to the tent with wet hair and tingling skin and their clothes scrunched up in their hands. On nights when Sabine turned in early, Riley and Will would sit by the fire and stare at it and kick the ends of logs in and talk like before.

One night a week or two after Will had washed in over the rocks down the coast, he crossed his legs and swivelled the end of his fire poking stick in the flames and said: D'yah reckon it's all over when we kark it?

Dunno... probly... why? Riley asked.

Just wondering, Will paused, you know when I was caught inside that day and the rock ledge was right there and the whitewash coming at me, I really thought I was history... For some reason I looked up to the sky and in my head I asked for help... until then I didn't think I believed in anything. Only time any of us went to church was when we had the funeral for Dad but that was different... family isn't religious or anything... one of my aunties is but we don't see her... she lives in a big house near the river, borrowed money from Mum and Dad ages ago for a business or something that she didn't start and hasn't paid it back and keeps away... anyway, what was I saying?

You were in a pretty bad fix mate... maybe you just thought it wouldn't do any harm? Riley said.

Maybe.

Never been a fan of churches, Riley said. If you ask me priests are a bit weird. Some of them are probly alright. I forget which one it is but they can't have sex or get married or anything. That's a recipe for problems in my book... for me nature is pretty amazing as it is.

Yeah true... I'm not talking about churches at all, not too sure what I mean really... I dunno, when it's so easy to die it'd be good to know that there's more to it than just becoming dust. He added after a while: be good to know Dad is still going in some form... things were pretty bad back then when he died.

Yeah I know.

The mull all the blokes were into, you know when I worked on the weekends, seemed like it was the only thing that helped me forget about the old man.

Haven't thought about all that stuff much really, Riley said after a while, I can see you as a hermit in a small hut up a mountain somewhere fighting off the local village girls! he joked.

Hah... yeah I know... it's a bit strange coming from me. I guess when you've got time to think and you spend it all in the elements... I don't know how I didn't drown or get smashed up on those rocks that day... you should've seen it mate.

Must've been full on if you were shaken up by it, Riley looked over at him and then back down at the fire.

They raided the esky of its beers and talked into the night until the fire became a powdery mound of ash and black coals.

* * *

The weeks merged into months. Wetsuits faded and became brittle in the sun and started to fall apart on the shoulders and near the base of the zip. Seams stretched. Cold water leaked in more and more. Towels became stiff and gritty and felt like sand paper. When they picked them up off the fence they kept their hung shape and sundried pleats and had to be bent and cracked like cardboard.

Every now and then they went exploring. The four of them climbed high up a sand dune one afternoon when the wind was light and sat down in the fine white sand. Tiny specs right up near the peak of the mountain. As they sat hunched about with the setting sun on their faces, Will surveyed the coastline through binoculars. They talked about the breaks in the area and Will found white water down the coastline a bit and handed the binoculars around and they speculated about what it might be like. When they had finished their beers, Sabine led a ski-less ski downhill and the four of them jumped one after the other down the steep sand slope in a line, propping from side to side zigzagging down the hill and Riley tackled Sabine at the bottom.

Three of them piled into Will's car with their boards on a blue morning a few days later with a smaller swell and the wind blowing from the north. They headed out of the campground and started off down the road where they had dropped Squid off ages ago, to try to get to the place they'd seen from the top of the dunes. Randall stayed at the camp and wished them luck. A kilometre or two down the sandy track, they stopped when a bloke appeared in the distance in front of them, standing in the white light of the beating sun with his legs thrust apart and a shotgun hanging down by his side threateningly. They looked at each other for a moment in silence and reversed back to the intersection and headed home.

They never made it down there. Like Randall said, no one did.

They went down to The Bay a few more times and rode that long left again and some places other travellers coming from the east had spoken of which were harder to find and required a long hot fly flicking hike cross country. They pulled up at a long right hand point late one morning. Unridden waves reeled down alongside the black boulders lining the shore for hundreds of metres. Seals were basking in the hot sun and when Will joked about their blubber melting on the rocks and slicking into the ocean for the great whites, their enthusiasm faded and they slipped back into the car and got going.

Travellers came and went out at The Point. Some stopped over for a few days on their way east or west, others for a longer time. Bedraggled strangers struck up conversations about the conditions and speculated about what may be coming. Talking about what it had been like recently and other places ridden along the way to The Point. Sometimes for hours. It instantly united them. Newspapers brought in by new arrivals were quickly distilled down to the page with the weather report. Synoptic charts were carefully pawed over and the details of the coming conditions quickly circled the campsite as people met on the beach or at lookouts or coming out of the spiralling rock walled open air toilets clutching their byo roll of toilet paper. Faces lit up at high-pressure systems sitting over The Bight and lows spinning deep in the ocean off to the southwest. The love of surfing ran through them like a visceral thread, bringing unlikely people together, mostly in harmony. Randall was by miles the longest resident and was generally deferred to around the campfire on matters relating to The Point.

* * *

The Panel Vaners headed back to Moana a bit earlier than they had planned. After Kurt's drop in on a local at the right, they'd been given the ultimatum. It was in the afternoon when the sun was low. He said he didn't see him and rode off over the back of the wave as soon as he heard the yelling echoing at him from someone riding inside the tube. But the local bloke with a greying dark beard, bristled tight like steel wool, followed him. He didn't even finish riding it and paddled across, sat up on his board next to Kurt and looked him hard in the eye and shook his head slowly and pointed at the shore and said with a deep authoritative calm: That's fucked mate, you're in, right now... pack up your things and get going. You'd better not be here in the morning.

Kurt sat looking after him for a few seconds as he paddled off. He never looked back at Kurt. Kurt went in.

Randall saw the whole thing and dropped over to see The Panel Vaners later that night. As he walked by, two of Pepper's puppies they'd adopted scampered over and twisted through his legs and reached their paws up to his shins. He picked one of them up and tickled the warm furless skin on its blotched pink stomach and started talking to the Panel Vaners.

After a while Kurt asked: So d'ya reckon we gotta fuck off tomorrow or what?
Yeah... that was what I came over to talk to you about... I know it was accidental and you got off the wave straight away but you'd better do as he says mate. Bear is a serious unit... if he comes over with the boys in the morning and finds you guys still here it won't be pretty... there's stories about him. You don't wanna stay around for a fight with the locals out here.

The next morning the Panel Vaners, with the puppies curled up timidly low and tight on the passenger seat floor, spun their tyres and saluted goodbye to The Point with an unseen pair of doughnuts on the cricket field to Guns 'n Roses thudding and fuzzing beyond speaker capacity and whipped billowing clouds of dust over the campsite for a few minutes before it patiently resettled in the low light of dawn. Bear did come around later that morning. Squid was sitting next to him in the front of the old brown ute. They both had their arms cocked on the window-sills. Another three men were standing up in the tray back of the ute holding onto the rim of the roof. Several thick tree branches stripped of their bark protruded out of the back of the tray behind. Will saw them drive slowly and quietly around the campsite a few times looking for The Panel Vaners. They stopped at Randall's place and then rolled away.

* * *

The cooler nights and mornings, lighter wind days and strong swells of late Autumn settled in. Around the campfire after dinner one night Will announced to Riley and Sabine that he was going to get a lift back west with Randall in a few days. It came out of the blue. Riley looked closely at Will in the low light and then glanced across at Sabine who looked back quickly at him and over at Will and then down at the fire. After a pause he said a little hurriedly: Sure mate whatever you want.

After a few moments of silence, he asked: Any reason?

Nah, just like to get back and do a bit of work and save some money… reckon it'd be good for you two to have some time together anyway.

Don't go because of that, it's good all of us being around… wouldn't be the same without you round here, Riley said.

Yeah, nah, reckon it's a good time for me to get going though… I've lost track of how long we've been out here… I feel good, this trip has got me back on track, like all that stuff is behind me… I want to get on with things, make up for lost time, do a bit of work, go travelling overseas in a while. You know, do something different.

Things were a touch uncomfortable around the camp for the couple of days before Will and Randall headed off. Sabine thought she was the reason why Will was leaving and kept a low profile. Riley had a mixture of feelings. He thought he probably hadn't hung out with Will much after he'd got together with Sabine except in the surf and maybe Will felt a bit in the way, a bit like a third wheel. Spending time and exploring just with Sabine would be great though and they wouldn't have to worry about being so quiet on still nights. But he'd be losing his best mate. Will over compensated out of character to try to make them feel that his leaving had nothing to do with them. It was all a bit awkward.

But the decision was made also for Riley and Sabine a couple of weeks later when the bloke from Queensland got eaten at the left hander at the base of the fishing cliffs late one afternoon on a steely Easter day. Riley and Sabine left. Everybody did. Even the new arrivals who'd just driven over for Easter. The place was eerie and unsettling after the attack. Suddenly the dangers which they knew all along were there but were something that just wouldn't happen, actually had.

Riley and Sabine were over the dune getting things ready for dinner at their campsite when it happened. The story was that his two mates had just gone in and walked up the beach and stopped at the top of the low sand dune to wait for him to catch his last wave in. When they turned and locked back out to sea, they saw wild thrashing in the water. Then everything went still for a few seconds. Then there was more thrashing and bits of shark and surfboard appeared momentarily above the grey surface of the water. They dropped their boards on the sand and one of them ran around the limestone cliffs to see if he could see his mate while the other one bolted in to get help.

Riley was the first person he came across. Riley got straight in his car and skidded off to town. The cops phoned for an ambulance from a bigger town an hour or two down the road and came straight out to The Point with their lights blazing and sirens blaring. The bloke's mate on the cliff never saw any of him in the water. They never found him. The whole camp looked for traces of him on the surrounding beaches for a few days. Even the locals let people go down the track near their shacks to check the coast down there. A couple of bits of board washed in with serrated teeth marks ripped through the foam and fibreglass but that was it. His mates were shaken up pretty badly. Especially when they got back from calling his family in town. Everyone was. No one went in the water.

The campground soon became deserted. It felt like a morgue. In a way it was. Over the next few days, car after car, piled high with gear and mixed feelings and painted in salty sea spray and desert dust, shuffled slowly and solemnly behind each other out along the dirt track.

The locals stayed on. It was part of the place. It went with the territory. It was going to happen from time to time. Like it had before. Besides they had nowhere else to go.

Part III

16.

Saya melihat ombak... surfing.
Tidak ombak di sini.
Selatan dari pulau ini?
Saya tidak tahu.
Perahu – selatan dari pulau ini?
Tidak tahu... maaf.
Ok, terima kasih.
Tidak apa apa, selamat jalan.
Selamat tinggal.

Will walked slowly away. The old man stayed sitting under the palm tree. Tough husked greying coconuts lay about near him in the sand where they had fallen. He watched Will and drew on his menthol cigarette.

Will's boards, bags and boxes of supplies were piled up on the road where the wide planked wharf of the little port ended. He shoved his phrase book back into the front of his backpack and heaved it on his back and headed off down the potholed dirt road.

It was a few months now since he had left the south east of the island of Java. He'd more or less been on the road the whole time.

*   *   *

The jungle grew thickly around the long sweep of Grajagan Bay. Right up to the very edge of the coast. Just a few metres in, it was dense and dark and impenetrable to the sky, crammed with tropical almond trees with glossy green leaves and other trees flowering pink and white pom poms and bearing gift box fruit, thickets of wild bamboo with stems as wide as legs and towering eighty feet or more high and vines wrapping themselves over everything. On the shoreline, parallel to where the main wave broke along a sharp shallow reef just off the coast, a narrow walking track had been cut into the jungle and wound its way through the vegetation, covered with fallen leaves and dry bamboo sheaths. A myriad of insects screeched and pulsed in the trees.

The jungle was real. Huge monitor lizards strode and flicked their way through camp every few days with all the time in the world. Every now and then a python showed up in the area and frightened the life out of everyone. From time to time barefoot brown skinned locals pinned down the diamond shaped head of a luminescent green mamba with the forked end of a long stick. The deadly snake was proudly paraded through camp held tightly by the head and tail for travellers to touch and photograph. They said you had less than two minutes if it bit you. The dangerous part was not so much the initial catching of the snake, although that could always go wrong, but the moment of releasing it back into the jungle. When the time came, a crowd of locals and surfers would follow along a track leading deeper into the jungle away from the coast and gather round in a small clearing. They'd watch as the local captor twisted and retwisted the snake from the tail so it would first have to focus on uncoiling itself in the air before it could try to fling itself back at its tormentor. Then the snake was flung away with both arms in a flash of writhing lime and the crowd got ready to bolt.

Green fowls with colourful fantailed plumage strutted busily along the tracks near the fishing village in the south and through camp. There were stories dating back of leopards and panthers taking nearby villagers' goats and chickens and leaving footprints on the beach but they hadn't been seen for a long time. On the long trek around the bend of Grajagan Bay to another wave, Banteng twitched about nervously on the foreshore and darted off into the forest. Wild boars snuffed along the reef at low tide. Leaf monkeys cawed and screeched out of the trees and all the sounds of the jungle echoed over the sand and water with increasing animation at the end of the day. The jungle was not some artificial place you drove away to in a tourist bus on a sightseeing tour for an hour or so. It was right there. Engulfing. At all times.

The camps had been set up a few hundred metres inland from the beach. Wooden huts with small porches at the front were raised off the ground in amongst the trees. Inside the dark rooms, mosquito nets hung over low wooden beds, patched with coloured cotton here and there to stop up holes. The beds had threadbare sheets and foam mattresses heavily compressed from years of use. The itching usually didn't start until day two or three and then it settled in for the duration. Dog-tired bodies turned and rolled again and again in the still tropical night heat and gave in to raking and gouging at their skin, leaving it pocked with bloody craters promising infection from the warm coral water. Food was plentiful. The kitchens, stacked with local people, were kept busy making nasi and mie goreng, banana pancakes and cheese and tomato japples all day.

The wave out the front of the camp was made up of a series of overlapping long sections with fabled names like Kongs, Money Trees and Speedies. Tales of huge days where it broke continuously from one end of the long reef to the other circulated, handed down through an untraceable lineage of friends of friend's. Each section was unique and had its moment of glory each day when the tide was right for it. A long deep G-Land tube lit up by the afternoon sun like a shimmering emerald could never be forgotten. One was never enough though. The exhilaration of the ride out there was like a drug, an addiction that could never be quite satiated. Dusk's soft colours descended quickly into blackness close to the equator. Surfers waiting for one too many last waves were caught out stumbling along the jungle track in the blackness with the sounds of the jungle closing in, trees shaking and things thudding unnervingly to the ground.

Living in the middle of the jungle on the doorstep of one of the world's best left-handers had been made easier by the camps over the years. But that was also the problem. Multiple camps had sprung up since the pioneers had first trekked in years ago. There were Americans, Europeans, Brazilians as well as the omnipresent Aussies and the odd Kiwi. Word was well and truly out about the place and it was busy in the water most days. Hungry surfers jostled for position and pushed each other deeper and deeper. Tactics were employed.

The almost complete lack of girls out there added fuel to the fire. Every now and then a pretty girlfriend would arrive wide eyed and dishevelled into camp after a journey that had been a fair bit more demanding than she had been led to believe. She'd be continually watched by fifty revolving pairs of eyes pretending not to as she went about her day-to-day activities. While she sunned herself on the beach, queues of toey strangers would file slowly past on their way in or out of the surf pretending not to look, others would hover in the vicinity and a few would just go and sit right down next to her and start up a conversation while her man was out in the water, hoping somehow there might be half a chance and if there wasn't at least they would've had a good look.

After Will had been there for a couple of days, he got a few tips on timing from Gibbo over a beer on the porch one evening and fell into a rough routine where the numbers in the water seemed more manageable. It meant that they didn't always catch it when the conditions were at their best but least the mood was better in the water then. When the surf was big and serious and some stayed on the beach, they could go out more at the prime times. Regardless of the numbers though, they would always go out for the flawless late afternoon session and stay out until they could barely see and the numbers dwindled to a handful.

Gibbo had the hut next door to Will. He was a blue collar bloke from Newcastle. Salt of the earth. He told Will that he was on a trip through the islands for as long as the dough he'd inherited from his Granddad passing away lasted. It was his brief ticket out of the everyday grind of the steelworks. Every one said he was mad throwing the towel in when things were a bit shaky at the factory with the recession and he should put the money away for a rainy day. But there was no way in hell he was going to let a chance like this go. Besides, as he told Will, his Granddad had said to him before he died that he was putting something aside for him and had looked him in the eye and made him promise to do something special with it.

The day after Will had first spoken with Gibbo, he lay down on his sagging mattress for a rest in the afternoon and pictured his own Grandfather sitting down to afternoon tea as he did each day in his small sitting room where the green carpet was worn thin and smelt of tobacco and all of the cabbage, potatoes and chops cooked over the decades. His nobbled vein risen hands would be resting on the wooden armrests of his favourite chair. Every now and then he'd wobble a scrawny flecked arm over to the small round table near his knee and take a sip of tea. Then he'd jiggle the cup back onto the saucer and gingerly take a bite at one of the arrowroots and re-adjust his false teeth as he looked out at the hazy world passing by his front window through watery old eyes pooled in pale pink rimmed sagging lids. Will told himself he'd write him a letter one of these days. Tell him what he was up to, tell him how he wanted to help Joe that day.

After the initial ten days he had signed up for, he'd stayed on for another ten or so. Towards the end it had started to feel like time to do something different, something off the beaten track. Back to Bali didn't feel right. He wanted to make it up as he went along. Do some solo travelling. He'd pulled his map of the islands out one night, spread it out before him on the bed and studied it by torchlight. He'd poured over the bays and points of the southern coastlines of the islands to the east and west, looking for areas open to swell and protected from the trade winds. He'd drawn tentative circles in pencil around a group of small islands off the coast of Sumatra and around a big island which lay disconnected from the main arc of the island chain in the opposite direction away off to the south-east and decided to sleep on it.

*   *   *

On the way into the village from the port, Will passed a black sow with dehydrated flanks and five dark haired piglets sniffing and nosing clumsily at plastic bottles and other rubbish lying by the roadside. The limestone road was wide and dusty and where it bent a few hundred metres down the way, a group of children played with an old bike tyre. Lining the road were small shacks walled with corrugated iron and concrete blocks, some painted, most left drably grey. Down a track off to the side, traditional huts with walls of woven split bamboo and roofed with thatching stood above the ground on wooden stilts.

Two well groomed uniformed men were sitting on pink plastic chairs under the shade of a low leafy tree outside a grey corrugated iron shack a few houses after the start of town. A plywood shutter was propped open at the front of the shack by a length of wood above a bench top counter. Three jars were lined up with packets of crackers and sugar sweets inside. The walls of another jar were lightly smeared with oil and sugar from round sweet breads. Next to the jars stood cloudy recycled bottles of fanta and sprite. Inside the shack, behind the bench, pairs of brown eyes peered out of the dark interior. The men waved Will over with authority.

As he walked over, a few mangy dogs lying in the shade nearby rose up on their emaciated haunches and started up a howl, took a few frail steps and bared their teeth unconvincingly at him from tight skinned skulls. The man in the blue uniform spoke sharply and bent down as if to pick up a stone and they cowered and quietly slunk off to lie back down in the dirt on their withered sides. The man in the green uniform put his hand out to Will and said hello in English. Will shook hands with them.

Where you come from? The man in the green uniform asked in English, concentrating hard. His veins protruded on the sides of his close shaven head.
Australia.
What you do here?
I'm looking for surf... have you seen any surfers here?
Surp?
Ombak besar, Will moved his hand up and down.
Tidak... tidak touris... sometimes we have boat with sail.

After a slight pause the man in the blue uniform looked at Will and stood up and said: You come with us to police station for little bit please? You have passport?

Yes, Will said a little uncertainly, can I get my other bags? They're over there, he said pointing to the wharf.

They walked slowly back down the road to the start of the wharf together, talking in a mixture of English and Bahasa. When he saw Will's things piled up on the road, the man in the green army uniform stopped and looked back towards the small shop and yelled out, making a pushing motion. A cart appeared swiftly out of the shadows pushed by a young boy in a pair of faded red shorts with a thong on one of his feet.

They loaded the cart up with Will's things and the boy looked proudly around as Will helped him push it back up the dirt road. He beamed at the pack of smaller kids who ran out onto the road and were circling the cart and helping to push. Villagers appeared on the side of the road, looking out from the shade of the trees. The uniformed officers swaggered regally in front of Will and the cart and their growing entourage. After a little while they stopped at a squat concrete building and dismissed everyone with a lazy wave of the hand.

Will left the cart on the street and followed the officers up the few steps to the porch of the building. Dry cement oozed out thickly in places between the concrete blocks and was missing altogether in others. A broad crack ran the length of one of the walls on a meandering diagonal. On the small porch was a large plywood desk. The blue uniformed policeman sat down behind it and lit a cigarette and motioned to Will to sit down on the chair on the other side. He leaned back and drew on his cigarette and studied Will. The man in the green uniform perched on the low concrete wall of the porch and adjusted the position of his gun and holster around his waist. He lit up a cigarette with a flash of his silver lighter. On the desk sat a rusted typewriter. Over the policeman's shoulder a short gloomy corridor led inside the building. A small room ran off either side, fenced floor to ceiling with thick vertical rusted iron bars. Some were missing in one of the cells.

The policeman tapped his cigarette over the porch floor, slid open a drawer of the desk and pulled out a single unlined sheet of paper and a pencil. He asked Will for his passport. Will dug it out from his backpack and handed it over. He licked the nib of the pencil and wrote Will's full name and other details slowly down on the piece of paper in uneven capital letters and folded it up and put it in his pocket and leant back and smiled: Mistah William where you want to go?

Will pulled a creased map out of his backpack, unfolded it and spread it out on the desk and pointed at the coast in the south west part of the island.

17.

Hi Bates it's Riley.

G'day Riley, how's it going?

Good mate, how bout you?

Yeah, no wucken furries.

Hey, I'm looking for Will... is he around?

Nah mate, he moved all his stuff back to his Mum's place a while ago... he's gone to Indo.

Riley was quiet for a few seconds.

You still there Riley?

Yeah, sorry mate... when did he go?

Dunno exactly... probably a few months ago now.

Really... Geez lucky bloke, Riley tried to sound relaxed, did Miranda go with him?

Nah, they had a pretty big bust up and he left pretty quickly after it. He'd been thinking of heading off for a while anyway, Bates said.

Yeah he talked about it round Christmas time... but sounded like it was still a way off then... what happened with Miranda?

Not sure exactly, Will didn't really say. I came home from work one day and found his wetty cut up in pieces out the front of the house... his favourite board had been stabbed with a knife about a hundred times on both sides... all her stuff was gone. Bloody hell... what'd Will do?

Nah nothing, he had three more days at the mines before his rotation finished and he was due to come back... I called him that night and told him about his stuff 'n everything and he was quiet for a bit and then asked me if I could put it in the bin for him... that's all he bloody said. He was pretty good about it when he got back. Fuck'n hell if that was me I would've been mighty pissed off... dunno what I would've done.

Yeah... I know, wetty probly doesn't matter much but he loved that board.

He's better off without her if y'ask me. She was pretty to look at but when she stayed here she'd whine a lot, you know, about him not spending time with her, that all he wanted to do when he got back from Up North was go surfing. Said he was addicted to it and nothing else mattered. She used to complain about him to me sometimes, you know when he'd left at the crack of to go for a dawnie and hadn't told her nothing about it and didn't come back from the surf til night time 'cos it was going off and the breeze didn't come in.

Riley paused for a moment: Yeah, right... do you know whereabouts in Indo he was going?

He talked about going to Bali first and checking it out for a bit and then he was maybe gunna check out G-Land... after that he wasn't sure... see what happened when he got there.

Yeah... cool.

What've you been up to... still Down South?

Yeah still Down South… shacked up with that French girl I met about a year and a half ago. Renting a place in The Bay together. Lucky bugger… much work down there?

Yeah… there's a bit of building work… enough to keep us goin. Sabine's been working a bit as well. She's gone back to France for a few weeks to see her family for some of their Summer… get out of Winter Down South for a bit. What've you been up to?

Same old same old. But good. Not surfing that much. Knee's still buggered. Should be back out there in a coupla weeks the doc reckons. Bloody better be. How's the surf been Down South?

Waves were really good in Autumn and early Winter. Hard to get any work done. Me and everyone else was in the water all the time. Starting to get a bit rude down there now. Wind's been howlin from the west and northwest all week.

Yeah… same up here… good time to shoot north.

For sure, don't think I'm gunna get there this year but. You going? Riley asked.

Yeah in a month. Thomo and a few of the other guys are going up as well.

Hope you get some swell… bound to get some good days this time of the year.

Yeah, I know, I'm hanging for it.

You don't know how long Will was gunna be away for do you?

Nah, think a while… give his Mum a buzz they'll probly know more about what he's up to.

Yeah, good idea, thanks mate… I'm probably gunna come up in a week or so, I'll give you a buzz and we'll catch up for a beer or something.

Yeah no worries Riley, that'd be good, see yah then.
See yah.

Riley put the phone down and muttered "bloody hell he's gone already". He went to the fridge, snatched a can of beer out and swore when it spurted out the top over his hand and down onto his jeans. He licked the beer on his hand and walked over to the couch and flicked the television on and slouched down. He stared blankly at the screen as the rain pelted down on the tin roof and lashed the glass and the northwest wind rattled the windows in their old wooden frames and gusted in under the gap below the front door.

* * *

A week later he had a break between jobs and drove up to town. He called in at Will's Mum's house on Sunday afternoon. He walked round the side to the back deck without knocking like he'd always done. Max barked and raced down the stairs, sniffed around his legs and lifted his upper lip in a crazy grin while his whole body wagged about from side to side. Then he stood up on his back legs and put his front paws up onto Riley's chest and licked Riley's hands as he took his paws and placed them back down on the grass. Riley got down on his knees and put his arm over the dog's shoulder and patted its black flank and let it lick and nuzzle his neck and ear and sniff his head all over.

G'day everyone, Riley smiled disengaging from the dog and walking up the stairs onto the deck where Will's family were sitting around the table in the afternoon sun.

G'day Riley... Max is pretty pleased to see you, Tom said.

He shook Tom's hand: Geez Tom, you keep getting taller every time I see you. You'll be bigger than me next time, Riley joked, how's the surf been up here?

We've had a few really good days down at the beach... Point was fun in Autumn but packed. It's crazy out there these days. Mainly surfed down the beach a bit. Will and I had some good days up the coast round Easter time before he left.

Yeah it's good up there in Autumn... everywhere's good really.

He leaned down and kissed Emma on the cheek. Hi Emma, nice to see you... still studying?

She flushed: Yeah, in my last year now.

Will's Mum stood up and hugged Riley as he walked towards her: It's good to see you Riley, we miss you round here, how are things Down South, how's that beautiful girl?

Hi Kath, she's good, great actually. Went back to France for a few weeks last Friday. See the family and stuff.

How's your French coming along?

Badly... I've got a few more words. Her English is so good, don't need to learn French now.

You're going to marry that girl, I can tell.

Cut it out, Riley said laughing.

Thanks Tom, Riley said as Tom handed him a cold beer. He sat down and took a sip.

You know Will's gone travelling? she asked.

Yeah I heard... spoke to Steve Bateman the other day. Have you heard from him since he left? Riley asked.

He called for Tom's birthday in early May from Bali... sounded like he was having a great time, surfing mostly and meeting other travellers... what is it now... July, so we haven't heard from him for a couple of months. But he said he was going to go to a place in the jungle on another island... what was it called Tom?

G-Land, Tom said.

Yes, that's right... he said he probably wouldn't be able to get in contact for a while. But I was just saying this afternoon that I was surprised he hadn't called by now again. He wasn't going to stay in the jungle for too long.

G-Land is s'posed to be pretty remote... there's camps there for surfers though so he'll be with others... the wave is s'posed to be amazing so he may have got hooked on it... how long is he gunna be away for all up?

When he left in April he was planning on being away for Winter... coming back in September sometime... when he called though he said life was pretty cheap over there. It'll be good for him to have a break from that girl.

Yeah Batesy said it was a bit of a bust up.

Yes we don't really know what happened... Will didn't say much... all he said was she wanted more from him than he could give. She was a pretty thing but fairly firey at times... you know... determined... what was it you said Tom?

High maintenance, Tom grinned.

She wasn't really a beach girl, didn't like the sea much or sand and said there was no way she was going to wait around on the beach while Will surfed. Will was ok with that I think... she liked shopping... always looked very nice.

Emma laughed: I liked her, she was fun... but yeah she wanted Will to go along with her some days and used to get upset when he said he wasn't into it and would rather go surfing... God can you imagine Will shopping, he was lucky to go once a year... she kept trying to get Will to change his hair style and dress more stylishly, you know, get him out of his shorts and thongs... But Will just stayed as he was and kept surfing and the new clothes stayed in the drawers. We didn't see that much of him either, he was pretty focussed on surfing.

Tom said: Yeah if you ask me it was really the surfing... she said he was obsessed by it, probly right... she thought he liked surfing more than her and when he started to talk about going overseas on a surf trip for a while, you know at least a few months, by himself... things went pear shaped between them pretty soon after.

*   *   *

A few weeks later Riley reached in and pulled the mail out of his box at the post office in town and flicked through it. He stopped at an envelope with his Dad's handwriting and slid his finger along the fold at the back to open it. Inside was a short note from his Dad and a postcard. The postcard was dog-eared and lightly streaked with dirt and smelt of cloves and tobacco. On the front of the card, green terraced rice paddies fell in layers down a hillside carved out of jungle pressing thickly forward on all sides. Here and there workers stood bent over up to their knees in the fields under broad brimmed conical hats. Will's scrawl spread out across the back unevenly:

Gday Riley, been in Indo for a few months. Had some good waves in Bali. Hectic but fun. G-Land was good – great wave, long hollow left. You'd like it. In Padang waiting for a dodgy ferry to go out to some offshore islands in a few days. Not sure if there's waves out there. Better be – been a mission to get here so far overland from G-Land, more to come. Hope this makes it and everything is good with you and Sabine. Take it easy mate, Will.

The postcard stayed up on the fridge as the cool months passed and the warmer ones came around, held in place by a magnetic blue wren. It caught Riley and Sabine's attention every now and then at first and they thought of Will up there roaming islands in the middle of nowhere as they opened their old fridge door and stared at its scrappy contents. After a while though, it melded into the collage of flyers for music shows, waves cut out from surf magazines, bills to pay, the rental agent's magnet, photos of Sabine's sister's new born baby, reminder notes and other things that flapped on the front of the fridge in the wind. It became part of the furniture, just another picture their eyes habitually flicked over each day without further thought, surviving up there as other things came and went and the seasons passed.

The place was bought the following year by a family from the city to use as a beach house. When they were packing their things up to move to another rental just up the hill, Riley took the postcard down. It was stiff and dry. Its edges curled outwards and the lush greens were sun bleached to washed out blues. He turned it over. The black ink was faded in places and illegible in others. Every now and then he'd heard on the grape vine that Will was still away. He tucked the postcard inside the freezer door with the other things that were to go back up on the fridge and got on with packing.

18.

Hi… how was your day? Sabine said happily, turning to look at him over her shoulder from the corner of the room. She was sitting before an easel, sketching in pencil onto a white canvas. A polaroid photo of a blood red sunset was taped onto the top of one of the corners. A corridor of afternoon sun slanted in through the salt-sprayed window across the room, lighting up a hazy stream of slow moving dust.

Ok… getting there, should be right by the time we go away, Riley said putting his keys down on the table and walking over to lean in to kiss her on the cheek and neck.

What's this one? He asked with his chin resting on her shoulder looking at the pencil lines on the canvas.

This Bay at sunset a few days ago. I decide to do a series of it at sunset at a few times during the year… you know, the seasons. Same aspect but the sun sets in different places in each season and the light is very different… each painting be similar but bit different.

Cool idea. He looked around at the walls of the open room of

the shack packed full with her unframed paintings and sketches:
We're gunna have to get the landlord to extend the house to
fit your paintings in soon, he smiled.

Yes, I know, I was thinking… maybe I have an exhibition
when we get back from France. What do you think?

Yes sure, why not… most people who come to our place like
your stuff, others will as well… where would you hold it?

I'm not sure yet. Maybe I see if Carmel wants to show some
pottery and we do something together.

Riley stood up behind her.

Hey The Point looks pretty fun. Wanna come for a surf? He
put his hands down onto her waist and slid them up to tickle
her ribs.

She laughed and squirmed and pushed him away.

Maybe… will it be ok out there for me?

Yeah should be… come outside and we can have a quick look,
Riley said, sliding the old glass door open slowly so it didn't
fall off its runners and stepping out onto the deck. Sabine
rested on his back as he leant on the railing to look out to sea.

They watched for a few minutes.

Tide's pretty low, Riley said, it's not a very thick swell so
there's waves breaking out there in the middle of the reef that
aren't that big. It'll be kinda like that surf we had out there a
few weeks ago 'cept that there's hardly anyone out this arvo.

A set swarmed over the rocks scattered out to sea off the other
point to the south in a wash of foaming white spires and then
bent into The Bay towards the granite headland to the north.
Deeper inside The Bay, a cray fishing boat slowly rose and

rolled and fell on its anchor as lumps of swell surged through. Out on the flat rocks at the end of the point, a surfer stood patiently with his board under his arm, silhouetted black against the falling sun, waiting for a break to jump off and paddle out. The first wave of the set reared up on the reef and cascaded down and then steamed along towards the channel, deep mossy green from the soft Autumn sun. Unridden. Someone caught the second wave in the set and they watched his tiny black form swoop down the face in the distance and pull back up into a crouch as the wave folded around him, nearly hiding him. He held the position for a long while in the dark hollows before being swallowed by the gurgling bend of the last section.

Carn let's go, I'll get the wetties off the line, grab your board and I'll meet you at the car, Riley said excitedly and trotted off down the rickety steps off the deck to the Hills Hoist which rose up on a tilt out of the long grass, amongst the rotting timber, bent bikes and rusted wheelbarrow of the yard of their rental.

It wasn't far but they drove around to The Point to save time. Standing on the flat rocks on the low rise up from the dusty parking area with the light southeast wind cool against their bare skin, they scrambled into their wetsuits shrunken thick and tight from merry-go-rounding in the sun on the clothesline. Sabine followed Riley down the skinny dirt track which wound its way between the waist high vegetation, beaten into gnarled submission by the wind. They walked along watching out for exposed roots and stones and broken beer bottles and glancing at the surf from time to time.

They crossed the strip of beach littered with periwinkles, branches of stale seaweed crisping and blackening in the sun and the scarred browning nose of a broken surfboard. Then clambered over the barrier of rocks, still warm underfoot from the day's sun. At the water's edge they picked their way across the slippery submerged rocks in the shallow water of the keyhole. As the water deepened, they slid onto their boards and struck out across the sea swirling milky froth and jade from the passing of the last set, senses sharply alive from the cool water washing over them, tasting the salt in their mouths, feeling its chill on their hands and heads as they stroked and duck dived their way through the broken waves over to the deep channel.

G'day mate, Riley said as they paddled along the edge of the breakers past a lanky bloke in a black wetsuit, hood pulled down low over his head, sitting a little down the line on the inside catching the wider breaking waves. He nodded at Riley and Sabine as they continued further on out the back to where another surfer was sitting on his board.

How is it Rod… looks like there's a few coming through?
Gday Riley, hi Sabine, yeah it's fun. There's been some good sets, not big but swell's hitting the reef right… fair bit of west in it.
Been out long? Riley asked, sitting up on his board.
Yeah, a while, had to call in sick today, couldn't let another good day go through to the keeper out here, he laughed. Had a few earlier as well, barely been a soul out all day… dunno where everybody is, probly good at lots of places… jus one more for me but… it's time to crack a coldy while I've still got

all my limbs. He grinned at them and brushed his hand lightly over the top of the water and they all looked out to sea.

Rod took the first wave of the next set, paddling out to meet it and swinging round quickly under the rising peak to glide onto it, stand up and disappear over the surging ledge. The one after doubled up and rolled through wide and unbroken where they waited. They let it go.

How bout going for this one? Riley asked as the third wave started to draw up on the reef beyond them, the water shallowed by the waves that had just passed through.
Sabine looked at the rearing wave and back at Riley and shuffled nervously on her board.
It'll be ok, paddle hard… a few extra strokes and stay low on the drop, go on it's only water.
Mmmm, Sabine said uncertainly sizing up the rising swell line. She looked at Riley and he smiled.
Oh merde, she said and turned and kicked and paddled her way onto the wave and Riley watched the back of the wave and a few seconds later Riley heard the hooded bloke let out a whoop. Then he saw Sabine glide into the deep channel, before she lost momentum and fell backwards off her board. He watched her coming back out, checking out to sea over his shoulder now and again for a wave. As she approached her face was all wide stretched smile and white teeth and glittering eyes and glowed from the exhilarated blur of the ride and from the honeyed light of the late afternoon sun.

Over her shoulder the houses on the hillside of the little seaside town watched over the Bay, peering around and above each other and through the trees, bathed in the sunset light, pierced with blinding silver shimmers of the reflections on west facing windows like a hundred locked lighthouse beams. The light was clear, sharp, precious, as if the rest of the day was just a lens spinning slightly out of focus, a dress rehearsal for that brief perfect moment of rich pure clarity.

He smiled at her as she paddled nearer. Nothing needed to be said. But it was and she was still telling him about her ride in an animated flurry of French and English as he paddled onto the first wave in the next set and disappeared down the other side. They traded waves and stayed out after the falling sun had finally flicked below the horizon and in the end the hooded surfer also went in and it was just the two of them sitting next to each other out there in the grey water with their feet up on the decks of their boards out of temptation. They paddled hard out and over a rogue bigger wave which loomed large and dark in the fading light and stretched for the length of the reef all the way to the channel. They waited out there for a while in case there were others on their way, before paddling back in to the take off area.

They rode the last wave in together. Riley watched her from behind as she shot along and he whistled at her as they neared the end of the ride and she looked behind with surprise and lost her balance and fell off to the side and he laughed and dove off as well. They belly boarded in side by side on the whitewash of the next one and, when it ran out, paddled in over the still water, black from the falling night and the kelp covered reef below, past the curve of submerged boulders and the low red rock cliffs where a yellow coated fisherman stood above them with his line poised and reached the small beach in the final moments of dusk.

They tugged off their wetsuits on the flat rocks and stuffed them and their boards into the back of Riley's car and drove back to the house naked head to toe with shivering laughter and goose bumps and the heater on full bore. They hurried through the unlocked door of the house in darkness and left wet sandy prints across the floorboards all the way to the shower.

Their feet were the last to thaw and hurt and burnt as the blood pricked and needled back into them through unwilling vessels contracted tight from the cold. As they stood sharing the thin stream of warm water, his mouth ran down the side of her wet neck and his hands held the curves of her buttocks. She pressed her hips against his and leant her chest back from him with her hands around his neck as the hot water poured down to pool at their feet from the blocked drain they hadn't got round to fixing. He lifted her up and her dripping legs moved apart and wrapped tightly around his hips and she held his head to her slippery chest as her back pressed against the glass shower screen, opaque from steam and years of built up soap scum, while the precious tank water rained down on their faces and over their bodies and slowly rose up around Riley's feet.

After dinner, with the unwashed dishes piled up in the sink, Sabine lay down on top of Riley on the skinny brown couch and they fell asleep in jeans and jumpers and thick woollen socks in front of the red glow of the radiator creaking and tinkling on uneven metal legs on the old jarrah floor.

19.

Can you get that Riley? Sabine called out leaning over the stove stirring the pot.

Yep, sure.

Riley picked up the receiver and said hello.

Hi it's Kath here, Will's Mum. Is that you Riley?

Yeah, hi Kath, how are things?

Alright thanks. How about you both?

We're good. Having a quiet night in The Bay. Been working pretty hard to get a job finished before we go to France.

France! That's exciting. When do you head off Riley?

Next week.

That'll be nice. Will you meet Sabine's family?

Yeah, we're going to stay with them in Lacanau for a coupla weeks and then we'll travel round France for a little while together. Might even know a few French words by the end of it, he laughed.

How long will you be away for? She asked

Due back in mid July… how is Will going? Is he back yet?

No. Actually Riley that's what I was calling you about. We haven't heard from him for a long time, about two and a half years now.

Really? Riley exclaimed.

The last time was when he was in Singapore on a visa run just before Christmas the first year he was away. He said he'd been on islands off the coast of Sumatra, living in villages and surfing. When he got back to Indonesia he was going to try to get to some other islands. He said it was remote out there and it would be a while before he could get in contact again… probably on his next visa run. But it's been so long and his visa must have expired ages ago, she sniffed, you haven't heard from him have you?

Nah, not for ages. We got a postcard from him – but that was only a couple of months after he left. I don't think any of the other guys have either or they would've said. How long has been away for now… must be over three years?

Yes, that's right. Tom thinks if something had happened to him we would have heard… the authorities would've got in touch, but I don't know. If it's really remote… she trailed off.

Right yeah, geez he's been away for ages. What was the island he was heading for?

I can't remember now if he said. He probably did but it would have been an Indonesian name. I've been thinking of getting in touch with the authorities but I don't really have much information to give them and if he has missed his visa runs… I don't want him to end up in trouble over there… it's a bad place to get locked up, her voice quivered. I'm actually not too sure what to do… I've never been overseas but I was thinking of flying up there and trying to find him. The kids think I've gone mad…

I'm so worried and tired all the time now... I can't sleep at night... I couldn't convince you to head up could I to see if you could track him down? I'd pay for you to go, she asked hesitantly. Riley paused: I'd love to help you Kath but the thing is I've got this trip to France with Sabine in a couple of weeks that's all booked and paid for. S'posed to be meeting the family and all. Yes of course... sorry, she said quickly before he finished.

There was a moment of silence and then she asked softly, trying not to show her anxiety: What about after your trip to France? Riley thought for a moment: That wouldn't be too late for you? No... well I'm not sure... at least I'd know whether he's all right or not. Not knowing is very hard for me. I don't think I can take it very much longer, she said and suddenly unable to hold it back any longer, began to sob.

Riley was quiet for a few moments while she cried and then said: It'll be ok Kath, don't worry, let me talk with Sabine. We fly back through Singapore. My ticket may let me stop over there for a little while and then I could head down to Sumatra from there and try to track him down. If not maybe I could come back here and then go back up on another flight. I'll check... the job I was supposed to start when I got back – it's for a mate so should be ok to delay it a bit.

Thanks Riley, she sniffed.

No worries, I'll call you tomorrow night or the one after.

Ok, thanks Riley, and if you can go, as I said I'll pay for you.

Nah that's not necessary Kath but thanks for the offer. He's a good mate and I should've gone up to see him already. I'd be taking a board or two and I'd never hear the end of it if Will found out you'd paid for me to go and surf with him, Riley laughed.

Ok, she laughed tearily, thanks Riley.

No worries, I'll call you soon. I'm sure it'll work out.

Thanks Riley... Riley?

Yes.

When you call back... none of the others here know I'm asking you to go up, she said softly.

Ok got it, that's cool. We'll keep it under wraps. See you.

Bye Riley.

20.

Almost as soon as it had reached altitude and levelled off, the aeroplane started its descent towards Jakarta.

The middle seat in Riley's row was empty. By the window a diminutive old Indonesian lady leant against the wall of the plane with a thin blue blanket neatly skirted over her legs. Another blanket was shrouded around her head and shoulders. Heavily ringed fingers clutched it together at her small pointed chin against the cold air breezing through the cabin.

In the middle seat on the other side of the aisle, an obese ruddy skinned man in a short-sleeved shirt and a baseball cap had fallen off to sleep. The big pored flesh of his cheeks drooped to merge with the fatty folds of his neck and formed a wobbling cushion on his chest for his indiscernible chin. Plump freckled hands rested on a worn black brief case spread across his knees and his whole body rose and fell with the undulations of his heavy breathing, jiggling the collection of pens riding in his top pocket. From time to time a guttural sucking snore reverberated. His huge form spilled out across the armrests. Flabby rolls reached into the seats on either side where vastly smaller, grim faced Indonesian travellers folded themselves up tightly and turned away.

Riley walked down the steps off the plane with his backpack slung over his shoulder. Wet pools from the afternoon downpour steamed on the asphalt in the heat of the sun. The warm air engulfed him, hugging his skin. His clothes clung to him close and low, heavy with humidity. He followed the trail of passengers over the tarmac and into the terminal building. He walked down the long tiled corridor following the signs to Immigrasi and took his place in one of the visitors' queues behind a nervous cluster of Japanese tourists with matching bags and t-shirts murmuring and bustling about at chest height. Eventually he was motioned forward to the counter by the immigration officer who took his passport with disinterest and flicked through it with one hand, his stamp poised in the other. He looked up at Riley: Mistah, you mus get visa to come to Indonesia… is back up there, he pointed and handed back Riley's documents.

Riley looked where the officer pointed and back at the long queue behind him. The officer motioned again for Riley to go back to get a visa and then looked past him blankly and called the next person up to the counter.

Eventually Riley made it through immigration and found his black backpack circling alone on the carousel and his board bag lying on its side on the floor nearby. As he shouldered his backpack, a pack of boys in grey shirts with yellow name tags sewn onto their pockets: Taufik, Denny, Jery and others, rushed over towards him and a couple jostled to put his board bag on their trolleys while others gently tugged at the bags on his shoulders. Riley put his hands up and told them that he was all right and reshouldered his backpacks and picked up his board bag. The porters left without protest in a hubbub of Bahasa to swoop on their next tourist.

Riley slid and carried his luggage over the floor to the disordered customs queue where local people breezed through without stopping. A uniformed man motioned Riley over and took his customs form and tossed it without looking into the clear garbage bag with thousands of other unprocessed forms. He directed Riley to put some of his bags through the large black scanner where two attending officers sat on chairs smoking cigarettes with their backs to the screen.

He tugged his gear down the aisle, past the small boxed bureaus of money changers and hotel and car rental agents urgently beckoning to him with flashing teeth and arms extended through narrow slits below the glass partitions of their tiny offices.

Outside the exit a huge crowd of locals bobbed and weaved behind a wall of others pressed up against the metal railings. Arms reached up and waved above an incomprehensible whir of voices. As he passed through the gate, Riley was set upon by half a dozen taxi drivers reaching to relieve him of his luggage and bombarded with "Where you want to go Mistah, where you go", " I take you, cheap price", "Nice car, cold air". They quickly melted back into the crowd when they learned that he was only walking the short distance to the domestic terminal. Out in the street, cars and vans whipped in to stop at the curb and then pulled out again and shot down the road, bumper to bumper, straddling the lanes barely inches apart. Horns bleated unceasingly. People bustled in the humid heat and everywhere the smell of cloves cigarettes and car fumes mixed with the fragrance of the sultry tropics.

Riley had an hour or so until his flight to Sumatra. After checking in he stopped at a small shop filled with locals speedily pinching rice and noodles between chopsticks and fingers, drinking black coffee from glasses and smoking. On the wall above the counter was a row of old bubbling laminated photos showing steaming plates of food. He ordered nasi goreng from a smiling softly spoken lady with a gold-capped tooth and sat down to wait for it. He ate it slowly enjoying the spicy flavours. When he had finished, egg and all as well as the lettuce and sliced tomato on the side, he drained the glass of water and got up and handed back the pink tray and wandered off through the airport towards his gate number.

He drifted into a bookshop and hovered at the travel section. He bought a travel guide to Indonesia and a map wrapped in cellophane. Riley glanced at his watch and sat down on a bench seat outside the shop, pulled the map out of its wrapping and opened it up. The island of Sumatra lay large to the northwest of Java over a narrow passage of water. The island was longer than it was wide. Its northern tip was the upper end of Indonesia. He found Padang about half way along the southwest coast. A high mountain ridge ran the length of the island. Off the coast, clusters each comprising many islands of varying sizes, stretched to the northwest and southeast of Padang. He'd only counted forty of the islands by the time his flight was called. He leant back in his chair and shook his head and stood up and went back into the bookshop to buy a phrasebook.

As the aeroplane took off he looked out through the window at the blackening night and leaned over and pressed his face against it to peer down. The lights of Jakarta blinked and streamed below in golds and reds and silvers as scooters and cars, fishing boats and cargo ships all busily swarmed about the houses and roadside stalls, the big hotels with sleazy basements and ports of the polluted city.

Stewardesses with glossy black hair sleeked into French rolls floated down the aisles and handed out small plastic water containers with a thin film of plastic stretched tightly across the circumference. As Riley wrestled with opening his, treading that fine line between unsuccessful under exertion and wearing the contents from pulling too hard, a series of rumbles twisted through his belly. They were quickly overtaken by rising cramps seizing and jabbing at his lower insides and then a pressing urgency had him contorting himself out of his corner seat and hastily across the Indonesian passengers next to him and shuffling stiffly down the aisle. He shut the door of the cubicle and barely had time to pull his shorts down before a sharp explosion of wind and liquid shot from his backside and gatling-gunned the bowl in a series of loud uncontrolled bursts. All over his skin was cold and hot and clammy and foreign. He reached up and slid the metal knob across to lock the door.

As the acidic squirting continued, he propped his elbow on the narrow sink bench next to him against the torture unwinding in his belly and rested his sweaty forehead in the crook of his arm and tried to fend off fainting, breathing hard his own rank toxicity in the confines of the tiny space. Soon parts of his body no longer acted under his direction. It was as if some alien force had stepped in to run the show, to clinically empty him and he was just a pained, sweating bystander.

Eventually, miraculously, the pain subsided. He waited for a little while before he limply tidied himself up and got up and washed his hands. But as he unlocked the door, another wave of cramping pain shot through him and he slid the knob back and slumped down hastily for another round.

When he finally emerged from the cubicle, he was weak and dehydrated. He kept his head down as he brushed through the people queuing to use the toilets. After his next cubicle visit, which came after only another fifteen minutes or so and had him jumping the small queue that had formed in the meantime, the other two passengers in his row thoughtfully shuffled over to give him the aisle seat of their own volition. Crumpled low in his seat, he sipped water and feebly waived away the stewardess poised by the trolley packed with meals and drinks, covered his face against the nauseating smells and sounds of others eating around him and tried to sleep between cramps and dashes to the back of the plane.

After they had landed and been welcomed to Pah-dang over the intercom first in Bahasa and then in English which sounded like Bahasa, the middle aged Indonesian man sitting next to him looked over at Riley and smiled and said as they taxied to the terminal: Drinking and teeth – only bottle water. No ice. No eat unless peel or long cook. You ok soon. Jus bottle water, cooked rice.

After the next four days during which he was bedridden in an ordinary hotel in Padang with slow motion images of what he'd eaten and drunk at the Jakarta airport flicking and replaying teasingly across his mind, too weak to do anything except pick up the receiver and ask for rice and bottles of water, crouch across the tiles to the toilet and shower and only his guide book to read, those words became his mantra.

* * *

On the fifth morning, he woke up early, hollow and hungry. He watched the ceiling fan circle round above him for a while before he padded over the cool white tiles to shower with his mouth closed up tight. The lift was out of order still and as he slowly and weakly made his way down the stairs, a vague memory came to him of struggling up them a few nights ago with his bag of boards, helped by a small Indonesian man tortoised under his large backpack.

The hotel was across the road from the river. Its small lobby was at street level and had three levels of rooms for rent above it. Inside the lobby, gleaming white tiles were continuously mopped clean and the pace hotted up when the afternoon thunderstorm's muddy wet street feet hit. Deep cracks ran down the walls and across the ceilings. A relative of Riley's airport taxi driver beamed proudly out from behind the carved wooden counter and gave him directions to a place for breakfast in broken English.

The air was still cool as he left the hotel early that morning for the first time. He walked slowly along the potholed walkway next to the river.

He'd found the hotel in his guidebook when he was already laid low inside it with his stomach cramped and twisted. The guidebook talked up its proximity to the river. But it was far from scenic. Rank odours of rotting vegetables mixed with those of human waste and diesel and decay, like a dump on a hot day. It shimmered in unnatural olive greens and, at its surface, plastic bags and bottles and thongs, parts of leather shoes and bits of wood and cigarette butts and other rubbish drifted slowly downstream towards the ocean through whirling rainbow coloured oil slicks. Colourful wooden boats planed slowly along the river leaving wakes of foaming scum. Others bobbed and knocked into each other on both sides of the river, tied up to short makeshift rotting timber jetties. People bustled urgently on foot or scooter along its edge. Here and there skinny men and women in loose torn rags stood apart with hand lines fishing into the dirty river from narrow bridges swaying precariously under the weight of the passing traffic. Away off in the distance, others squatted from place to place amongst the rocks and mud of the riverbanks, backsides bared to the rising sun.

Riley took the second turn on the left as directed. He found the place a short walk down the road past a row of shanty shops with dusty blue and orange tarpaulins strung across the pavement. He peered into the dark interior of one of the shops as he passed and a lady wearing an apricot hijab smiled at him. In the window of the place next door was a sign 'Rumah Makan Padang – Bagus Makan' and below it stood a glass cabinet with two long wide wooden shelves with a myriad of small bowls of food. The door jingled as he went in. It was empty. He sat down at a table in the breeze from a fan on the counter.

After a few minutes, two young girls shyly appeared from the back of the room and, without asking, began to lay before him an array of small white bowls: one with a peeled boiled egg sprinkled with red powder, another with a couple of tiny fried fish half the size of his hand, a bowl of finely chopped red chilli, a bony wing and drumstick from a scrawny fried chicken, rice, an unfamiliar green vegetable, a thick red curry with bits of mysterious meat lurking at the surface, tofu in more red powder and other dishes and a bowl of water. There were cold drinks in a fridge next to the counter and he ordered a sprite from one of the hovering girls.

The cold effervescence played on the roof of his mouth and his tongue and the sugar rushed through his empty body. He swallowed his malaria tablet with the next swig and breathed in the spices and surveyed the plates of foreign food assembled in front of him. He was starving but wary of his shrunken stomach. He picked at the familiar fried chicken with his fingers, left the fried fish with images of his walk still fresh in his mind, ate the boiled egg after dusting the red powder off and had a few pinches of sticky rice. As soon as he'd rinsed his hands in the bowl, the girls silently slid over and started clearing away the bowls. He got up when they had finished and one of them wrote a number down on a piece of paper at the counter and told him what it was. He looked at the writing and handed over some rupiah, got some change and stepped out, sweating from the chilli and a little bewildered, into the rising heat and humidity.

On the way back he stopped at a rickety trestle table covered with fruit and vegetables still dusted in dirt. He bought some bananas and a few hard green skinned balls from the old man sweating contentedly in the half sun under a ripped beach umbrella. As he handed over the fruit, the man said something to him. Riley assumed it was the price and he held out a rupiah note and the man's face lit up and then he pulled himself together and nodded gravely as he took the note. He gave Riley a few more bananas, picked up a green coconut and sliced off the top of it with a few blows from a bush knife, showed him the little hole to drink from and handed it over instead of change.

21.

A week later, Riley was finally at the port waiting to board the only ferry out to the islands with his gear and cartons of supplies at his feet, an addiction to Padang food, a few words of Bahasa, a phrase book and no wiser as to Will's whereabouts. The only inkling he'd got was from a tired old Australian bloke sitting hunched over on a stool with a fair few drinks under his belt at a bar on the seafront one night. He'd looked at Riley through narrow dark slits between eyelids puffy and jaundiced from hard living and then down at the photo of Will which Riley had put down on the bar after they'd spoken for a while and mumbled that the face rang a bell. But any memory that he might have had of talking with Will had been long since washed away by nightly floods of beer and whisky.

From where he waited on the low concrete wall Riley watched as goats and buffalo were tugged and whipped up the gangplank onto the orange ferry and disappeared into the hull. A stream of vans and small trucks followed. Pallets of caged piglets and chickens and roped down cargo were winched up off the asphalt and swung around onto the hull at the bow, precariously above the heads of workers and passengers walking past or standing idly by.

As dusk gave way to darkness and the lights came on at the port to summons whirring balls of thrilled and fascinated insects, the ship's horn sounded and set off a stampede of people rushing with bags and boxes. At the bottom of the gangplank a man stood authoritatively collecting tickets and slowly allowing people to pass. Little children caught up and slipped through the forest of legs to find their parent's pair.

Riley was the only foreigner there. He decided to wait until the scramble died down before lugging all his gear across to the gangplank in a couple of journeys. When he eventually made it on board, all the seats inside and the places outside with any fresh airflow were taken and the ferry was underway. He found some room outside on a small side platform of the lower deck. He put his things down and settled on the metal floor with his back against the wall of the throbbing engine room and the air around him hot and loud and thick with diesel fumes and damp from the salty spray as the old laden ferry ploughed slowly out through the bay. He regretted not paying whatever it took to get a sleeping cabin.

Nearby, a gloomy faced family sat close to each other cross-legged on reed mats, eating rice with their hands out of folded pieces of paper. The father said something to the others and they all shot sideways glances at Riley and went on putting pinches of rice into their mouths. After they'd finished eating, they passed around a bottle of water and then lay down on their sides and pulled dark sarongs up over their heads. From time to time people came out from inside the cabin area and leant out over the rail as the boat chugged along, up and over the undulations of the swell in the black night.

Where you come prom?
Riley looked up from the floor at the smiling moustached face of a man dressed in dark trousers and a shiny black jacket. One of his black shoes rested on a crossbar of the ship railing. He held a cigarette between his thumb and forefinger and put it to his mouth.
From Australia. Do you speak English? Riley asked.
Ya little, I'm a teacher.
Riley stood up and came alongside him and leant over the railing into the sea air.
Pirst time in Indonesia?
Yeah, it's all new to me.
Smoke?
No terima kasih.
You like Indonesia? He asked smiling.
Ah yeah, haven't been here that long so haven't seen much yet, but seems good. Riley put his hand to his belly and smiled with a slight wince: Was out of action for a few days.
Ya, that can be bery bad. Jus drinking bottle water. He glanced over at Riley and said: Where you go?
I'm not really sure… I'm looking for my mate. I think he's still here. He's been in the islands for years surfing. I'm not too sure where he is but I thought I'd get out to the islands and take it from there. There's only one ferry out to the islands from Padang isn't there?
Ya, jus one boat… your priend name?

Will.

Surping... what is surping?

Surfing?

Ya.

Riley leant down, unzipped his board bag and pulled out a surfboard: surfers stand on these boards and ride waves which roll into the shore from out to sea, here have a look.

The teacher held the board with both his hands and looked at it: bery light, no break in wabe?

Sometimes, yes. Very fragile.

The teacher handed the board back: Your priend, he surping like you?

Yeah, Riley said putting the board back in the bag.

Where you stay?

I'm not sure. I was going to ask for a good place for a night or two at the port when we get there.

The teacher nodded and thought for a moment: My house in nuder place, small village, little bit far, north from port. My bruder's priend has a lodge near port, small wisma, maybe is ok for you. Not many places to stay, we no hab touris. I show you? Maybe he know your priend.

Ok, thanks, that'd be great, terima kasih.

What your name?

Riley, he held out his hand and they shook.

My name Adi. Please Mistah Riley, I go back to my pamily now, little bit sleeping. I wait for you when we stop tomorrow.

Yes, ok. Terima kasih. See you in the morning Adi.

The teacher walked across the deck to the door and held the handle and steadied himself as the boat lurched up and over the swell and then went inside. Riley stayed at the railing.

Out to sea, in the distance, the dim lights of small fishing boats flicked on and off as they bobbed through the crests and troughs of the moving ocean. Up ahead, two large vessels crossed the ferry's path. They were brightly coloured wooden ships, lit up with hundreds of multi-coloured globes hanging from wires zigzagging between bow and stern and from port to starboard and all over the multiple curved arms which spanned out over the water and dipped into the sea as the ship rolled. They looked like alien creatures, huge omnivorous insects from another world prowling the ocean for prey in the night. Riley watched them until they faded from sight, took a leak over the side and then lay down on the warm metal floor with his head and shoulders leaning against his big backpack and the small one held across his chest. He pulled his t-shirt up over his face against the fumes and closed his eyes.

The motion of the boat was regular on the windless sea and he managed to get some sleep despite the metal floor and the drone and fuzz of the diesel engine. When he awoke, day was just breaking. He blinked a few times as he lay there and then reached into the small backpack on his chest for his water bottle and sat up slowly to lean against the ferry wall. The family had gone. He had a drink and looked at the coast of the island as the boat moved past it. Behind slices of beach and treed marshes, the island rose into jagged heavily forested hillside. It was grey and misty in the first light. As the ferry steamed on and the light lifted, here and there he could make out a few thatched huts and smoking twists of small fires rising up out of the coconut trees and other foliage lining the shore. A few small boats lay peacefully at anchor just offshore.

The large squat ferry coninued on, muscling and bulldozing through the still water, on and on, its engine thudding and coughing plumes of black diesel into the sky, invading further and further into the tranquil bay. Its loud horn demanded and echoed back across the water: three long reverberating blasts heralding its imminent arrival, murdering the peace.

The isolated settlements eventually gave way to larger villages and the grey sky to blue as the sun appeared and when the ferry turned to starboard towards the end of the deep bay, the port town came into view from Riley's side of the boat for the first time. A rambling mess of corrugated iron shacks spread out along the coast. Warped doors and lengths of dirty cloth swung in the doorways. Wooden window flaps were propped open from house to house and everywhere clothes hung to dry on makeshift lines of string. Protruding above the buildings in town was a tall red church steeple bearing a white cross and behind it, the metallic dome of a mosque. The small town spread up and over the steep rise of the hillside. High above, volcanic mountains rose steeply into the blue sky.

Near the wharf, cars and scooters moved about amongst pushbikes and pedestrians preparing for the arrival of the boat. Horns bleated.

Bastards... they've flogged my bloody supplies, Riley said out loud as he flicked through his boxes looking for a snack. Shit all my noodles, rice, condensed milk... mozzie coils, matches, god knows why they left the rolled oats, must've missed em... raisins and peanuts gone...

He kept rummaging. The morning sun slanted in and heated the side of his tired, irritated face as the boat pulled slowly up alongside the concrete wharf. They'd taken a fair bit of stuff. He'd have to replace it. He stood up and looked around for his thongs and swore with disbelief, they'd gone as well.

He looked up at the sound of kids laughing and, as the ferry moored, watched four skinny local boys take turns leaping off the end of a broken strip of the concrete wharf. They jumped into the dirty water and burst up out of the muddy depths to spit out a mouthful of tea coloured sea and wipe their laughing silted faces with their hands before climbing up a fallen pylon and onto the wharf to do it all again, impervious to the broken glass scattered everywhere.

Adi was standing on the wharf below and waved up at him, then turned and spoke to his family and they waved also. Riley waved back. Adi came over to the side of the boat and motioned to Riley to pass his things down to him over the railing. On the wharf, Adi introduced his family and waved his arm and in a few minutes a small black horse pulling a colourful covered carriage, driven by a grinning shirtless boy, clipped slowly over.

We take becak to check lodge. Bery cheap. My pamily wait here with your bags.
Riley hesitated for a moment.
Adi looked at him, smiling: it's ok.
Sorry Adi, someone took some things from me last while I was sleeping.
Adi shook his head: maybe that pamily near you, we go look, talk to police.

No, it's ok, don't worry. Mostly food. They needed it more than me.

Our people no good sometimes, then smiled: Get your shoes and we go.

Ah, they actually took my thongs as well... is there anywhere I can buy some here?

Ya, he laughed.

Riley climbed into the carriage first and sat down with his small backpack on his lap and the canvas roof stretched taut across the top of his head. Adi got in next to him and said to the boy: Wisna Marwan, Jalan Ahmad, kasih.

The boy nodded and called out 'Hah' and slapped the small horse on the shoulders with the reins. The horse snorted and they moved off slowly. The gate into the port was off its hinges in the rubble to the side of the road. A man sitting on a stool in the small office at the exit, nodded at them through the open window as they passed out into the street and joined the light flow of traffic.

Along both the sides of the street, ramshackle shops propped against each other and displayed their wares on unstable tables and grass mats and in baskets on the ground. People sat idly by in the shade looking out onto the street, watching, waiting. Down the way they passed a woman standing by the roadside at a rickety set of wooden shelves bearing glass bottles of dirty gold fuel with plastic bag lids held down by rubber bands. The attendant in an old white t-shirt and grease marked blue trousers rolled up to his calves, was pouring a bottle into the woman's scooter and chatting with her, drawing on a cigarette bouncing about between his lips.

A bit further on, another scooter zipped past them driven by a man wearing a helmet. A three or four year old boy stood on the small landing in the space between his father's knees holding onto the handlebars with a big smile and cheeks pinned back in the wind. The mother sat behind the father and held him around the waist and their daughter sat behind her and did the same, their faces inclined identically into the breeze pulling at their black ponytailed hair. On one of the mother's shoulders was a bag bulging with supplies and slung off the other arm, at the bend of her elbow, was a metal laundry bucket out of which peered and flopped the wispy, black haired head of a small baby.

A boy riding a large rusty bike, standing up out of the seat so his bare feet could reach the pedals, came racing up behind Riley and Adi in the trotting becak with a huge grin and called out continuously 'Hello Mistah, hello Mistah, what's your name? Hello Mistah' and gleefully followed them like it was the best day of his life. When they stopped at a place for Riley to buy some thongs, the horse took the opportunity to raise its tail and drop a pile of manure on the road and the boy laughed and rode off in the other direction.

Another kilometre or so down the road, they pulled up alongside a neat single story concrete building painted light green. It was set back from the road behind a mango tree. Across the road was a primary school. Kids wearing red and white squealed and ran about, huddled under trees and wandered down the street. A neatly dressed man with short black hair streaked lightly with grey and parted on the side, was sitting in a chair on the porch looking out. He adjusted his glasses, rose up with a smile and put his feet back into his black sandals as they walked across the grass towards him. He shook Adi's hand warmly. Adi introduced Riley and Marwan to each other and they also shook hands and then Adi spoke with Marwan in Bahasa.

Eventually Adi turned to Riley and said: Marwan hab room and he say you welcome. Air cool not working but hab pan. Normal price pipty tousand rupiah one night with brekfas but you my priend so porty tousand.
Riley did a quick currency conversion in his head and said: Ok, terima kasih.
Riley pulled a photo of Will out of his small backpack and handed it over: Can you ask him if he knows Will?
Adi and Marwan leaned in and studied it closely and then spoke together for a time. Adi turned to Riley with a grin and said: Ya, he stay here before one time. He look different to photo. Old photo. Hab much hair, bery thin, skin dark like Indonesian. Hab good Bahasa. Only stay short time. He get many supplies por trip.
Really... can he remember how long ago it was that he was here? Riley asked Adi.
Adi and Marwan spoke and then Adi turned to Riley and said: He checking, we go get bagasi and you come back.

Back at the wharf, Riley thanked the boy for the transport. Adi translated the price and Riley gave him a bigger note which was roughly the equivalent of fifty cents and the boy beamed with gratitude. Adi called out to a white van parked off to the side of the wharf. It had dark tinted windows and silver reflective foil covering the front windscreen save for an eye level strip. It shot over. Adi's family helped Riley load his things into the back of the van and then Adi quietly told Riley what the price should be and held out his hand to say goodbye.

Why don't you all come with me in the van and keep going on to your village? Riley asked as he shook Adi's hand.
Thank you but is bery expensive. We take bus. Is no problem, Adi said and smiled.
How much? I can pay.
No, is ok Riley. Hope you see your priend.

Riley climbed up into the front seat. The driver turned the music up loud and looked across at Riley with a nodding grin. Below his sweaty forehead, one black eye peered through the hole where a lens was missing from his wrap around reflectos. He drove the short distance to Marwan's place hunched forward over the small racing wheel, swerving in and out of the light traffic with a hundred musical bleats from his horn and frighteningly fast, as if it were the final closely fought stretch of a formula one race. Riley sat pinned back stiffly in his seat, no seatbelt in sight, clutching his bag.

Marwan was sitting on the porch again when they pulled up. The driver helped him unload his things and carry them over. Riley asked him how much and the driver said something. At Riley's blank face he went to the front of the car and wrote on the back of a cigarette packet and showed it to Riley who laughed and shook his head and borrowed the pen and wrote down the amount Adi had said which was half of the driver's number. The driver said ok with a grin and Riley paid him and he drove off with another burst from his musical horn.

Riley put his things in his room and came back to the porch. Marwan picked up the guestbook from the table and opened it up to a page about a third of the way through the book. Riley peered at it. In the first column was the date of Will's stay and after Will's details was his signature. Will had been there nearly two years ago. Riley asked him if he knew where Will was going, forgetting that Marwan didn't speak English and Marwan smiled blankly back at him. Riley took his backpack off his shoulders, put it down on the table and pulled out the phrasebook and map. He looked through the book for a little while to find what he wanted to say and pointed at the map and asked: Tolong, di mana Will sekarang?

Saya tidak tahu, Marwan said. He then pointed at an island on the map which lay back down the long deep bay the ferry had sailed up and away off to the south and said: Will situ sebelum di sini.

Riley found a pen in his backpack and Marwan wrote what he'd just said down on the inside cover of the phrasebook and Riley looked up the words. He looked through his book and asked: Sekarang baru pulau?

Marwan nodded his head, shrugged his shoulders and smiled. Riley pointed at three other islands which lay further still to the south and asked: Di sini?

Marwan said: Ya and shrugged his shoulders and looked smilingly unsure.

Riley thanked him and went to lie down for a while. He switched on the fan and pulled the curtains and the room became darker. He lay down on his back on one of the single beds with his knees contoured to the edge and let his thongs slip off onto the ground. His hands rested on his chest and he closed his eyes as the fan picked up speed overhead and brushed warm air across him.

He woke in the mid afternoon and walked slowly down the street towards the port. It was still hot and humid. He nodded as he passed shyly smiling faces and earnest stares. He was hungry and stopped at a place on a corner not far from the port and had some steaming rice with red chilli and a whole fried fish. He steered clear of the glass of water and the fish's glazed eyeballs.

At the port, he walked up a flight of stairs to a wooden shack raised high up off the ground overlooking a small harbour. The orange ferry was still tied up at the main wharf nearby. One side of the harbour was a natural rock outcrop extending out into the bay with vegetation tenaciously growing out of the black volcanic rocks. Potholed walkways formed the other two sides and a calm stretch of water allowed the boats to pass. As he mounted the stairs, he looked down on the colourful wooden boats jostling together, side to side, almost filling the small harbour. Here and there fishermen slowly inspected and repaired nets and patiently tinkered with ancient outboard motors and smoked and talked across the boats.

He stooped to walk through the doorway into the shack and peered about between the posts and small packets of snacks strung from the ceiling on string. A pretty girl with long black hair and perspiration beading on her forehead and upper lip was behind the counter arranging cool drinks and a bowl of tiny peanuts on a tray. She smiled at Riley and slid off to deliver the drinks and nuts to four men engaged in a card game in smoke filled dimness at the back of the room.

Do you speak English? Riley asked when she returned. The men at the table looked up at him and stared for a moment and went back to their cards.

She shook her head and smiled and said: Tidak.

He pointed at the fridge and held up his forefinger said: Satu cold sprite terima kasih.

While she got it out of the fridge and took the top off, he dug the phrase book and the photo of Will out of his bag. He put the photo down on the counter and worked out what he wanted to say: Saya taman. Nama Will. Anda tahu?

Riley had a drink. She looked at the photo and shook her head shyly and said: Tidak... saya ibu, bekerja besok.

Riley reached across and picked up the pencil lying on the counter and motioned her to write down what she'd said. She wrote down 'Diah' in small neat letters. He tried again, phonetically writing down what he thought she'd said. She laughed and the men up the back glanced up and then quickly went back to the tattered cards in their hands. She corrected him. He looked up what she had written down in his book and said: Besok jam?

Besok pagi, she replied.

Ok, terima kasih, he smiled.

22.

The ocean raged. Grey walls of water reared up into steep peaks and broke and crashed with rushes of white foam. Violently. Striking out at the lurching boat. Overhead the dark sombre sky poured down torrential rain and in the east towards Sumatra it thundered and cracked and strikes of lightning burnt down from the heavens magnesium white.

Water poured into the boat off the roof and leaked through holes and makeshift patches and gushed over the sides and stern. The engine was almost powerless as, again and again, its meagre propeller was thrust out of the sea with a high fast whir and then buried too deep with a low slow labour in the rough seas. The driver held on hard to the tugging tiller with both hands, water running down his grim face, saturated. Two other boatmen in clinging wet jackets bailed furiously with a cracked plastic jug and a small white bucket.

Riley scooped water out with a bowl he found floating in the bottom of the boat. At the bow, a covered storage area was filled with the passengers' bags and supplies, stowed on a raised platform wrapped in greasy tarpaulins and tied down hard with oily rope. Just back from the bow, a boy was holding onto the anchor rope, being tossed about like a rodeo rider, desperately trying to keep a look out.

Four female passengers wearing large green garbage bags over their clothes with holes ripped for their arms and heads, sat gripping the bench next to them. Their shoulders were low and rounded, heads bowed forlornly against the endless drenching and the stagger and thump of the boat. One was weak and folded limp from seasickness and a larger woman pushed her own body against her, pressing her to the side of the boat to jam her in. Riley stayed as he was in his t-shirt and boardies. Wet through. His spray jacket was rolled up in a ball in his backpack. Inaccessible. Ineffective anyway. His board bag was lashed on its side next to him on the benches and showered with water like everything else.

They had left early that morning under a blue sky and a light wind blowing from a little north of the rising sun. Diah and her mother had come down the stairs and onto the wharf to wave the boat off. After the first day, Riley had come back to the port the next morning and, over the following days, had eventually found a boat that was willing to take him south. It wasn't the same boat that had taken Will down that way the year before. People thought that boat had stayed down there as best he could tell.

The wooden boat was painted in light and dark blues, open decked with worn bench seats straddling it from one side to the other. Its thin plywood roof was painted white and supported by posts and covered two thirds of the boat from the stern. The hulls pulled together narrowly at the bow which rose up much higher out of the water than the stern.

Riley had climbed aboard one afternoon and, after introductions from the mother, had spread the map out on one of the bench seats of the boat in the shade and sat on another and looked over it with the wiry boatman. The island had been confirmed with a grease smudge from the boatman's pointing forefinger, a series of nods and a blur of babbling Bahasa. The price was written in pencil below the island on the map. It was hefty. The mother had said it would be. Riley had told him his name and they had shaken hands. Riley had paid the boatman upfront so he could buy fuel and supplies for the trip and he had stared at the notes for a few seconds before folding his hand around them and walking smartly off, holding them a little stiff and apart from his torso as if they didn't really belong to him.

As they'd manoeuvred out of the tightly packed harbour a week later, bound for the island away to the south, some of the fishermen had grinned, teeth missing all over the place and yelled out to them in Bahasa from their boats and from where they squatted on the wharf gutting the previous night's fishing haul, amid cackles and laughter. Comments had been shot back from the boatmen on Riley's boat and more laughing and banter had followed as they coasted out into the bay.

They had headed south, the boat skimming across the lightly rippled water, back down the long deep bay Riley had come up on the ferry nearly two weeks before. As they neared the entrance to the open ocean at the southern end of the bay, clouds had started to gather off to the east over the green mountains of Sumatra, obscuring their summits, softly shadowing the rest. It had looked like a postcard then, far from threatening.

Outside of the protection of the bay, the wind was stronger and, at first, as they ventured further into the open ocean, small waves started to slap against the sides of the boat and the occasional misty spray flicked up and over it. Clouds hurried overhead. For hours it stayed like that and they made good progress. Then it all changed with unpredictable speed. Light grey clouds amassed and then shut out the blue altogether and became dark, hanging lower and lower. Sumatra and the island they'd left soon disappeared from sight as grey walled squalls rained down all around. The sea and sky merged in colour. The wind blew hard, sending washes in over the sides of the boat and whipping rain at them, hard and horizontal. Then a huge squall heaved and blustered and for a long time, they knew nothing beyond the hulls of the boat as heavy sheets of rain belted down and the storm harangued them at sea level. Even the bow was lost from sight for a time.

It was not very long after they had emerged from the second total whiteout that the boy lost his footing and then his hold on the rope and was flung against the side of the boat. Then overboard.

The driver cut the engine and started yelling. The women raised their saturated heads with alarm. As the driver leaned against the side of the rocking boat and peered desperately out into the tempest holding a coil of wet greasy rope, Riley quickly pulled a surfboard out of his board bag, flicked the leg rope on and dove over the side.

He struck out hard. Even if the boy could manage to keep his head above water for a while, there was little time to find him before they would both disappear from sight of the boat and then, in this churning ocean, it would only be a matter of time. It was risky. Stupid really. He pulled fifteen strokes in one direction, scanning the rough rising crests of the waves for the boy. No sign. He turned. Two strokes. Six strokes. Ten strokes. Twenty strokes. Still no sign. He changed direction again and kept paddling. Then a few metres away he fleetingly saw a raised arm. Then it disappeared from sight below the waves. Riley paddled frantically. Then the arm reappeared and, for a moment, he saw also the boy's panic-stricken head on the crest of a wave.

He got to him and the boy grabbed desperately at the board and tore at Riley's arm to scramble on. Coughing. Spluttering. He held on tight with his arms around the front of the board and his chin raised up on its deck. Riley slid back down the board to counterweight the boy and then half sat up and yelled and waved with one arm while the other held the board. He could see the boat and hear the engine between washes of the waves. It had to come to him. They couldn't paddle. It was side on to them, moving slowly. He couldn't tell if they could see him in the rain sheeted haze. He waved wildly again and yelled hard to hoarseness. Then it slowly started to come around, circling towards them, bouncing up and down in the huge sea chop.

When Riley had jumped over the side, he hadn't given any thought to how they would get back in the boat. He'd just gone. And as it came near, rearing up and down like a wild brumby, he saw the difficulty of getting close enough alongside to hand the boy up and clamber up himself without getting crushed by the boat. No lifejackets. No lifebuoys. Only an oily length of rope. Several times he lunged at the rope. He got it in his hand on the third throw and, as the boatman gave out more length, he showed the boy to hold it at the knots and prized one of the boy's unwilling hands off his board and thrust the rope into it, then the other. The driver and one of the boatmen pulled hard on their end of the rope and dragged the boy quickly through the water, his face raised to the pouring heavens, disappearing underwater now and then.

When they got him alongside, one of the boatmen leant out over the side while the other squatted down and held onto his legs. He got his arms under the boy's shoulders as the boat dipped into a trough and they scratched and scraped him on board. The women, gathered on the opposite side for balance, peered over their shoulders nervously. The boatmen lay the boy down on his side on one of the benches and held him for a few moments as water ran out of his nose and mouth and he threw up and coughed and pulled air into his constricted lungs and wheezed. He closed his eyes and curled his knees up towards his chest shaking. One of the women moved over to hold the boy.

The rope was thrown out to Riley. He let it stay in the water and pointed and motioned for them to tie one end to the boat and then re-throw it to him. He would be too heavy for them to haul in. They pulled the rope back in and re-threw it. He tried to explain. They understood and tied it off and threw it out to him again.

He paddled to the snaking rope, grabbed it after a few lunges and pulled himself nearer to the boat. A couple of metres away, with the rope loosening and tightening in the undulations of the waves, he paused and looked around at the sea and slipped off his board and waited, riding the crests and troughs for a short while, kicking with his legs under water to stay afloat, the board tugging at the end of the leg rope around his ankle. The boatmen were assembled on the side watching him. As the boat dipped down into a trough he scrambled a little further up the rope and disappeared below the surface. With the rise of the following crest, he pulled hand over hand up the rope with all he had, water pouring down on him off the side of the boat. He threw one arm over the side. The boatmen lunged at him and grabbed an arm each and held on hard as the boat dropped down into the next trough. The water grabbed at his legs and torso, wanting him back, his board writhing madly in the sea under the falling boat. He held on through the dunking and, on the next rearing crest, got a leg up over the side and then they had him on board, tumbling onto the benches on his side as the boat twisted, hitting his head and bruising his shoulder and thigh in the fall.

He winced and lay there for a few moments, coughing up seawater while the boatmen wrestled with the board still attached to his leg. He sat up painfully and undid the leg rope at his ankle. As the board came in over the side, he saw the gashes and dents on it from where it had been struck by the boat. The driver shuffled over to Riley and leant down, his small dark eyes and lined brown cheeks dripping from rain and salty spray and tears of relief, and hugged Riley around the shoulders, softly repeating "terima kasih", "terima kasih". Then he stopped and let go and looked at the boy and back at Riley and said softly: Anak saya hanya.[1]

The driver clambered over the benches to the back of the boat to start the engine up. The two boatmen got back to bailing. The women sat back down. Two of them flanked the boy. The engine did not start. The two boatmen looked up at the driver. He tried again. The rain fell. The sea flew up around them and struck the boat and water ran in over the sides. The boat lurched. The boatmen bailed.

Riley got off his wet plank, leaned down into the bottom of the boat and picked up a container floating in the pool at his shins and helped them. The driver tried again. The engine didn't start. He reached into a ledge in the sidewall of the boat and pulled out a small rusty hammer and a skinny red screwdriver and started tinkering away when the rolls and turns of the boat allowed. One of the boatmen went down to him and they spoke together for a short while. The driver pulled out another old tool from the ledge and the boatman went back to bailing.

Riley looked up over the side of the boat. Grey walls of rain fell on all sides and merged with the sea spray haze and the storm clouded in low, obscuring everything. He looked at his surfboard bag and back at the driver working away and resumed bailing.

After a little while, the driver called out something in Bahasa and one of the boatmen scrambled up to the bow and awkwardly unravelled the anchor line as the boat bounced around. He tossed the small anchor overboard and let the line run out until it reached the final knotted confusion permanently affixed to a post at the bow. Riley kept bailing. He started to count each bail to try to measure time. Silently mouthing the numbers at first and then saying them out loud, losing count from time to time and starting again. Only a dim grey glow made it through the heavy dark clouds to show it was still day. Everyone was sopping, shivering from the wind on their wet clothes and skin. Hungry. Nauseous. Drained.

Riley opened his mouth to the rain every now and again. The driver continued to work quietly on the engine. Without the boat moving forward under engine, it thumped less hard into the oncoming seas and less water flowed into the boat. The three of them gradually made inroads on the water levels inside. When it had reduced to an ankle high spread, one of the boatmen went up and sat by the driver and he bailed as they spoke. The women and the boy sat huddled close together, some looking vacantly down, others with eyes closed, a dripping ripped orange tarpaulin now pulled around their stooped shoulders.

Eventually, hours later, the engine started up. The driver revved it a few times quickly and let it idle and revved it again and then called out and one of the boatmen hauled the anchor in. They got underway again, the lurching and belting into the sea and the cold sea spray showers now a welcome relief. Riley looked back at the driver steadfastly directing the tiller to god knows where and then leant down to resume scooping out the water and started to count again. The boatmen joined him.

Thousands of bailouts later, the dim light gave way to darkness. There was no gradual fade. It happened quickly. And at the fall of darkness, as if they were somehow meteorologically inseparable, the rain stopped as suddenly as it had started and the wind dropped away to half-hearted gusts for a short while and then to nothing. The sea settled and slapped and lapped at the sides of the boat without consequence. Their progress improved. The bailing finished. When the clouds finally disappeared and the stars showed overhead, the driver looked up at them for a while and then adjusted the direction of the boat and they continued on. Every now and then, startled flying fish broke through the surface and darted off across the top of the black water in an urgent winged glide.

After a time, a few lights flickered off to the west. Riley looked back at the driver and nodded in the direction of the lights and the driver shook his head and changed course slightly away from them and continued on. The lights fell away from sight.

Without warning the engine jerked and spluttered and then cut out altogether and the boat stopped. Everyone straightened up from their hunches and twisted stiffly around to look back at the driver. He was leaning down to pick up the fuel container to feel its weight. He shook it easily and looked up at them and they saw a flash of smiling teeth in the moonlight. He lifted it lightly up to show them and then changed over to a spare tank and glanced up at the night sky before he went to start it up again.

*　　*　　*

Deep into the night, only the moon's movement across the sky marking time, an island appeared faintly out of the darkness ahead of the boat's bow, its low-lying outline scarcely silhouetted against the glow from the night sky. The driver changed direction hard and slowed down. Riley peered out at the island now on the port side of the boat. No lights shone. Nothing. Black. Still. In the open water between the side of the boat and the island, a little way off, he made out waves breaking on a submerged reef, whitewash glowing in the moonlight.

Soon the boat altered course again to the south. The island grew quickly before them as they approached and Riley looked back at the driver who nodded in its direction and grinned. They coasted around a corner of the island and entered a bay. The tops of palm trees were faintly discernible against the skyline. Below the leaning trees, a long beach, the colour of wheat in the low night light, curved away out to another point in the distance. Out to sea from the point flashed strips of platinum whitewash. As they slowly pulled up in the still water inside the corner of the island, a low light became visible from time to time through the jungle on the island, unhurriedly swinging its way through the trees to the top of the beach. The driver turned the engine off and the boat drifted towards shore across the black silky water sparkling with a million reflected stars. Its bow soon skidded up onto the wet sand and stopped and then slid in a little more with the gentle pushes of swell.

Holding the lamp at the top of the beach was a bare-chested man in a dark sarong. The driver called out to him. He walked slowly down the beach towards them as the driver stepped along the side of the boat, holding onto the roof for balance. The boatmen dropped into the shallows and steadied the boat against the ebb and flow of the water while the driver and the islander talked up at the bow. Everyone else stayed sitting on the bench seats and waited. A thin strip of sooty smoke swayed out through the top of the lamp at the islander's side and its amber glow lit up the dark tattooed patterns on his body, the drawn skin over his high cheeks and angular forehead and left deep shadowed hollows for his eyes. Long black hair fell past his shoulders. As the driver continued to talk, the islander looked over at Riley a couple of times and opened his mouth into a leering smile, revealing rows of teeth sharpened to points, like the razored teeth of a shark, giving him a savage and menacing appearance.

The driver turned and said something to Riley. Riley didn't understand what he had said and leaned forward on his seat, peering out of the blackness. The driver squatted down and started to work on undoing the rope tying the tarpaulins around the gear stowed in the bow. Everyone else patiently looked towards Riley. He got up out of his seat and clambered forward and asked: Will… teman… di sini?
The driver turned and looked at Riley and grinned and spoke to him. Riley looked blankly back at him. The driver said something more and then pointed at Riley and then at the island and smiled again. None of the other passengers moved. Riley spread his hand out and pointed at them and looked back at the driver. The driver nodded his head in a direction

out to sea. Riley turned and looked where he had indicated and saw nothing. He paused for a few moments and then undid the rope loosely tying his board bag to the boat and shuffled forward with it over the benches.

At the bow he took his thongs off and threw them over the side onto the sand and passed his board bag down to one of the boatmen who carried it half way up the beach and put it down. Riley took his small backpack from the driver and jumped down off the boat and cringed and stumbled a few steps from the pain in his bruised hip. The driver handed down his big backpack and he walked up the slope of the beach across the fine sand, slid his feet into his thongs and put the backpack down next to his board bag. The driver offloaded his other supplies over the side and they piled them up on the beach next to his other things. Each time Riley put something down he looked up the beach and into the blackness of the jungle beyond for Will.

He walked back to the boat. The islander turned and faced him and Riley held out his hand apprehensively which the islander took and crushed in a hand much smaller than Riley's and said solemnly: Selamat datang.
The driver reached his hand down to Riley from up on the bow and said: Selamat tinggal and something else which Riley did not understand.

The driver then picked his way back along the edge of the boat to the engine and started it up. He called out to the boatmen who leant their shoulders into the bow of the boat and heaved it off the sand as the water washed in and then pulled themselves onboard over the sides. Riley and the islander stood on the beach and watched the boat reverse out and then swing and slip away out to sea trailing a white line in the dark water until it disappeared into the blackness and became only a distant drone.

The islander turned to Riley and motioned for him to go with him. He bent down and picked up some of the supplies with his free hand and headed off up the beach. Riley followed with his packs on his back, his surfboard bag slung across his shoulder and his arms full. At the top of the beach, he led Riley between a Pandanus tree and a fallen coconut palm and then onto a sandy track which wound through thickening trees and bushes, jet black beyond the reach of the lamp. The jungle was silent and still. The only sounds were their footsteps on the damp track, the faint far off rush of waves breaking and rolling in and the pattering of heavy drops raining down as they brushed against the wet foliage.

After ten minutes or so they rounded a sharp bend and the lamp eerily lit up the raised splayed roots and roped tentacles falling around the ridged trunk of a huge Banyan tree. A little way on past the tree, the jungle thinned to a clearing where the nightlight softly penetrated and dimly revealed a scattering of thatched huts. Through the smoky hazed doorway of one of the smaller huts, a young woman with black hair falling down her back, squatted low on her haunches next to a campfire, naked except for a sarong around her waist she'd gathered up above her knees. Beaded necklaces hung around her neck. Her face and tattooed arms and the flesh of her chest shimmered deep gold in the saffron firelight.

Every now and then she reached a long stick into a black pot sitting on the flames and stirred. The other huts were quiet and still.

He followed the islander further into the small village. At the steps of the largest hut, a white female dog lying on its side baring ribs and long emaciated teats, lazily raised its head off the ground at their approach and pulled its lips back to bare its teeth for a fleeting second before its head fell weakly back down onto the dirt. The islander walked up the steps, put Riley's things down on the floor of the hut and dragged a woven mat over. He put the lamp down next to it and motioned for Riley to sit. The islander sat down cross-legged opposite Riley with his knees touching the floor and stared at him. After a little while he spoke and then closed his eyes and started to chant. Riley watched him in the dim flickering light cast by the lamp.

Tattooed black lines ran around the top of his chest in parallel semi circles and continued to swirl up the side of his neck and onto the side of his face. A deep scar cut across his cheek. Lines of stars joined like barbed wire ran down one arm, spreading out from a point on the shoulder to rejoin at another point on his forearm. Across his legs were evenly spaced horizontal lines. His hands were gloved in tattoos. As the chanting continued, exhausted and starving, Riley's eyelids drooped down low until his eyes were no more than quivering bleary slits and his head fell down towards his chest and bounced partly back as he fought against sleeping, bobbing lower and lower like a ball in slow motion towards rest.

The chanting stopped as the hut shook lightly from weight on the steps and Riley lifted his heavy lids to a blur of the woman carrying a flat wooden dish bearing an unpeeled green banana and pieces of boiled yam and fish. She made no attempt to cover herself and, as she leant down to place the dish on the mat in front of him, her necklaces and breasts fell and she smiled gently at him. Then she stood up and walked back out into the deep night with soft pats of her dirty-soled bare feet.

The islander pointed at the food and said: Makan, makan. Riley wiped his hands on his t-shirt and picked up some pieces of yam and ate them quickly. He pushed the dish towards the islander who said: Tidak, tidak.

Riley ate everything on the dish under the islander's unwavering watch which broke only to chase away the skinny dog from the steps. When he had finished, Riley thanked the islander who flashed his unsettling pointed teeth and picked up the dish and the lamp, walked to the steps and turned and said: Selamat malam.
Selamat malam, Riley replied.

The islander left, plunging Riley into darkness.

He lay down on the thin grass mat above the rough floorboards of the hut and his eyes gradually adjusted again to the night. After a little while, he got up and walked over to his board bag, pulled both his boards out, wiped the damp bag off with a towel and lay it on top of the mat. Then he pulled a dry pair of board shorts and t-shirt out of his backpack and changed into the shorts and hung his mosquito net from the rafters above the mat. He opened a bottle of water and drank from it. He lay down again, tucked his t-shirt under his head, blinked a few times in the dark. He whispered: Will's bloody well not here… he would've shown up by now if he was.

He closed his eyes and shook his head slightly. Out of the silence of the jungle came a series of high-pitched squeals and guttural grunts. Riley opened his eyes and looked out into the blackness and lay on his back breathing shallowly.

23.

It didn't seem like he had been asleep for very long when two roosters raucously announced the new day. He stayed on his mat with his eyes closed and hands resting on his chest, listening to the earnest roosters and the subtle calls of other birds joining in and drifted off to sleep again. He woke again sometime later and turned to look outside as a scratching sound approached.

An old woman, tiny, loose skin falling, unclad like the others, bent, scratching leaves across the sand with a bamboo rake taller than she was, shuffled slowly into view. She stopped when she saw the mosquito net and stared at Riley, still holding the rake. Her hair was greying and pulled back off her round flat face. Where her front teeth would have once been, her top lip was drawn inside of her puckered bottom jaw and gave her face a sunken aspect. She went back to her raking and disappeared out of sight. Behind where she had stood, three huts sat apart from each other in a row, shadowed beneath tall trees. Grey smoke rose through the thatched roofing of the lower middle one. The other two were raised up on low wooden stilts. The walls were made from bamboo strips woven carefully together. On the roofs, layers of dry brown palm fronds were heaped thickly upon each other. Riley lay still for a while looking outside.

In a little while he heard the sound of young children playing in the village. He slowly crawled out from under the mosquito net and pulled his t-shirt on. He had a drink of water and slung his small backpack over his shoulder. From the top of the stairs he watched three boys tear around the village, rolling coconuts and dragging sticks in the sand, stark naked. They stopped when they saw him and bunched together in panic, then skittered off into one of the huts and peered out from behind the walls on either side of the doorway. A man appeared in the opening next to them. Riley pulled his phrase book and the photo of Will out of his bag and walked down the stairs. The air was still cool. A gentle breeze rustled the treetops.

He picked his way across the sand towards the huts. A white puppy fell in alongside him and darted at his heels fascinated by the clicking of his thongs. As he approached, the kids drew back further into the doorway. The man next to them continued to stare at Riley and called something out. The islander soon appeared from behind one of the huts. He raised his hand to Riley. Riley waved back and as he walked over a boy appeared on the small landing at the top of the steps of the hut wearing an ill fitting old blue t-shirt that swamped his shoulders and fell half way down his tattooed thighs. Tufts of black hair sprouted from his chin and above his lip.

Selamat pagi, the islander said to Riley.

Selamat pagi, Riley replied and nodded with a smile up at the boy who smiled back with sharp teeth pointed like the islander's.

Makan? The islander asked.

Riley nodded, terima kasih.

They went up the steps and Riley ducked his head to get in through the low doorway into the hut. Inside it was dark. The only furnishings were woven mats laid on the floor and a rough shelf at the back which held two sarongs, the kerosene lamp and a cooking pot. The islander motioned Riley to sit on the floor and he and the boy sat down as well.

After they had eaten, Riley handed over the photo of Will to the islander and said: Teman saya. Nama Will.

The islander pulled the photo close to his eyes holding it in both his hands. He showed the photo to the boy and they talked for a little while and then burst out laughing and the islander said something to Riley which he didn't understand. The boy then grabbed part of his shirt and looked down at it and back at Riley happily and said: Teman anda.

Riley understood and his eyes widened and he laughed along with them. He asked, pointing at the photo and then at the floor next to him: Teman di sini?

The islander shook his head with a smile and said: Tidak.

Riley's face fell. The islander watched Riley for a few moments and then stood up and motioned for him to follow and they walked down the steps with the boy following. Just beyond the bottom of the steps, the islander stopped next to the trunk of a coconut tree into which three long bladed bush knives had been hacked horizontally. He extracted one and the boy did the same and they headed off along the track through the jungle dangling their knives by their sides with Riley walking in between. Insects shrieked from the trees in rhythmic pulses.

After walking for a little while, Riley glimpsed the sea through the trees and soon they emerged onto the beach. Three roughly hewn dugout canoes were pulled up at the top of the beach at the base of a couple of coconut trees. Shafts of wooden paddles protruded out of their hollowed centres. He followed the islander down the slope of the wide beach, past their footprints from last night, to the harder sand at the water's edge. The boy walked behind him.

The beach was still cast in shadow from the trees and swung away in a gradual arc, groomed smooth by the last high tide. Palm trees and long branches of tropical almonds leant out across the sand. Fallen fronds and coconut husks lay at the high tide mark. Here and there a waterlogged coconut rolled about at the water's edge on the gentle surge of the sea. Close to the beach, the water was grey and silver in the shadows and smooth like a mirror. Further out, touched by the sun, scattered here and there next to the denim blue water of the reef, vibrant aqua pools glistened where the seabed was sand.

Away in the distance up at the point, waves reared out of the deeper ocean and broke one after the other. Riley stopped, mesmerised. The boy caught up to him and called out to his father who stopped and looked at Riley and smiled and waved him on.

He walked along, the moist air warming as the sun slowly rose higher into the sky behind the trees. The sea washed over his bare feet and ankles and the waves exploded in the distance out to sea from the point. Riley took a deep breath and slowly let the air back out. The muscles in his shoulders relaxed a little. He kept walking along with the islanders, breathing deeply in and out.

The beach narrowed closer to the point. They climbed over a large tree which had fallen across it and lay partly in the water and continued on. Riley watched the waves. After drawing up steeply out of deep water, they folded down, bursting whitewash, and then peeled along the reef in the offshore wind. Unridden. Sometimes gushing a cloud of misty spray out from inside the deep round hollows between the back of the wave and the falling lip.

As they rounded the point, an island came into view a long way across the sea beyond the waves breaking on the reef. It sat low on the horizon. The fringing trees were bathed in morning sun giving their foliage a golden incandescence. A thin strip of sandy beach was just visible between the coconut palms and the ocean. They kept walking around the point. Soon another island came into view in the distance. It was further away than the other island again and sat lower to the horizon off to the southeast. The islander walked up the narrow beach to the edge of the jungle and climbed up onto the raised root ball of a fallen coconut tree lying with the broken tip of its trunk immersed in the water. He motioned Riley to climb up next to him. When Riley had joined him, the islander thrust the bush knife out to sea towards the distant island and said: Teman anda di sana.

Riley looked at him for a moment and then out to the island. He pointed at the island: Teman saya, Will?

The islander nodded.

All of a sudden branches shook and rustled wildly above them and then the ground next to them shuddered with a series of heavy thumps. Riley was startled and battled with his balance for a few seconds before giving in to it and falling off onto the sand. The islander laughed gleefully as he stepped over to the base of the coconut tree to pick up the branch with four green coconuts. One of the nuts was leaking clear liquid into the sand out of a long split in its husk. Riley looked up the tree and saw the legs of the boy. His feet were turned on their sides, soles aligned to the curve of the trunk, toes gripping like fingers, knees splayed. The rest of him was buried deep in the green palm fronds. Then the boy wriggled out and peered down at them with the bush knife between his teeth. He slid down the tree and he and the islander set about knocking off the green husks of the tops of the coconuts with sharp precise blows.

The islander prized out the soft white coconut stopper from one of the three holes at the top with the knife tip and handed a coconut to Riley. Riley held it in both hands and put the hole to his mouth and leaned his head back and drank. It was cool and lightly carbonated and he held it there and sucked and drank and some ran out the sides of his mouth and down his chin and neck and he kept drinking until the nut was empty. He shook it near his ear to make sure. The islander took it from him and, holding it in the palm of one hand, brought the knife down hard along the middle with a dull hollow crack. He dropped the knife and it fell point down into the sand and he pulled the nut open with his hands and gave the two halves to Riley. Riley sat down on the sand and used his fingers to scrape off the damp milky flesh lining the inside of the shell and scooped it into his mouth.

Riley took his bag off his shoulder, placed it on the sand at his feet and pulled out his phrasebook. He stood up again and leant his back against the tree trunk and looked at his book for a few minutes.

The boy said: buku.
His father nodded wisely and said in a low voice: ya, buku.
Riley pointed at the more distant island and asked: Kapal?
The islander looked at him quizzically and smiled and said: Ya, kapal.
Riley looked at his book again for a while: Di sini untuk dibawa di sana?
Ya, kapal, the islander replied.
Kapal di sini? Riley tried another approach.
Tidak, the islander replied. Then he pointed at the first island they had seen when they had rounded the point that morning and said: Kapal di sana.
Kapal datang di sini? Riley asked after looking up his book again.
Ya, the islander replied, datang segera.
Riley looked up segera and flicked through his book for a moment and then asked: Kapan?
Segera, the islander smiled and tossed his coconut into the jungle behind, leant down and picked up his knife out of

the sand and motioned Riley to head back along the beach with them.

They walked back around the point. Their footprints had been washed away. Riley watched the waves breaking on the reef as they went along. When they arrived directly in front of the reef, he stopped. The others stopped as well. Riley looked at the islander and pointed at the waves, then at himself and then back at the waves and moved his arms in a paddling motion and squatted side on in a surfing pose and said: Surping?
The islander and the boy laughed loudly and mimicked his surfing stance. Riley laughed with them. Then he tried again: Teman saya Will… surping, ombak? and pointed at the waves again.
The islander nodded and smiled and said: Ya… teman anda di sana… ombak besar.

They walked together back along the beach. Near the track through the jungle to the village, two of the canoes were gone. Riley stopped in the shade of the Pandanus tree at the top of the beach. The canoes were heading towards a tiny atoll no more than a kilometre from the island. It was a mound of sand, surrounded by reef and raised above the level of the sea by only a couple of metres. He watched the canoes for a little while, looking back up to the waves breaking on the reef up at the point from time to time. The islander and his son nodded at Riley and kept walking on to the village.

Riley watched a good-sized set break in the distance at the point, each wave swinging in wider than the one before and breaking further down the reef. Then the same lines of swell continued on, sweeping down through the deep water to the atoll and broke on the reef to its south, walls of water standing up and running along towards him.

Riley turned and ran down the track to the village. He slowed down at the big Banyan tree and smiled and greeted people going about their morning activities as he walked into the village. At the hut where his things were, he pulled his wallet and passport out of his backpack and stashed them up in the thatched rafters on the inside of the roof and picked up his smaller surfboard. He inspected the wax on it. It was soft and sweating in the humid heat and, up the front where his chest lay when he paddled, it was black from his cold water wetsuit and melting. He reached up into the rafters and pulled a card out of his wallet and used it to scrape off the wax. It came off easily in long warm soft curls which he balled together.

He ran through the village bare footed with his board under his arm. Villagers stopped what they were doing and looked as he ran. Some grinned. A few frowned. A couple of brown skinned kids got over their shyness and squealed and babbled and fell in light-footed behind him on the track. By the time he reached the beach, their numbers had swollen to ten or so and they went along the hard sand by the water's edge with him, talking in a continual lively stream which Riley did not understand. Some ran on ahead and doubled back or dove into the water and splashed about and caught back up. They touched his leg rope and the hem of his boardies with their fingers, feeling the foreign material as they wandered along. They cautiously tapped the fibreglass of his surfboard and put their ears to it to listen to the hollow sound. Half way to the point, two of them gathered up their confidence and shyly slid their shoulders under the nose of his board and trotted on straight-backed, proudly looking about at the other kids. He strolled along the beach towards the point, surrounded by jabbering waist high kids, breathing the warm salty air, the sea washing in and out alongside.

When they reached the point, the tide was low. Parts of the reef were visible above the surface of the sea. Riley dipped his board in the shallow water at the edge to cool it so the wax would stick. He put it down on the sand, knelt down and rubbed wax on in small circles in the shadows of the encircling posse of kids squatting by his side. When he finished, he put the block of wax in the crook of a tree branch and looked about for a place to paddle out.

On the south side of the reef, he found a narrow deeper channel with a rippled current which led out through a break in the fringing reef. Riley leant over his board as he shuffled along in the shallow water, carefully placing his feet to avoid the long needle sharp spikes of the black urchins he could see waving threateningly here and there under ledges and in crannies in the reef.

When the water became deep enough, he lay down on his board and started to paddle. When it became darker blue at the end of the channel, he duck-dived and the water ran over and cooled his head and shoulders. He slipped off his board into the sea, face down, eyes closed, limbs spread and let it engulf him for a time. Out of air, he turned to float on his back and, as he as he lay there with his arms out wide to the sides, looking up into the clear midday sky, rising and falling slowly on the undulations of the ocean, the salt water washed and revived him like it always did, the sun warmed his face and chest and his tethered board gently twitched at his ankle.

Riley sat on his board out the back and waited out a few sets and, as they broke and peeled down the reef, he turned and followed them from behind, watching the lip folding over and over, the back of the wave almost the same height as the water level where he sat, powerful, drawing hard on the reef, spray from the light wind misting the sky, now and then holding a rainbow for a fleeting second.

A set appeared looming darkly in the deep water further out. Riley paddled out a little. The first wave broke deeper to the south from where he was sitting and ran part way down the reef invitingly. The next one loomed larger, its wall building towards him. He scrambled out to catch it and, in the end, went too far. It dropped away into deep water where he was and then heaved up onto the reef ledge closer in and exploded down the line. The last two waves in the set bent in with longer intimidating walls stretching far away off to the north and broke wider still, running along closer to the boiling, gurgling shallower part of the reef. They looked unmakeable. In time he would work out that they were the good ones. He missed the whole set. He looked back to shore as he rose up and over a line of swell and saw the kids in the shade of the trees, looking out.

Riley caught the second wave in the next set. The surface of the water glistened as the wave approached and he paddled hard into the rearing wide wall as it gained height and speed.

He pushed up to his feet and dropped down the wave, water draining off the reef and rushing up the face, a kaleidoscope of vibrant colours pooling and swirling from the tropical reef and sea life below. He leant into a bottom turn with his back to the wave, leaning hard on the inside rail to stop the board skipping out and as he rounded out of the turn he looked up over his left shoulder at the wall bending in up above him and drove up high into the pocket and spun his board and body into a turn and then fell weightlessly back down with the lip to the bottom and did it again further down the line, absorbed in the fluid motion. At the end of the wave, as he skated his board over the back of it to avoid the bare reef in front, he looked to shore and caught a glimpse of the kids leaping up and down on the sand in different directions, stark naked and waving their arms about squealing.

He fell off his board backwards into the sea and laughed under water with his mouth open and his eyes closed, spread out like a starfish above the shallow reef for a few moments, tingling, elated.

As he bobbed up and looked around for his board, the next wave in the set was grinding hard, top to bottom, down the reef towards him, draining more water off the reef. He had no time to reel his board in. He swam hard, desperately scrambling to get further out, watching the lip axing down towards him, his board trailing on his leg rope behind like an anchor. There was no way he was going to get out past it before it broke so he stopped and urgently looked about for deeper water and dove as the whitewash from the broken wave steamed in. It reached down and got hold of him underwater and tossed and dragged him about and drove him in. He felt his arm scrape against sharp coral. He pushed and pulled at the water with his hands to try to stay away from it. It got him again on the same arm and he kicked out and caught the top of his foot on another bit of reef.

He came to the surface to see the next wave rifling along the reef. There was very little water where he was. He lay flat with his arms and legs splayed and looked down for a second and breast stroked quickly to a gap in the reef nearby. He ducked underwater and his knee grazed the reef as the spent whitewash rolled over him. After it had passed he hurriedly swam back out over the shallows and climbed on his board when it was deep enough and paddled hard out the back before the next set came.

When he made it out of the impact zone, he sat up and looked at his arm. There was a long cat scratch on his forearm which wasn't too serious and two parallel deeper cuts on the side of his upper arm which were dripping blood. His knee was also bleeding. On his foot a flap of pink skin waved about in the water above a gouge about the size of two thumbnails. He looked up the reef as the next set started to bend in and then back over his shoulder at the group of kids looking out towards him and paddled back out.

The kids stayed for the whole of his surf, hooting at the spectacle. When he disappeared behind the curtain of the wave on a few, they were equally as exuberant whether he made it back out of the barrel or was swallowed by it. When he finally came in, they ran down to the water's edge and gathered around him talking excitedly and pretending to surf, squatting with their arms out.

They led him back to the village along a shady jungle track which wound between the trees, following the sweep of the beach, never far from it. The sandy earth was soft and scattered with leaves. Whole coconuts and broken husks spilled off to the side. Green vines climbed and tangled around tree trunks. They ducked under branches reaching out across the track in places. A flock of birds took fright and fled from the treetops as they rounded a bend. Insects throbbed on all sides. A few of the kids ran ahead and every now and then disappeared off the track into the jungle to reappear down the way.

Later that night, not long after darkness had fallen, he lay down on his back on top of his board bag mattress inside the dark hut with iodine drying maroon on his cuts, his shoulders tired from paddling and a belly full of fish, looking up into the darkness. His skin was damp and sticky in the humid air. The mosquito net was pulled down around him and the ends fell about on the rough floorboards, weighted down in places with flat white rocks the size of his hand which he'd found nearby. He lay still in the heat, his arms by his sides, palms up and his legs slightly spread. The sweet scent of the frangipani trees near the steps wafted over on the faintest breath of wind. Outside the night was still and quiet save for a locust like chant and diminishing cries from a baby. He turned his head on the side. In the earth floored hut across the way a small fire smoked and flickered. Now and again the islander's woman wandered in front of it.

The villagers were unfamiliar, unsettling in appearance but unassuming, kind, simply making space and allowing him to fall in with them. He'd thought very little about what looking for Will would actually involve before he arrived in the country. He'd been pretty naïve really. But even if he had thought about it, there was no way he would have imagined any of this. Images of the day's simple freedoms flicked through his mind. He thought about Will living like this day in day out here and now on the island across the sea, if he was there.

24.

The following weeks passed in a similar way to the first days. Riley stopped asking when the boat was going to come. The islander always responded in the same way: 'segera' – 'soon'. Riley didn't think he knew. He couldn't see how he would. There were no phones, no radios, no calendars. Out there time went by unmeasured. Each day merged into the next. Just as it always had. The island was small, connected by narrow sandy walking tracks through the jungle. Thatched huts for sheltering from the elements. Only the occasional dugout canoe paddled slowly by. No boat came. There was nothing he could do about it.

The islander's family had eventually let him contribute some of his supplies to their meals. They mostly ate together sitting cross-legged on the grass mats on the floor inside their sparse hut. Riley's tightly strung legs didn't last very long in the pose and he shuffled them about regularly while the family sat still with straight backs and their knees elastically on the ground. They had three children – two girls either side of the age of the boy as far as Riley could tell. One of the eyelids of the younger girl was inflamed and red and closed over. She peered timidly out of the other one. The eldest daughter had her mother's high cheekbones and deeper set eyes. She left her long black hair loose to dry when she came back from bathing in the sea and it cascaded half way down her bare back. Like the others, her small firm chest was uncovered. Riley tried not to let his gaze fall.

At meal times they usually ate in silence. When they communicated they did so very simply. The islander told him the names of the things he was eating and he practised out loud, often with laughter from the family. He studied his book. When he'd asked them how long Will had stayed there, the islander had smiled and said a long time. The eldest daughter had looked down and stopped eating for a little while, then looked up at Riley and smiled shyly at him.

He went to bed not long after darkness had fallen and got up at dawn with the village. The tide was constantly changing. Over the course of a day and night, it came in twice and went out twice. Each day a little later. Riley fell into its rhythm. He surfed the reef up at the point when it had more water over it with the fuller tides. During the day when the tide was low, he spent time wandering through the village and out along the tracks through the jungle.

One day he went with the islander and his son all the way across the flat island to the east side where the trade winds blew. Off the beach, there was a natural pool in the reef and they waded out into the choppy water and collected fish from the bamboo traps suspended in the pool on long stakes driven into the sand and reef. After they had scaled the catch together on the beach, they walked back around the northern side of the island. The boy wandered along the shoreline and from time to time flung his small net out into the water which swished and leapt and bubbled with tiny fish as the net landed. He pulled in scores of sardines which he stored for the walk back in the hollowed out inside of the bamboo pole he carried.

They ducked in off the beach part way around the northern side of the island and went along a wide track through the coconut trees. They stopped at a deep hole in the ground with rocks piled up around its edge. The islander looked down into the well and then proudly over at Riley and said something to the boy. The boy rested his bamboo pole against the trunk of a tree and draped his net over a branch. He walked over to the well and lowered an old plastic bucket down on a long rope to the dark pool of water lurking below and carefully pulled it back up to the surface. The islander invited Riley to cup his hands into the bucket and drink from it. The rest of the water was poured into two smaller buckets hanging off either end of another bamboo pole which the islander lifted up across his shoulders.

They left the well and continued on to a large clearing where there was a plantation with banana trees and papaya and the huge glossy green leaves of yams and other vegetables. They startled a few wild pigs which grunted and squealed and thrashed off guiltily through knee high escape holes they'd bullied into the surrounding jungle. The islander carefully put his water buckets down and slipped into the grove and cut a huge bunch of stubby green bananas off a tree which whiplashed back, freed from the weight. Riley stepped in and picked it and the islander grinned as he flinched at its unexpected weight.

*   *   *

On a cloudy afternoon sometime after he'd lost count of the days on the island, Riley rubbed some wax onto his board on the beach, overseen as usual by intrigued villagers and paddled out through the channel to the reef. The swell had risen a little from the day before and the waves were flawless on the rising tide. He watched them go through unridden as he paddled back out after each ride. Parrott and angelfish and other colourful sea life swam around in the clear water below him. A turtle popped its head up and looked around furtively and swam on past with short thrusts of his webbed feet, narrowly avoiding being picked up by a set wave.

As the afternoon progressed, the sun fell further to the west and slanted in onto the back of the waves, lighting up the folding lips into sparkling crystal the colour of icebergs. The onlookers gradually left in dribs and drabs and shuffled unhurriedly down along the beach or disappeared into the jungle and in the end he was alone up at the point. The wind dropped out altogether at sunset. He sat peacefully and watched the sun fall into a haze of low cloud and hover just above the horizon, large and round and crimson, as if suspended. Waves came and went as he looked on. The base of the red sun soon disappeared in the clouds and only the top half remained. Then it too gradually vanished altogether. The colours in the sky darkened and the light tinged grey green.

With disbelief at first and then unmistakeably as it became stronger, the drone of an engine and the slap of a planing hull sounded across the windless water for the first time since he'd arrived. Sitting up on his board, alert, Riley saw its dark outline low on the ocean coming from the southwest. He called out excitedly and whistled and waved his arms vigorously. Then he got off his board and held it up and waved it about above the water. The boat went past to the north out beyond the reef. He got back on his board and sat there looking in the direction of the boat. And then in the blurred grey light he saw it swing in towards the island down at the head of the beach where he'd first arrived. Shortly after, he heard the sound of the engine slowing.

Riley quickly looked out to sea as a wave appeared. He paddled hard and dropped into the dim depths. As he came out of his bottom turn, he reached down and grabbed the outside rail of his board with his right hand, guided his board part way up the face of the wave and thrust his left arm into the water beside him and held on as the wave folded over him. He shot along encased in its blackness, two trails of white jetting along behind from the pressure of his inside rail and his hand on the water, the sound of the echoing wave roaring all around. At the end of the wave, he lay down on his belly and rode the whitewash from the next one in the set all the way in over the reef to the beach. He stood up quickly on the sand and undid his leash and ran along the beach with his board tucked under his arm and his eyes fixed on the boat as it putted into shore. A handful of people had already gathered at the water's edge and a few others were standing higher up the beach.

He saw the boat move away from the beach again and ran faster and called out but the noise of the boat drowned him out. Then the boat stopped in the deep water nearby the beach and he made out the watery flick of a rope pulling taut out of the water and all the way to the trunk of a tree at the top of the beach. An anchor splashed out off the back of the boat and a man dove over the side and started to dog paddle slowly in. Breathing heavily, Riley smiled and slowed to a walk as he recognised the boat.

The islander was standing at the top of the beach, finishing tying off the boat as Riley approached. The islander's son ran off towards the village. Riley ducked under the rope and the driver, his son and the boatmen greeted him on the beach like long lost friends. The driver said something to Riley which he didn't understand. The driver pointed to the south and said with a grin: Pulau teman besok.
Riley nodded and said: Ya, bagus, terima kasih banyak.

The islander walked down the beach to collect them, then led them back up the beach and along the track to the village.

When they reached the village it was in turmoil. Dogs were skittering and barking wildly and the islander's son was giving chase, wielding a bloody bush knife. More blood was streaked across his chest and cheek. Two other boys were also on the run, swerving all over the place in the near darkness. Villagers were standing by shrieking, lips stretched wide above rows of filed teeth and howling at the spectacle. Across the square, darting and stumbling at the head of the pack in the last moments of dusk, was a headless chicken with its wings spread and blood spurting horrifically out of its open neck. Eventually the crazed implausible scurry suddenly stopped and the chicken keeled over on its side not far from the thatched cooking hut where the fire burned. It lay still with a final reflex flap of its wing. The boy yelled at the scrawny dogs setting upon it, dealt out a few savage kicks and they yelped and slunk slowly off. The boy reached down and reclaimed the limp runaway bird for the farewell feast in the uma.

25.

By mid morning the following day, Riley was paddling across a shallow turquoise lagoon towards a right hander breaking a fair way offshore. He had had to get into the sea. Had to try and get his head straight.

The island had looked beautiful from the sea as they approached. Several times the size of the one he'd come from. Rolling hills covered in trees fell to the edge of the fringing beach. Just off the coast an idyllic small island with an encircling beach sat glimmering in the sun and all around, the sea sparkled. As the boat had come in, he had scanned the ocean for places to surf, looking for Will out in the water. There had been whitewash breaking and rolling promisingly away in the distance in a number of places and, in the passage leading to the small island, a wave had peeled along gently for a long way.

The boat had dropped him off and left. The driver had had an animated conversation with two of the villagers on the beach after they had arrived. Riley had had no idea what they were saying. The boatmen had got on with helping Riley get his things off the boat. Finally the driver had walked over to where Riley was waiting and told him that his friend was on the island and said he'd come back for him in a few weeks. He couldn't come back earlier he'd said. Riley had carefully checked all that he'd said in his phrase book and had marked out the days with the driver in the sand.

The reception from the villagers on the beach had been cold. They had led him begrudgingly along the beach, past a handful of dugout canoes and up into the trees along a track and pointed at a decrepit thatched hut on the outskirts of the village. Then they'd wandered off, leaving him there. Inside, the roof was open to the sky in places and floorboards were missing and broken. It smelt acrid and musty, of stale urine and chicken manure. The thatched roof had rustled urgently when he had walked in. Riley had put his things down and gone for a walk through the village. It was larger than the village on the other island and the huts stretched along a shady dirt track parallel to the coast. People sat on porches and stared at him as he walked past. Others kept on doing what they were doing without looking up. There was no sign of Will. No one had answered him when he approached and when he showed the photo of Will they had peered at it for a second and then withdrew. The place had a strange and inhospitable feel.

As he paddled out to the reef later that day, Riley tried to understand his situation. He wasn't sure exactly how long he'd been in the islands looking for Will. It was over a month, getting towards two. Now there'd be weeks out here and still no sign of Will. That was if the boat came back for him. He was in another beautiful place and it felt like a prison.

Sabine would be back in Australia now. He pictured her on her way home from work driving down the long hill into The Bay in the mid afternoon, slowing down to glance off to the west at the sea like they always did, talking to the guys working on the house next door as she pulled up. She'd go for a walk out through the dunes and along the narrow track to the big granite rocks strewn over the beach if the waves weren't right for her, rugged up against the cold in the turtle-neck jumper she'd found at the op shop for a dollar fifty. He saw her hands folded on her pillow near her cheek as she drifted off to sleep. He wondered how long she'd wait for him if he ended up getting stuck out here.

The night before he'd gone to bed with an exhilaration that had come from putting his trust in strangers, people more foreign and remote than he could have imagined and becoming friends with them almost without talking. Things had somehow come together. He'd felt certain he was going to arrive on the island the next day and surprise the life out of Will.

Eventually he neared the peak and watched the waves march in with a long wall and break on the shallow brown reef swirling below and then pocket before tapering off next to a deep channel. It reminded him of a place he surfed sometimes Down South. For a while Riley forgot about his situation and concentrated on getting to know the spot. He guided his board through sometimes three turns on a wave. It was a consistent swell and when he stopped and sat up on his board, it was to take a break, not to wait for a set to come. He looked around at his surroundings and as the morning went on, he started to feel a bit better about his situation. The sea always put things in perspective. Things could be worse. In the afternoon, he'd go for a walk and check out the other villages and see if he could track Will down or find a boat and take things from there. One step at a time.

He became hungry and took one last wave. As he kicked out at the end of it, something caught his eye. When he surfaced out of the water, he pulled his board under him, sat up and looked back towards the island. In the distance, a dugout canoe was slowly coming closer. Riley stayed sitting astride his board in the deep water. In a little while, he made out the bare torso of a man sitting inside the canoe wearing a broad brimmed hat. It looked like it was made from palm fronds. The ends flicked out wide, casting his body into shadow save for a pair of skinny brown arms moving in the sunshine with the gentle motion of paddling, alternating from side to side, gliding across the water.

Soon the canoe came near enough for Riley to see that there was a surfboard bridging the hull in front of the paddler. The paddler slowly lifted the paddle up above his head with one arm and tilted his head way back and, as the sun lit up the blond twists of his long unkempt beard and the golden ribbed hollows of his lean chest, he released a primitive cooee at the top of his lungs and Riley knew it was Will and knew that Will knew that he was Riley because that was the sound they had made since they were kids and Riley echoed the sound and, still sitting on his board, raised both his arms high above his head, his throat lumpy and his chest full and a bit tight and riding a torrent of warmth and elation and relief and a thousand other emotions.

Riley watched as Will stopped paddling a little way off, tossed a large piece of coral attached to a rope overboard to anchor the canoe in the deep water, took his hat off, slid his board over the side of the canoe and eased himself into the sea. Riley paddled over towards him and they sat up on their boards and shook hands with huge grins and Will looked out at him from eyes blue like they had absorbed all the colours of the ocean they'd looked at for so long, the skin around his eyes creased and stiff, lines wrinkling down his cheeks and disappearing into his wild beard, matted coarse hair long and bleached beyond white, falling past his shoulders and cut off in a straight line just above his white eyebrows.

Still holding Riley's hand and looking at him, slowly and softly, Will said: Riley.
Eventually he let Riley's hand go and shook his head and looked down and closed his eyes. Then he looked at Riley again and smiled and slowly said: It's good to see you.
Can't believe you're actually here, Riley said and rushed on: there's so many islands on the map. People recognised you from an old photo, god knows how. It's been quite a journey to get here mate.
Will watched him speak and lay down on his board and said quietly: That's the idea… let's catch some waves before the tide gets too low.

They paddled out to the take off area side by side in the deeper water, talking and watching the waves breaking along the reef as they went. Riley had to paddle a little harder than usual to keep up with Will. Will's board was tattered and yellowed. His skin was sunned to islander and black tattooed lines ran up one of his arms. His body was lithe and thin and dressed in a pair of old ripped blue board shorts that were now too big and held in place around his scrawny waist with a fibrous tie. Here and there his limbs and back were dotted with red divots, raised claw like stripes and swollen pink lumps from sea ulcers and coral scrapes.

Thanks for dressing up for the occasion, Riley joked.
Will looked over at Riley and gave a friendly grin and slowly said: These are all I have left. I tried surfing in a sarong but it comes off all the time. Usually I just leave my sarong in the canoe and don't wear anything. There's never been anyone else out with me. This is the first time. I saw you catch waves from the shore... you've still got that distinct surfing style, he laughed. It's good to finally see you mate. Hey, what's the story with the village? Riley asked.
How do you mean?
I dunno, they seem pretty unfriendly compared to the other island, Riley said and pointed in the direction of the island. Did you go there before?
Yeah, that's how I knew to come here.
The people here are protective. You're with me. It'll be ok now. Did you see the boat come in? Riley asked.
Yes... from a distance. Did you ride the wave over at the other island? Will asked.
Yep, that wave is amazing.

Yes, it is, Will said softly. There's a few places here that you'll like as well, he added as he stroked smoothly onto a wave.

Sitting up on his board and looking over his shoulder, Riley watched the nose of Will's board appear above the back of the wave amid a shower of spray and then disappear and, further down the line, saw his head and shoulders and an arm swinging gracefully back from the open face towards the breaking wave with more spray. They surfed together for a while, trading waves with barely a chance to talk. When the reef began to show above the level of the water on the inside from the falling tide, they clambered aboard the canoe and placed their boards across the hull. Will handed Riley a roughly hewn oar and they paddled the canoe slowly back to shore.

They dragged the canoe up onto the beach above the high tide mark and Will looked up at the clouds and then turned the canoe on its side and put the paddles inside.

We've moved your things to another hut, come and I'll show you where it is, Will said tucking his board under his arm and wandering off between the low dunes towards the village. They walked barefoot along the wide sand track in the shade of the tall coconut trees. It was a different village with Will at his side. People waved from thatched huts on stilts lining the track and passers by grinned filed and absent and rotting teeth and exchanged greetings with Will. Nude kids flocked around them, now excited by the presence of the new stranger. Some reached up and grabbed Will's hand and Will held theirs and spoke to them gently as they walked along for a little while before they skipped off.

Along the way, Will stopped at his own thatched hut. It was the same as the others in the village. He looked up and put his board down out of reach from overhead coconuts. Riley did the same. At the side of the hut a woman was pulling dry sarongs off a line strung between two coconut trunks and draping them over her bare shoulder. Will called out and they walked over towards her. He said something to her and Riley heard his name and she smiled and reached out her hand and Riley took it.

This is Rani, Will said.

Hi Rani, apa kabar? Riley said and they both looked at him for a moment and then the three of them burst out laughing. She had beautiful dark almond shaped eyes and long shining black hair pulled loosely together behind her. She hadn't got at her teeth. Her coppered skin glistened with light perspiration from the humidity and falling onto her full bare chest, were necklaces made from tiny colourful shells.

Will said something to her and she handed him one of the sarongs. He wrapped the sarong around his waist and stepped out of his shorts and put them down with his board and they continued on.

She's beautiful, Riley said after a few steps.

Yes, she is, Will smiled at him. She is pure all the way through. I am learning from her, learning everyday from these people.

How old is she?

Will looked at him for a moment and then said: I'm not sure. I think she is probably seventeen or eighteen. People don't keep track of their ages here. We don't talk about age much. After a certain time it becomes hard to tell, you can really only try to guess the number of decades people have lived for. There's your place there, Will said pointing to a hut a little further on the other side of the road. The family has gone to Padang for a while.

After Will had shown Riley his hut, he told him that he wanted to introduce him to the village elders. They walked on and not far down the road, flanked on three sides by low walls of white coral and towered over by tall trunked coconut trees, was a long hut with neatly thatched bamboo walls similar to the one Riley had stayed in on the previous island. A cylindrical wooden gong was suspended on thick fibrous rope from a rafter on the porch.

Riley followed Will up the steps and inside, cross legged on grass mats in the dim light, six older tattooed men sat peacefully chewing, opening their reddened mouths now and again to spit into a small wooden bowl at their sides and mumble to each other and pick up another small nut from a larger bowl in the centre. Will spoke to them softly and they all looked at Riley and nodded and mumbled. Riley walked around and shook their hands and they regarded him carefully. Will and Riley sat down on the floor. Will spoke to them some more and more nodding and mumbling followed.

There were long silent periods where no one spoke. It was dark and cool inside and all that was audible was the sound of their breathing, chewing and spitting.

After a while they got up and headed slowly down the steps. As they started to walk back through the village, thunder rumbled overhead. The sky was dark and low above the swaying treetops and in a few minutes it started to rain, heavy full drops striking their skin and bouncing off the earth below, sending grains of sand up onto their shins. Will stopped and stood there in the middle of the wide track, with his arms out beside him and his head tilted back as the rain ran over him and fell into his mouth. Riley stood by as more and more villagers left their huts and found places open to the sky and did the same and naked kids dashed to splash in familiar puddles. Bowls were placed on the ground to catch water. All around them thunder shuddered and the rain slapped and slid through the trees in a continuous onslaught, deafeningly, shutting out all other sound.

Soon they continued slowly on in the drenching rain. Near Riley's hut, Will told Riley that if he wanted to get into something dry and come over, they could eat together.

Do you surf everyday? Riley asked manoeuvring his chopsticks around a twist of noodles he'd contributed, jabbing a piece of fried egg on the end of one stick and wrapping his mouth around most of it.

Will slowly finished his mouthful: Not everyday. When it's good I usually go out. In the season when the bigger rains come, the waves aren't as good but outside of that it is good a lot, he smiled gently. But there are things I need to do... to help feed us... work in the plantation... spearfish. Sometimes some work on the huts. Every now and then I get sick and don't have the strength to surf.

What do you do when you get sick out here? Riley asked.

Mostly just rest and take what the islanders give me. They make medicine from the plants on the island. I am slowly learning about it from them. I don't have any western medicine left now. Not so long ago I had a bad fever and my body sweated and ached all over. I don't know what it was... probably dengue fever. I was laid low for a while with that. Had no energy and lost a bit of weight... Just coming out of it properly now.

How do you get dengue fever? Riley asked.

It's like malaria, not as bad. You get it from mosquitoes... there is a swamp inland from here, many mosquitoes. Put spray on if you've got some and maybe cover up. Did you bring a net?

Yes, Riley said putting his empty bowl down on the grass mat in front of him. I've got malaria tablets as well.

That's good, they are very bad at night here, much worse than the other island... It's nice to speak English again, he smiled and reached over and refilled Riley's bowl and put some more into his own and drank from the rainwater bowl.

How long has it been? Riley asked.

I'm not sure... let me think, he closed his eyes and thought for a while. He opened his eyes: The last time was when I was in Singapore for a visa. That was a while ago now. I spoke with my family in Australia then as well I think. What month is it now?

August.

August... it's been a few years then. It's amazing how the language just stays there.

Can you get a long stay visa out here so you don't have to leave? Riley asked.

Let's talk about that a little later on, Will suggested, lying down on his back on the grass mat and closing his eyes, I might have a rest while it's still raining. If you want a rest you can lie down here as well if you want or back at your place. We can go and catch some prawns up in the hills this afternoon.

Yeah ok, I'm on for anything. I might go and sort out my stuff, Riley said getting up, I'll see you a bit later.

Yes, I'll come by. Thanks for coming out here to see me, Will said, with his eyes closed and his hands resting by his sides.

Riley smiled at Will and shook his head and walked down the stairs and started to run across the road in the rain. Half way across, he stopped and slowed to a walk and let the water drench him.

26.

What's the wave like? Riley asked, pulling his paddle through the silky water at the side of the canoe, his bare back warming under the early morning sun.

It's a long hollow left, Will said from behind him. You've got to pick the right one and go as fast as you can to make it. Its got a very long wall and looks like it's going to close out a long way down the line but some are makeable.

How do you pick 'em?

I'll show you when we get out in the water. We should start to see it in a little while.

They glided over the still water in silence for a while with only the sound of their paddles dipping in the water and the occasional cry from birds swooping and circling over the sea. From time to time the birds climbed high into the sky and then peaked, pulled their wings into a tight tuck by their sides and arrowed down into the sea for small fish.

How much longer are you gunna be away for? Riley asked.

How do you mean?

You know, when do you think you'll come home?

This is home for me now Riley, Will said slowly.

You're never coming back?

I'm not sure about never but I've got no plans to go back.

Really?

Yes.

What about your family?

Yeah, I think about them sometimes.

I saw your Mum before I came up. She's close to the edge mate, not hearing from you or anything.

Will was quiet for a few moments. Then he looked over at Riley: It's not possible to get in contact out here and a long journey to get somewhere where you can... she broke a promise.

How do you mean?

She used to two-time Dad when he went away Up North to work. He didn't know. No one did except Emma and I. When he died and things, I, was heading off the rails, she promised me she'd never the see the bloke again out of respect for Dad... to make up for stuffing up when she had him. Before I left I found out she'd taken up with him again, probably never stopped seeing him.

Bloody hell, really, Kath? Geez you kept that quiet. I thought it was the girl you were seeing that made you get away so quickly. That's what the family thinks and it all happened around the same time but no, not really. Miranda was good to me, too good, wanted me all the time, away from the sea. It's nice to be wanted but I couldn't give her that commitment, she'll make some bloke happy though. But I needed to get away. Was going anyway, but when I found out, I had to go straight away.

Yeah, don't blame you. Kath... it's hard to believe. Guess no one really is perfect.

I don't begrudge her wanting to have the company now, I'm okay with it.

After a few moments silence, Will continued: There are a lot of places and people in the world, it's good to see different places... meet different people, have new experiences. I've got another family here on the island now. Living differently, day by day, in nature... it's hard sometimes but it feels good... feels like I'm really living.

Especially with good waves around, Riley joked.

Yes, that's what got me out here in the first place but it's not the thing that's keeping me here now. The people out here live simply, take each day as it comes. They know their environment... take what they need and save the rest for another time. It's good for the soul.

Will paused and then went on: Not all of the people are like that though... sometimes a fishing boat from the big islands comes out and in the night you'll hear explosions – they let off dynamite and damage a lot of coral and all the fish in the area float to the surface stunned or dead. Then they go round and scoop them up in a net and take them away. They kill the reef and ruin the habitat for the fish.

You don't get bored out here... feel like your mind is drying up, with no news... or work or anything? Riley asked.

Sometimes I used to think how good it'd be to see a movie, read a book, have hot chips from that place we used to go to near the beach, I used to long for a cold beer... but as the days passed those cravings disappeared and all the other stuff... it mattered less and less and I guess I've now replaced it with other things… learning their language, how to build huts, fish traps, growing fruit and yams, finding out about the different plants… how to make use of what we've got in the islands.

They paddled on for a little while in silence.

Out here you get plenty of time to think about things… see things differently when you're away from them for a while… when I last left the island – ages ago, when I went to Singapore, I picked up a newspaper while I was eating something. I'd been out of touch for ages… I didn't even make it through the headlines of the first three pages before I felt sick at all the disasters and fighting and bickering around the world. I folded it up and put it in the bin. Then I noticed people racing around the city… chasing around after each other's money, flat out.

They kept paddling.

Yeah big cities are pretty full on, Riley said.
It's not just big cities… it's five days work out of seven for the average bloke in the west, more for many. Kids study hard at school to try to get a good job and then they slave away and get big debts for houses and cars and slog it out for another forty years. Some get caught in a cycle of wanting more and having to work harder and longer to be able to afford it… and dream of taking a long holiday. It seems like something is missing in all that, like things are the wrong way round. I don't want to live like that.

The fishing line went taut. Will put his paddle down and picked up the hand reel and started to pull in the line: they might manage to sneak a week off here and there... go away to lie by pools and sleep, try to forget about work... do nothing, to get the energy back and try to make it through another year.

Yeah I know, I don't get how people get fired up about going away on holidays where they're just gunna do nothing, Riley said. It's a waste... but they're probably so tired from working so hard and haven't got that many interests left, maybe it's all they can muster.

Riley grabbed the tail of the small tuna as it came in over the side and put a knife into its head. He took the hook out and put the fish down into the water sloshing about in the hull of the canoe. They paddled a few more strokes. Riley pointed at a thin strip of whitewash away in the distance: Is that the wave out there?

That's the end of it, it starts a fair way higher up the reef. We've still got a way to go, but the tide should start to go out any time now and help take us over to it. We come back in the afternoon with the incoming tide... When I need a mental challenge I can get it out on this wave when it's a good size, he laughed. You'll see it at a good size today I think. The moon's full at the moment so we've got big tides... feels like there's a new ground swell.

They kept paddling, both looking fixedly at the whitewash grinding down the reef in the distance.

You know, just what you were saying earlier, Riley said, there's a lot of people and not that many places like this, not everyone can do what you're doing... if you get more people out here it wouldn't be the same, couldn't handle it.

Yes, Will said.

After a while he continued: there are more places like this than people think. Not just other islands but coastlines and mountains, places where you can live simply. But you're right, it'd spoil it if it got too busy out here.

They took a few strokes in silence.

I guess I'm not saying that everyone, or really anyone, should do what I'm doing... just that it feels right for me and I'm not really missing the west's approach... living for now, taking things day by day, doing the simple things... everything the village eats, it has grown or caught. What we shelter in, we've built from the jungle.

Doing what you're doing... you can't really get out and see the rest of the world, you need money for that... you're pretty much trapped here, Riley said.

I know... you're right, but I eat well here and now sleep soundly on a grass mat on the floor. It's simple. I'm fine with just this forever if that's what ends up happening. I'm happy here Riley.

Reckon it's gunna stay like this? Riley asked.

Don't know... people say the Government is putting pressure on the islanders... trying to move them to the main centres. Every now and then Government men come out here and I hear later what they've been saying.

Don't you talk with them?

No, I'm usually in the hills when they come.

Why?

It's a long story Riley.

They paddled on.

Will continued: one day a boat with surfers and cameras on board may come by and discover it... or the greenies will come and throw a floodlight on the place. They'll all probably mean well but it'll be the beginning of the end for the people out here... it may take five years, maybe twenty five. I hope it stays as it is for as long as possible.

They were quiet as they paddled closer to the reef, watching the waves spin along. This is probably close enough, Will said after a while, you get rogue sets out here... we'll watch it for a few minutes before we put the anchor down.

Look at this set, Riley called out as the first wave rolled in towards the reef and reared up and then broke top to bottom and reeled along, spitting out spray from its hollow inside for hundreds of metres and pivoting on the reef until it had turned through more than ninety degrees from where it had first begun to break. Then the next wave in the set did the same thing and the next one after that.

Riley was silent. He shook his head and looked over his shoulder at Will who looked back at Riley with a broad grin.

Bloody hell mate, no wonder you stayed here. I thought the wave on the other island was good but that's the most perfect wave I've ever seen... anywhere.
It's a pretty amazing set up isn't it. You're going to go as fast as you've ever gone on a wave today. It's a bit deceiving... they all look makeable from here but some are too fast. The bigger it gets the more makeable it is. When it's only head high out

here it's very fast. When it's double overhead and bigger, it slows down a bit but it's more intimidating paddling into the waves and taking off.

How big do you reckon it is?

It's a good size. Probably double overhead... a bit bigger on the sets. How big is your board? Will asked.

Six six.

That should be good.

What's yours? Riley asked.

Six three.

Do you have a bigger one?

No, just this one left now. My bigger board has been busted for a while.

I brought some repair stuff. I dunno how it would fit with your philosophy on living using only the resources from the island, Riley joked, but you can use it if you want.

Hah, yep thanks, Will laughed, heaving the coral anchor over the side, I have to make an exception for surfing otherwise I'd be riding coconut trunks.

They paddled towards the line up. The water's surface was now lightly rippled by a gentle breeze which brushed the faces of the waves as they rose up on the reef and the lips threw out a little further and more crisply, making the barrels more open as the waves folded over and over on themselves all the way down the line.

There's a take-off point around here where the wave bends, Will said and sat up on his board about half way along the length of the reef. It's makeable from further up the reef as well but I tend to just ride it from here... it's so long already from here.

Ok, no worries, Riley said, which ones are the ones to go for? As the wave comes in, look down the line at it. If the wave looks bigger or the same size down the line as it does where we are here, you'll probably not make it. You want ones where the wall tapers off a bit down the line. This one, he said as a wave with an immensely long growing wall that looked like it reached hundreds of metres all the way to the canoe bent in towards them, I'd leave.

A few more waves went through.

That's a good one, Will said, see how it looks smaller down the line than here.

Out at sea the dark lines of a bigger set appeared.

Paddle down the line a bit and sit a bit wide and watch this set, Will said, starting to paddle out. If there's a good one I'll show you what you could try when taking off, paddle hard, get up quickly and stay high to get speed and then drop down the face and tuck in and race the barrel for as long as you can. It's not a wave for big turns, he said over his shoulder, just go.

The first wave in the set steamed in, rising higher and higher on the reef, the wall reaching endlessly out past them to the northeast. Riley watched Will sitting up on his board, with his head tilted slightly on one side, his hands holding onto the nose of his board, sizing the wave up. In one snap manoeuvre he was lying down and paddling furiously with his chin down low and his feet churning the water behind. He picked the wave up and got to his feet quickly as the lip started to feather and throw just inside him. He raced across the top of the wave on his backhand with three long high side skates and then shot down the face on an angle as it started to bowl beneath him and the last thing Riley saw was Will enclosed deep inside the tube in a crouch, the fingers of his left hand leaving a light trail on the smooth water next to him, his eyes fixed down the line and a huge smile stretched across his face.

Yeahhh, Riley yelled out loud as Will flew past. He looked over his shoulder at the back of the wave rocketing along, wisps of spray fanning over the top. Riley lay down onto his board and paddled out to where Will had sat and carefully studied the next wave in the set. It looked longer than the one Will had taken. He let it go. The next one looked longer still. He looked over his shoulder again at the waves rifling down the reef as far as he could see. Will's wave was still breaking in the distance.

The first wave in the next set looked better and he went out to meet it. It was on him more quickly than he'd expected. He paddled hard and got to his feet in a low backhand crouch with one arm buried into the wall and the other hand simultaneously grabbing the outside rail of his board as the wave encased him. He stayed locked in that stance making small adjustments to the position of his board on the face and peering through the opening in the folding wave as it changed size and ran along, a crushing roar echoing all around him. Then he became so deep that he lost sight of the opening all together and only saw the silvered white of the falling lip. He navigated his board through the tunnel as it revealed itself to him, section by section, flying along, taking shallow breaths inside it, until finally the wave overtook him and the churning foam ball behind swallowed him up and bounced him off his board.

When he surfaced, he looked around and saw the wave shooting off, in the direction of the rising sun. It was the longest and deepest backhand barrel he'd ever had and he hadn't even ridden a third of the wave. He climbed back onto his board and duck dived under a few smaller waves and made it unharmed back out to the deeper water. He sat up on his board and looked down the line and saw Will still a couple of hundred metres away paddling towards him.

They stayed out for most of the morning. Riley started to make a few of them all the way through to kick out at the very end. They barely spoke to each other except in whoops and whistles as they shot past each other, one peering out of the round tube and the other paddling up the face looking in. When the tide became a bit low, Will headed back to the canoe and Riley followed on the next wave. They had something to eat and a lot of water and rested and talked as they sat in the canoe watching the waves roll through unridden.

Let's go and catch some fish while the tide's low, Will said and tugged at the anchor, we'll go inside the end of the reef where there is less swell and come back here in a few hours with the incoming tide if the wind is still good. You can use my spear gun and I'll use this one, he said pointing at an old piece of wood shaped a little like a rifle with a slightly crooked rusty spear and brittle black rubber.
He pulled again at the rope: Looks like the anchor's got a little stuck. Can you hold the rope here Riley... when you feel

four tugs in a row like this that means it's free and you can start to haul it up.

Will put on an old dive mask and dropped over the side of the canoe, took a few deep breaths and disappeared with a few kicks into the darker depths.

* * *

In the late afternoon, after another long surf, they left the waves and paddled the canoe unhurriedly across the sea back towards the village. The light wind had dropped away altogether and the water reflected the golden hues of their bare arms and shoulders dipping paddles into the sea at the sides of the canoe as the sun fell towards the ocean behind them. Light ripples radiated out over the still sea from their strokes. Slicks from the motion of the hull and the balancing arm of the canoe sliding through the water swirled gently away. They pulled the water slowly. Contently tired after a full day in the ocean. The skin on their faces glowed from the sun and saltwater and all the waves they'd caught and seen each other ride and the hundreds which had gone unridden. Half a dozen dead fish, each with a small bloody hole piercing the flesh behind their heads, and the rest of the tuna which they'd partly eaten raw before the afternoon surf, the red flesh still warm and quivering as they'd put it in their mouths, swilled around their hips and feet in a dirty pool of seawater.

They paddled along as the day fell away. There was no rush. If they got back after darkness had fallen, it didn't matter. There would be light enough from the moon to get back to

the beach. After a while Will said quietly over the rhythmic swish and trickle of their strokes: It's been so long I'd almost forgotten how enjoyable it is surfing with someone else.
Yeah, that was amazing out there, Riley replied. It all feels a bit like a dream to me. I keep expecting to wake up Down South, pinned to the mattress under layers of old blankets with the Winter north-westerly howling outside and shaking the hell out of the front windows... That's the best wave I've ever surfed mate.
It was a good size for it today.

They paddled along quietly for a while.

There's another one... a right, on the other side of the island, on its day it's probably better, Will said softly.
Riley looked over his shoulder at Will behind, grinning back at him from under his woven hat: You taking the piss?
Nah, I'm not... it's quite a way out beyond the right we surfed the first day, needs a different wind to the left today... I surf it every few days at this time of year... we'll go there, Will said.
Riley shook his head: It's a good life you have out here.
Each day I try to appreciate how lucky I am. Getting sick is hard though. People die out here. I'd probably already be gone as well if I didn't have a mosquito net.
I've never seen so many of 'em, Riley agreed. They were so thick the night after that really rainy arvo, they formed a black cloud swarming around my net. I lit them up with my head torch. You could see the cloud moving around trying to find an opening in the net, could hear them... they were bloody loud. If I'd had any flesh touch the net during that night, reckon they would've drained my whole body of its blood.

You know I've got anti-malarial stuff... probably got more than I'll need, you can have some if you want.

Thanks, I'll have a look. Some of those tablets make me feel terrible, others are ok. Maybe good to have them put away in case someone gets it and we can try to knock over the worst of it with a big dose. When you're out in the islands for a long time, it's not really possible to take tablets every day.

They paddled along in silence. Into Riley's thoughts again came the face of the islander's eldest daughter when she had turned and looked back at him from the bottom of the stairs on the last night he had spent at the other island. He'd been lying on his side looking out across the village after the chanting had finished. Everyone had left the uma and gone to bed. She'd come timidly up the stairs and paused on the top stair for a moment. Then she had walked softly across the floor to where he lay. Filtered moonlight shining through the trees had caught the side of her face, the tip of her shoulder and curve of her bare breast and then the smooth chestnut coloured skin of her naked hip as she dropped her sarong to the floor. Riley had been taken aback and had too quickly said: 'tidak'. Then he'd apologised and had come out from under the mosquito net and picked up her sarong and handed it slowly to her. She had looked at him for a time with an innocent purity. After she'd wrapped the sarong back around herself, he'd hugged her, her chest warm and firm against his and her hips moved in to touch his. Then he'd led her by the hand down the steps and watched her walk away until she disappeared into the night shadows.

Must've been hard leaving the other island... taking a chance and coming here, Riley said after a while.

Yes it was… the people there were kind… patient. That wave is good. The same family that helped you, looked after me… became my family. The parents had me call them Aman and Bai. I'd been to the bigger island to the north of it beforehand… you probably wouldn't have seen it on your wild boat trip… I found some good waves there as well. So I thought there was nothing to lose by coming here and there was a good chance that there would be waves here as well… this island looked bigger, more room to grow… I'd been there for a long time.

They paddled closer to the main beach. A few pigs were fossicking around in the last of the daylight with their snouts hovering above the sand, piglets more or less in tow. A handful of villagers sat side by side on the upturned hull of a canoe lying on the sand under coconut trees. Two young girls walked along at the water's edge holding hands and swinging their arms. The sounds of their singing drifted out across the water.

Will continued quietly: Actually, there was a young girl on the island. As beautiful as I've seen anywhere in the islands. Aman and Bai wanted for us to be together. You'll know her, she was their eldest daughter. But I'd spent so long with them, they'd become my immediate family, taken me into their home, treated me like their son. It didn't seem right.

27.

Riley stood on the side rail of the driver's boat, holding on with one hand and waving with the other at the islanders gathered together on the beach under the trees. They stood squinting happily into the morning sun. Dogs lay at their feet and others ambled about the beach. Naked infants clung onto necks and bigger kids stood formally still with protruding bellies, looking at the boat.

Will's face was shadowed under his broad hat and from a distance, he was distinguishable from the others only by his height. In all other respects he was an islander. He stood behind Rani, looking over her shoulder with his hands resting on the bare skin of her brown belly. Riley watched as Will lifted his hat off his head and waved it in long high sweeps above him, grinning wildly out of his scruffy blond beard and then placed it back on his head and gently rubbed his hands across her belly again. She laughed and leant back into him and placed her hands on top of his.

As the boat gathered speed and rose slowly up to head away to the north, the wind from the motion brushed across his skin and spray flicked up at the side of the boat and the salt stung the cuts and ulcers on his skin. Riley held on tightly with both hands and kept his eyes fixed on the beach, photographing the sight over and over again in his mind. When the islanders had become specks on the beach, he ducked under the canopy, sat down on one of the bench seats and looked out of the side of the boat at the ocean and the rising sun.

He put his hand in the pocket of his shorts and pulled out the cowry shells Will had given him. As he turned the shells over in his hand he thought of the time he'd spent on the island. Each day had passed with an easy rhythm. Languidly. Dreamily. Interspersed with intensity. Mealtimes, legs stretched out on the floor. Bush knives in the plantation. Talking with the islanders. Circles of excited villagers peering in at their spear fishing catches. Waves shared. Hollow, empty waves. Endlessly long. Will laughing, from a long way down inside. A little crazy but patient, honest, content. No planes, cars, roads, television, news, shops. No money. Nothing except the sounds of the sea and the wind, of animals and people going about things just as they'd always done. Time. Hot groggy afternoon naps splayed out on a mat on the floorboards, sweat pouring off skin, praying for a breeze, a breath of wind, anything but the sultry stillness of the early afternoon. Downpour dancing. Kids everywhere. Many strong, some too thin, some very sick. Having nothing and everything. Pure laughter. The turtle feast on the beach under the half moon surrounded by bonfires. Boiled meat and entrails. Tattooed bodies dancing and swaying in the centre and chanting to the side, beating sticks and fog horning farewell shells.

And Riley realised Will had never asked him how long he was going to stay or when he was leaving. He just accepted things as they happened. Riley would stay or he would go. The only thing he had quietly asked, after they had shaken hands and clasped each other around the shoulders on the beach that morning, was to come back again someday soon and ride the boards he'd left there. And he'd softly added, waving his arm to include the surrounding islands, that if it were possible for Riley to keep the islands quiet, he'd be grateful.

In a while they rounded the point of the other island and the familiar shadowed sweep of beach came into view. A set broke at the lefthander and Riley laughed out loud and the tight skin of his sunburnt face creased into a smile which stretched and split open the thin surface of his burnt swollen lips, sizzling blood out of the cracks. As the boat neared, villagers started to gather in the shade down in the corner of the beach.

Riley returned to the beach from the village with a huge bunch of bananas. His passport and money were safely retrieved and shoved into his backpack. He stopped in the shade of the big Pandanus tree and looked down at the villagers on the beach near the boat. The islander's daughter stood off to the side with her legs in the sea. He watched her and licked away a trickle of watery blood from his lip. He turned to look at the waves rolling through up at the reef beyond the point.

The driver left the islander and walked slowly over. He stood in the sand next to Riley and looked out to sea, pulling on his mangled cigarette. After a little while, he glanced over at Riley and grinned and said: Mistah Riley, kita naik ke perahu besar atau kembali ke teman atau tinggal di sini?[2]

Glossary

1. My only son.

2. Mistah Riley, we go up to big boat or back to friend or stay here?

About the Author

The author was born in New South Wales towards the end of the surf mat era. He has spent a lot of days in the sea and roaming coastlines all over the place. This book was written during time spent recently in the South Pacific islands and in the south west of Western Australia. He lives near the sea in Western Australia with his wife, two young children and their pup and gets in it whenever he can. This is his first novel.

www.intothesea-novel.com